A Deadly Mission

by

Judith Campbell

Mainly Murder Press, LLC
PO Box 290586
Wethersfield, CT 06109-0586
www.mainlymurderpress.com

Mainly Murder Press

Copy Editor: Jenna Sprankle
Executive Editor: Judith K. Ivie
Cover Designer: Patricia L. Foltz

All rights reserved

Mainly Murder Press
www.mainlymurderpress.com

Copyright © 2010 by Judith Campbell
ISBN 978-0-9825899-5-3

Published in the United States of America

2010

Mainly Murder Press
PO Box 290586
Wethersfield, CT 06109-0586

Dedication

Creativity is a gift of grace. At the same time, I cannot create without the loving support (and forbearance) of my husband Chris; the love, chiding, and encouragement of my two sons and their wives; and the unmitigated joy given to us by our five grandchildren.

It is to you all that I dedicate this book.

Acknowledgments

There's a verse in an old camp meeting spiritual that says, "If you get to heaven before I do, just dig a hole and pull me through."

No one achieves much of anything worthwhile in this life without a little help from their friends—or in my case, a lot of help, encouragement, and professional advice. The creative journey can be a lonely one, but I am thankful that mine was not. I want to thank and acknowledge all of you who have held out your hand in support of this project.

Thank you to Cynthia Riggs, mystery writer extraordinaire, and one of the most generous and supportive women I have ever encountered; to the core members of my Oak Bluffs Library Writing Group, Philisse Barrows, Charles Blank, Debbie Dean, Laurel Chapman, Joyce Lockhart, Kay Mayhew, Peggy McGrath, Stephanie Michalczyk, and Barbara Peckham; to master storyteller, Susan Klein, and Jennifer Caven who read and edited a number of drafts in varying stages of disrepair; to friends, Melody and Frimma, who have stayed on the rollercoaster with me from the beginning; and to my beloved husband, Chris Stokes, best friend, and editor extraordinaire, (even if he does speak English, and I write in American).

Finally, although we've not met, I want to acknowledge mystery writers, P.D. James, Elizabeth George, Anne Perry and Faye Kellerman, as mistresses of their craft and writers who have carried genre writing to the level of fine art. I am humbly proud to follow in your footsteps. I am grateful to you all,

Rev. Dr. Judith Campbell, the irreverent reverend

One

The trash collectors knew better than to touch the body of the young woman they found sprawled in the alleyway behind the flower shop. While the younger of the two ran off to get help, the older man stayed, trying not to stare at the emaciated figure lying at his feet. The thick, sweet scent of rotting leaves and broken flowers spilling out of the trash container beside them smelled like death, like his mother's funeral.

From where he was standing, the man with a teenage daughter of his own could see a white plastic band around the dead girl's wrist and the glint of something shiny in her hand. Her only article of clothing was a hospital johnny tied in a ragged bow at the back of her neck.

Later that day, the Medical Examiner for the City of Cambridge would pry a silver cross engraved with the words *Jesus loves you* out of her cold, stiff fingers.

Two

Brother David was pacing, circling the room like a wolf stalking its prey. Despite the early summer heat, the windows in the upstairs room were closed, and only a small fan, grinding away in the corner, did anything to move the humid air around the people at the table.

David was an intense, restless man with the thin, muscular body of a distance runner.

"The answer to your question, Brother Aaron, and any other question you might have, is always going to be here."

He held up an open Bible and began reading aloud, stabbing at the page with his index finger and punctuating the words with the squeak of his sandals on the polished oak floor.

"For this cause a man shall leave his father and his mother, and shall cleave to his wife; and they shall become one flesh. And the man and his wife were both naked and were not ashamed."

He paused and looked at the four people seated around the table. Spittle was collecting at the corners of his mouth.

"Everything we know and live by is in this book. We are called to leave the material world and enter into this fellowship of believers so we may follow in the footsteps of Jeshua ben Josephus and like him, do the work of His Abba, Yahweh. The Bible tells us that when the time comes for a man to have a wife, a wife will be made available to him."

"And it came to pass, when men began to multiply on the face of the earth, and daughters were born unto them, that the sons of God saw the daughters of men that they were fair; and they took them wives of all which they chose. Genesis six, verses one and two," said Aaron looking up at the wiry man who was now standing over him. Aaron cleared his throat.

"But if some of us, uh, feel we might be ready to have wives, shouldn't we be able to say something?" The seated man looked down and began picking at one of his fingernails.

"For us, this means ..." said David, ignoring the question and glancing briefly at the woman sitting away from the others near the end of the table. "This means that when the time is right for a man to have a wife, the Abba of this Christian Fellowship will provide one."

Aaron nodded but said nothing. It was best to go along with David when he got like this. Sister Miriam and Brother Joshua, sitting opposite Aaron, exchanged a quick look but remained silent.

"Our Abba is wise, Brother Aaron. You need to trust him." David moved nearer the window, his voice returning to a more conversational level. "There's one more thing. Before we adjourn, we need to set a time to review our new member policies." He hesitated and cleared his throat. "As you know, earlier this year, we had an aspirant who became too zealous in her preparation. Her death was an accident, of course, but such things could reflect badly on us."

David closed the Bible and began walking toward the woman who had seated herself a little apart from the others.

"Meanwhile, Sister Sarah, have you made all the arrangements for the summer Praise and Glory Concerts on Boston Common? Permits? Newspaper advertising? Campus posters?" He paused. "Anything I might not have thought of?" He emphasized the personal pronoun.

Like the other woman in the room, Sister Sarah was dressed in loose-fitting, modest attire. As David approached, she tucked a dark wisp of hair under her headscarf.

"You've covered everything, Brother David." She turned and looked at the man now standing next to her. "Am I right in assuming we won't be doing the Bible study groups until the fall, unless, of course, you want to try running them in the summer? They've been effective."

"Thank you, Sister. We've found the concerts work best for the summer population. The other is more labor intensive and better suited to the traditional academic cycle, but you're always thinking, aren't you?"

Sarah shifted in her chair, edging away from the electric heat of the man. She began tracing a long, thin scratch on the surface of the table with her fingertips.

"Thank you, Brother David, but may I be excused? I think the heat is getting to me."

Three

Professor of Religion Olympia Brown and her long time friend, Father Jim Sawicki, had just returned from their end-of-semester lunch date. She had been rattling on about her expanding plans for the tumbledown antique farmhouse she'd recently purchased, while he, the ever-prudent Jim, suggested she consider doing some of the more necessary repairs before actually taking up residence. Olympia was explaining how she couldn't afford to maintain two houses when she saw the white envelope taped to her office door.

After unlocking the door and offering Jim a seat, she heaved open a resistant window to let in some air.

"So we both know what I'll be doing this summer," she said, settling into her own chair and ripping open the envelope. "I'll be digging through two hundred years of accumulated ... Jesus, Jim, listen to this."

Her hands began shaking as she read the contents of the letter aloud.

To members of the Meriwether College Community,
We regret to inform you that on May twenty-seventh of this year, first-year student Sonya Wilson died as the result of a tragic accident. At the request of her family, funeral services were private. The college plans to honor her memory at this year's commencement ceremony. Donations may be sent to

*the Sonya Wilson Memorial Scholarship Fund, established
by her parents and the College Board of Overseers.*

"This is such a goddamned whitewash," said the
Reverend Doctor Brown, mashing the letter into a
crumpled wad and flinging it across the room.

"Really, Professor!" Jim leaned back and arched a well-
groomed eyebrow.

"Oh, shut up, Jim." Olympia started to raise her hands
but then dropped them back on her lap. "I'm sorry, but it's
not funny. This is the official word on that freshman they
found dead last week, Sonya Wilson. I told you about it."

Jim nodded.

Olympia ran her hand through her short, salt-and-
pepper hair. Anything further about the possibilities and
eccentricities of her new old house would have to wait
until another time.

"The whole thing started last January. Sonya started
hanging out with a religious group called The Boston
Christian Common Fellowship. By February break she was
losing weight, a lot of weight. I tried talking to her, but all
she would say was that it was Jesus' will, and The
Fellowship was watching over her."

Jim started to say something, but Olympia ignored him
and kept on with her story.

"I called the Dean, but he said students go on crash
diets all the time, and unless it was a life-threatening
situation, confidentiality policies forbade his contacting a
student's family."

Olympia blew out a long breath in exasperation and
pushed at the perennial clutter of papers on the desk in
front of her.

"When I approached him a second time, he actually called me into his office and told me that my job was teaching and providing spiritual support for the students and nothing more. He said that if I went ahead on my own and contacted her parents, there could be, as he put it, consequences. He's got a power thing with me, Jim, but that's another story."

Jim listened. His time would come.

"I had no idea it was so bad. I should have done more to try and help her."

"I'm not so sure you could have," said Jim. "Religious fanatics are just that, fanatic, without reason, unreachable. So are anorexics, for that matter, if she was, in fact, anorexic."

Olympia tried to steady her voice. "The day before she died, she got so weak she passed out and landed in the hospital, but she managed to sneak out during the night. The next morning, her body was found behind a flower shop outside Harvard Square."

Olympia took off her oversized glasses, held them up to the light, made a face, and began polishing them with the edge of her blouse.

"I never told the Dean, but I actually went down to Cambridge Police Headquarters myself and asked to see the report." She shook her head. "The official cause of death is listed as complications due to anorexia nervosa."

Olympia shook her head and looked at her friend. "But that's not the whole story, and the administration isn't talking. Nobody wants to deal with what led up to it and ask how such a thing could have happened at lily-white, upper-middle-class Meriwether College."

Olympia was pouring out a semester's worth of anger and helpless frustration to the one man in the world she trusted, an intensely private, drop-dead handsome, gay Catholic priest.

The two met years earlier at Harvard Divinity School a few blocks away from where they were sitting. He was the student chaplain at nearby Allston College, and she was a professor of humanities and chaplain at Meriwether, a small women's college located in a pricey residential section of Cambridge, Massachusetts.

What began as casual conversations about their respective jobs slowly evolved into a deep and trusting friendship. Two late-career clerics with widely divergent theologies discovered they shared a profound commitment to making a difference in the lives of the people they served despite the consequences. They also shared a penchant for challenging the religious and academic establishment.

She was a mid-life and round-in-the-middle remnant of the sixties whose casual dress and easy manner belied a sharp intelligence and a ready wit. By contrast, he was much taller, more conservative in both personality and style of dress, and inclined to periods of quiet introspection.

The priest looked at his friend, knowing what was coming next, but courtesy and habit decreed that he ask.

"What are you going to do?"

Olympia straightened up in her chair. "I'm convinced her weight loss and death are related to that Fellowship group. I want to know what it was these people said or did that killed her."

"Would you believe their residence is literally right down the street from Allston College?" Jim leaned back and crossed his legs at the ankles.

"You're kidding."

"I'm not, but that doesn't mean I know anything about them. I see them all the time walking around in their old-fashioned clothing. They supposedly have a street ministry to the homeless. At least that's what they say when anyone asks."

He was absentmindedly straightening the papers on the table next to him.

"Too bad you missed the College Chaplain meeting last week. That very group was the subject of the conversation. A cult expert from Harvard Divinity School came to speak to us."

"Really?" Olympia looked surprised.

"She said that despite the folksy appearance, it's a very slick and private operation, and once people really get hooked into it, they don't often come back out. From what anyone can find out, which isn't much, they're much more controlling and reclusive than the Moonies." He shook his head and continued. "She even hinted that your Sonya Wilson may not have been the first."

Olympia snapped to full attention. "You're saying there might be other kids who have died?"

Jim threw out his hands in frustration. "Trouble is, there's been no way to prove anything. Accidents happen, and dead students don't talk. The Coalition of College Chaplains is trying to find a way to prevent them from recruiting on college property."

"So we have the summer to find out all we can before they start up again in the fall. Am I right?"

Jim peered over his glasses. He'd seen that look before. "What good do you think that's going to do?"

Olympia started counting off on her fingers. "Maybe save the life of another student. Maybe prove that Sonya Wilson's death was the direct result of her involvement with this group." Her cheeks were flushed, and her voice was rising. "And find out for myself the real reason why Meriwether College is so determined to keep me from asking questions nobody will answer. A memorial fund in Sonya's name isn't enough, Jim. That's a goddamned smokescreen. Something's going on, and I want to know what it is."

Olympia shook a finger in mock warning. "Can't have any negative publicity, can we? Can't have anything that could affect the bottom line, which I'll tell you right now is not the students. It's the law of the profit. I don't care what the damned dean says."

"It's not like you to sound so disillusioned."

"More like fed up, Jim. When I first started teaching, Meriwether College was everything I ever wanted, a small liberal arts institution with a commitment to educating women. I thought I could make a difference here." She shook her head. "It's not like that anymore."

"You're serious."

"I am serious," said Olympia. "Sonya Wilson died on my shift. I'm convinced the college could have done more, and I should have done more myself, but I didn't. So that makes me part of what failed her. I tried, but I lost her."

The priest reached over and laid a gentle hand over her clenched fists.

"You're still trying to find your daughter, aren't you?"

Olympia nodded and blew out a long sigh.

"I suppose it's one of the reasons I entered the ministry, part atonement, part rescue operation, and gratitude for getting a second chance with my two boys. Somebody somewhere has given my daughter a life I couldn't give her when she was born. I'll always keep looking for her, and so I guess I'll always keep trying to rescue lost kids."

"Don't you think that after ..."

Olympia shook her head and interrupted him with an impatient wave of her hands. She was gaining momentum. "Let's get back to this Boston Christian thing. We start by learning all we can."

Jim smiled and nodded. "Then what, *kemo sabe*?"

Olympia grinned. "I can't answer that until I know what we're dealing with. There's time before the students come back in the fall. I won't be working on my house every single minute of the day, you know."

Jim chuckled and shook his head. "I'm not so sure about that. I've seen you do three things at a time, and that's on a bad day."

Olympia nodded in complete agreement.

"If you think about it, that house of yours is really another one of your salvage projects, isn't it? Different day, different tools, but a salvage project nonetheless. You can't help yourself, can you? And when the hell did you take up carpentry?"

"I'm learning as I go. You know, on-the-job training."

Jim groaned. "Tell you what. Give me a day and a time, and I'll show up with hammer in hand. If you make dinner, I'll bring the wine. I need a break from the college and St. Brendan's."

"You could stay over, if you don't mind the mess. I can clear off the sofa." Even though there was no one to hear them, Olympia lowered her voice. "Between you and me, Jim, the place can be a little creepy, especially at night. I hear noises, and it's not the cats. I swear I can hear footsteps or the sound of a door opening. I've never lived in a really old house before." She looked over her glasses. "Actually, Jim, I think I've got a ghost."

"I didn't think anything spooked you, Olympia."

"Not spooked, Jim, more like curious."

His smile was gone. "What do you mean?"

"I'm not sure. Sometimes I get the feeling someone's standing beside me, and I know damn well there's no one there. The cats are picking up on it, too."

"How so?"

"Animals can sense things. Come see for yourself, then you tell me."

"Okay. Call me when you've cleared off a couple of chairs and a table. My days of sitting on the floor and eating spaghetti out of the pot with chopsticks are over."

"Jim?"

"What now?"

Olympia took a deep breath. "I've decided to try and contact her."

"Contact who?"

"My daughter."

"Do you think that's wise after all this time? What about your boys, your ministry, your position at the College?

"I have to, Jim. I can't get on with my life if I don't."

Jim looked at his long-time friend. "You've never told me her name."

"They wouldn't let me name her. They told me it was better that way. When I held her that one time, she was Baby Girl Brown, but in my heart, I've always called her Faith."

Four

July 12, 1859

The dank sea mist continues, three days now. I can barely see the tree my father planted by the northeast wall. I'd hoped the summer's warmth would bring him some relief, but this wretched dampness only makes the cough grow worse. It's more like November than July. I lit a fire just to try and keep him warm, but to no avail.

Last night he said, "Don't sell the house."(Oh, I can hardly bear to write these fateful words.) He insisted that I promise him, and so help me God, I did. More anon.
LFW

Olympia ignored Jim's advice about waiting and by mid-June was camped out in the kitchen of her historic handyman special. The plan was to work her way out from the center of the antiquated mess, cleaning and restoring one dank, musty room at a time. *I might have at least waited until I had hot water,* she thought as she filled the dented aluminum preserving kettle that once was her grandmother's.

She heated the cooking and bathing water on the stove, and when she got desperate, she begged showers from nearby friends. In between, she washed herself standing on a towel at the old soapstone sink, her wet body warmed by the wide swath of sunshine that flooded into her kitchen. Despite the primitive nature of her living conditions, The Reverend, Doctor, Professor, Olympia Brown had never been happier.

Jim was right about one thing, though. She couldn't resist a rescue mission, and this time she had landed herself a doozy with a story to tell. When she first sensed the presence of something besides her in the place, she told herself it was the obvious consequence of living in an old house with so much clutter and forgotten history. But eventually, Olympia could no longer deny the fact that her cherished "antique charmer just loaded with character," as it had been advertised, was really a falling-down heap of a house with a resident ghost.

Now, four weeks after she'd moved in, she was sitting cross-legged in the middle of the aluminum folding cot she had pushed against the window wall in the kitchen, working her way through a mug of cooling coffee and reading the paper. The story was on page three.

Allston College sophomore dies in freak accident.
Allston College sophomore Gregory Vanderloop died accidentally yesterday while practicing for an upcoming swim meet. Indications are that Mr. Vanderloop was taken violently ill while swimming laps in the college swimming pool. It is believed that he must have aspirated water and drowned. By the time fellow swim team members noticed he was not moving, it was too late to revive him. He was pronounced dead at St. Elisabeth's Hospital in Brighton. Police officials have ruled the death an accident. At this time, funeral arrangements are incomplete.

Olympia reread the headline. Jim was the Chaplain at Allston College.

With a rush of guilt she realized she had been so wrapped up with the house that she had not given much thought to investigating religious cults. So when the phone rang, Olympia jumped, kicked over her coffee, booted the cats, and grabbed it on the second ring.

It was Jim. "Olympia, I think we've got another one."

"Another what? What are you talking about?"

"It's in this morning's *Globe*. I tried calling you earlier, but the line was busy. One of my students drowned yesterday. He was practicing for a swim meet."

"I just read it. Did you know him?"

"I did. The article in the paper doesn't mention that he was a member of that Boston Christian group we've been trying to investigate. He came to me on the Q.T. because he'd become disillusioned and was trying get out. He said they were pressuring him to stay and actually starting to threaten him."

Olympia could hear the strain in her friend's voice.

"They couldn't revive him. He left campus in a body bag."

Olympia shuddered. "Jim, we've each had a student with ties to this Boston Christian group die in a freak accident within the last eight weeks. Do you think there's a connection?"

"Could well be," said Jim. "After your freshman died, I tried talking to a couple of them, members of the Fellowship, that is. I kept it casual, just asking about what they were doing."

"And?" prompted Olympia, looking around for something to do. She picked up a sponge and started wiping down the wooden counter next to the sink. "What did they say?"

"Nothing," said Jim, "just lots of sweetness and Christian platitudes coming from long-haired people wearing loose-fitting clothes. It sounded memorized. There's no way to get next to them unless you're a member."

"Or thinking about becoming one," said Olympia. "Maybe we could approach it from that angle. What are you doing tomorrow? I may have an idea."

"Greg was really bright," said Jim, not responding to her question. "He was a double major, pre-med and religion. He used to come in to my office and discuss theology and medical ethics. For a while, I thought he was headed for the priesthood."

"Can you meet me tomorrow morning at the Divinity School Library around ten?" said Olympia.

"Why there?"

Olympia laid down the sponge, made her way around the clutter in the middle of the floor to the refrigerator, and took out a bottle of diet soda. It was still early but already too warm to think about any more coffee.

"Didn't you tell me you met a cult expert from Harvard last spring? Besides, the Div School's got to be a warehouse of information on religion and everything connected to it. They must have a huge database. I'm still a virtual illiterate when it comes to those things, but somebody will be able to help us. We've only got five weeks before the students come back in September."

"Point made," said Jim. "I'll shift a few things around and meet you at ten."

"Meanwhile," said Olympia, "ask around, see what else you can learn about your student's death. Call the police and the first responders. You're a priest, they'll talk to you. Then, changing the subject, "If you want to make good on that offer of a hand and a paint brush some time, I could use it. I need your perspective on something that may or may not be going on down here."

"Like what?"

"Remember me telling you the place was kind of spooky?"

"Mmm, yes."

"Well, now I'm convinced there's a spirit here, and I think that he or she doesn't like me poking around."

"You need your priest friend to come down and do an exorcism?"

"I don't know what to think. Something's going on, strange sounds, sudden cold spots in the middle of this heat. Every so often the cats totally freak, you know, arched backs, bottlebrush tails, spitting and hissing, and there's nothing there."

"I think this house project is getting to you, Olympia. It's not like you to delve into the paranormal. I've known you for too long. You're the Reverend Doctor, Ms. Nuts and Bolts, Show It to Me and Then Maybe I'll Believe It lady."

"I'm a minister, Jim. I believe in God, don't I? That's about as paranormal as it gets. I tell you, something or someone that I can't see is making a fuss down here, and I want to know who it is."

From the change in his voice, Olympia knew she'd made her point. "Okay. Are you going to be home all day? Might as well give me directions."

Good old Jim. Olympia caught the sight of her grateful grin in the shiny curve of the coffee pot.

"I'm not ready for paint yet but I could sure use someone to hold a rubbish bag for me. You were right about one thing. This place *has* turned out to be one hell of a lot more work than I bargained for. What do you want for dinner?"

"Why don't we go out? You sound like you could use a night off, and I know I could."

"Bring your sleeping bag. You can crash on the couch. That way, we can drive into Cambridge together. I'll take the bus back. We can catch each other up on this cult business as well as think about what to do next. I'm afraid I haven't accomplished much in that department."

That evening, when they had come back from dinner and were sitting at the kitchen table sipping their wine, whoever or whatever it was that was hovering in the dusty corners of Olympia's two-hundred-fifty-year-old home chose to remain aloof.

Just like a damn kid, thought Olympia. *When you want them to perform, they never do.*

The following day, when they had finished up at the Divinity School Library, Jim let Olympia out at the train station in Harvard Square, but instead of taking the train to South Station and catching the bus home, Olympia got off in downtown Boston. When she came up out of the cool damp of the underground, she turned right, walked across a sweltering concrete plaza and into Boston's City Hall, and took the elevator to the department of records.

She had given birth to Baby Girl Brown exactly thirty three years ago. Today, on her birthday, she would give permission for her daughter Faith to open the records and contact her, if she so wished.

Five

By mid-August, Olympia and Jim had little more than a few statistics and some basic demographic information regarding the Boston Christian Common Fellowship. She was tired and frustrated with their lack of progress, and on a more personal level, she was lonely. Jim was her best friend, but he was gay. She hadn't had a real date in over a year, and from time to time, even ministers need a little action in the private life department.

Olympia looked at the cat calendar on the kitchen wall. Classes began in a week and a half. The kitchen still needed finish carpentry, and she was awaiting the delivery and installation of a woodstove. This she would hook into the fireplace that was the focal point of the room next to the kitchen. One day, she would scrape off the hideous pink-beige paint a previous owner used to cover the original brick surrounding the fire pit, but that would be a winter job.

Olympia knew that before she started one more project, she needed a break from everything domestic and academic. Her ghostly housemate was still in sporadic evidence, but she'd come to accept it. *Or maybe it's the other way around, and my vaporous friend is beginning to accept me. Will I ever know?*

On a calculated impulse, she picked up the phone and asked a neighbor to feed and water the cats for a couple of days. Then she dug around and unearthed a dusty but serviceable tent, her sleeping bag, and a few basic cooking supplies. Thus equipped, she drove due north to a campground on the Maine coast just north of Portland and a whole world away from anything religious, academic, personal — or spectral. She had discovered Pinewoods years ago, and for all the right reasons, she had kept the information to herself.

That night, wearing baggy jeans and her favorite worn-at-the-elbows plaid shirt, Olympia made her way out of the woods and joined the other urban escapees around the community campfire. She was sitting on a tree stump, trying not to spill a mug full of wine and keep her marshmallow from turning into volcanic dust, when an Englishman named Frederick Watkins claimed the log to her immediate right.

He had thinning hair, gentle eyes, a charming accent, and, she soon ascertained, he was single. At the end of a companionable evening, the two repaired to their separate sleeping quarters but agreed to spend the next morning together exploring local hiking trails and getting to know one another a bit more. By lunch time, they both agreed it was unfortunate that London, England, and Brookfield, Massachusetts, were so far apart.

Later still, while splashing through tide pools and admiring the dramatic, rock-bound coast of New England, Olympia offered to drive him to Boston when she went back. "It's right on the way, she said, "and we can continue the conversation."

On the four-plus hour meander to the city, Frederick peeled oranges and held Olympia's coffee as she negotiated the intricacies of the uncharted scenic byways of coastal New England. By the time she dropped him off in front of Boston's historic South Station, they had exchanged phone numbers and addresses, astrological signs, and more than a few stolen glances.

His first letter arrived in less than a week, and on the following morning, Olympia stopped off at the local post office and mailed a guardedly enthusiastic response. Then, with an enormous smile on her middle-aged face, she climbed back into her ancient VW van, shifted into first gear, and drove north to begin her twenty-seventh first day of school.

Six

In Cambridge, a late summer heat wave held everyone and everything in its sweaty grip. Olympia Brown was wearing as little in the way of clothing as she dared, a sleeveless linen tunic over a pair of loose-fitting slacks, and still she felt the sweat following the downward curve of her spine and soaking into the waistband of her underwear. She wanted to run around and shake herself dry like a dog at the beach, but she opted for fanning herself with the attendance folder

She stood, leaning against the chalkboard, watching the new freshmen trickle into the classroom and smiling when one or another of them looked up and caught her eye. They were so young and trying so hard not to look that way. College fashion changed over the years, but the anxiety of their newness never did. Within days they would learn the routine, know where everything was and who to go to for what crisis, but today they moved cautiously, trying to slip into the academic world as though they had always been there.

I wonder if Faith went to college, and if so, which one? Might I even have had her in a class and not known it?

Meriwether College had been founded in the 1920s as a two-year finishing school for the daughters of socially prominent Boston and Cambridge families. The original campus was a cluster of converted, mid-Victorian mansions located in a fashionable part of the city. Over the years, as the curriculum became more rigorous, the grand old homesteads that served as the first classrooms were gradually replaced with more modern structures or relegated to the status of dormitory or faculty offices.

More recently, as both the enrollment and the endowment dwindled, so did the pace of progress. Rather than move with the times, the board of overseers and the college administration were becoming more and more conservative and restrictive. Academic freedom was being replaced by academic caution.

Olympia was thinking about all of this as she went over to the window, turned the speed on the fan up another notch and stood directly in front of it. She held her arms away from her body, cooling herself down in the noisy breeze and giving the inevitable latecomers a few more minutes before she began her annual first-day ritual.

Listening to the light ripple of female voices over the clatter of the fan, she recalled the day less than a year ago when Sonya Wilson walked into this very same class. The dark shadow of the girl's death hovered in the empty hallways and would continue to do so until the questions surrounding her disturbing death were resolved.

Olympia looked toward the door one last time, took a deep breath and picked up a blue folder. As she moved to her accustomed spot in front of the chalk board next to her desk, she was more and more certain that this would be her last year in academia Added to that, her relationship with the Dean had become all but intolerable, armed neutrality held in place by her tenured position and his administrative rank.

Olympia pulled herself back into the present and squared her shoulders as the students shifted and then straightened up in their seats.

"Good afternoon, ladies," said Professor Olympia Brown. "I think there still might be one or two students who haven't arrived, but I think it's time we got started." Whereupon, as if it had been planned, the last student entered and slipped into an empty seat near the back.

Despite the oppressive heat and the current fashion of shredded jeans and bare midriffs, the girl was modestly dressed in an ankle-length skirt and long-sleeved flowered blouse. She had dark, intense eyes and hair the color of oak leaves in the fall, but today, her damp, coppery curls were plastered to her neck and forehead.

Catching her eye, Olympia said, "Why don't you sit up here nearer the fan? You'll roast sitting back there in the direct sun."

"I'm used to heat, Professor." But she stood up and moved to the front of the room, away from the safety and anonymity of the back. "I'm sorry for being late. Things move so fast here. I'm not used to it all yet." She flashed an impish grin at Olympia. "I think even the clocks go quicker east of the Mississippi."

She took an empty seat in the front row, carefully leaving as much space as she could between herself and the girl seated next to her. "Is this one okay, Professor Brown?"

"Much better, and you can call me Olympia, everybody else does. What's your name?"

"Bethany Ruth McAllister, Professor." The words tumbled out in a self-conscious burst. Then the overdressed young woman bent over, burrowed into her backpack, and came up with two pencils, a ball point pen, a notebook, and finally a Bible. All of these she set out in a row on the table in front of herself, building a wall and setting the stage for her first day at college.

Looking down at the girl, Olympia wondered about the significance of the clothing and the Bible. Clearly she was making a statement, but what was it? Taking a second look at her loose-fitting clothing, Olympia wondered if the girl might actually be a member of that fellowship group she and Jim were trying to investigate. No, it couldn't be. She was too innocent and eager to please. Olympia dismissed the uncomfortable thought and began calling out the names on her list.

On that particular first day of school, she was in no position to anticipate what awaited the modestly clad young woman with the riot of rust-colored curls and her restless, middle-aged, professor. Right now, all that concerned Olympia was learning their names and not passing out from the unrelenting heat of the early September day.

Seven

In all her life, Bethany Ruth never felt so far away from home. This was a cherished dream, hard earned, and finally come true, but now that she was here, could she keep up? Everyone around her looked like they knew what they were doing. Her father told her she had one year to prove herself, and if she managed it, then maybe she could stay for another.

In her home town of Stillwell, Oklahoma, Nazarene girls like her were raised to be good wives and mothers. A college education, when it was possible, was usually reserved for boys, who would be expected to support a family. With the encouragement of teachers who recognized her potential, Bethany Ruth persisted and eventually persuaded her parents to let her try, but only because it was an all-women's college with a strong emphasis on religion and ethics in the curriculum.

She accepted the challenge, earned herself several scholarships, and filled in the rest with student loans and a work-study grant. Now, with her Bible on the table in front of her and her heart hammering in her chest, she was prepared to do her best.

When Professor Brown finished calling attendance, she stood at the front the room, held out her arms and smiled. Bethany Ruth liked that smile.

"Welcome, ladies. My name is Olympia Brown, and my job this semester is to help you to understand the relationship between the humanities, the arts and religion. I believe the best way to go about your introduction to a subject like this is to actually get in there and get your hands messy." She held up a paint brush in one hand and a bottle of yellow poster paint in the other.

Bethany Ruth joined the collective groan as Olympia covered her ears in mock horror and said, "Quiet, all of you." She pretended to be yelling, but she was really grinning at them. "I promise this won't hurt a bit. I haven't lost a student in years.

Oh, but I have.

"Before we actually begin, I'd like each one of you to stand up, say your name, where you come from, and something about yourself you would like us to know. Who would like to go first?"

Bethany Ruth examined the cuff of her blouse. There was no way she'd be first. She would play it safe and listen to the others, then decide what and how much to say about herself and her life back home. When it was her turn to speak, she stood and turned to face the rest of the students seated around her.

"My name is Bethany Ruth McAllister." She was suddenly conscious of her midwestern drawl. "I come from Stillwell, Oklahoma, and I was raised in a good Christian home with my two older brothers and my two younger sisters. Before last week, I'd never been anywhere farther east than the state of Ohio, and I feel very blessed and excited, and to be honest, just a little bit scared to be here."

Professor Brown nodded, so Bethany Ruth continued. "I have a dog named Betsy, and I taught arts and crafts at a summer Bible camp to earn money to get here." Flashing a quick smile at her teacher, she sank down into her seat, blew out a long breath, and slowly traced the gilt edge of the Bible with her finger.

When the students had all spoken, the Professor took her own turn.

"You already know my name. I'm an ordained minister, I live with two cats in an antique farm house about an hour south of here, and I have two sons, both in college. Besides being a Professor, I'm also the college chaplain. So, if you ever need someone to talk to about anything at all," she pointed to the doorway behind her, "my office is right through there. Drop in any time, or call and make an appointment."

Bethany Ruth felt better. She liked knowing something about her teachers. It made them seem more like real people. Not only that, Professor Brown liked animals, and she was the college chaplain. If she ever did need someone to talk to, this was who it would be.

"And now," said Olympia, walking toward the supply closet in the corner, "I'll need someone to help me pass out materials."

Before Olympia finished her sentence, Bethany Ruth was standing next to her ready to receive the first carton of supplies. As though they had always done it, teacher and student handed out pencils, paints, brushes, paper, and for each and every young woman in the room, a brand new box of Crayola crayons.

The cautious mood in the room evaporated, and the wary, self-conscious students who had entered the room not twenty minutes earlier were now acting like happy children. They were all tearing open the packaging, feeling the brushes, testing the pencils, and more than a few of them smelling the crayons before dumping them out on the table and trying out the colors.

After a few minutes, Olympia asked them to take out a pen or a pencil and please open their notebooks to the letter A for art. Bethany Ruth watched as a few students actually started to look for the A section, but at least three others besides her caught the joke and giggled.

"Gotcha," said Professor Brown with a wink and a broad grin, "and just for the record, that will not be on the exam."

Bethany Ruth smiled for the second time that day.

Eight

By late September, classes were well under way, and Bethany Ruth was appointed as Olympia's student assistant. To outward appearances, the shy young woman from Bible-belt Oklahoma seemed to be settling into college life. If Olympia had a concern, it was that the girl spent too much time hanging around the classroom and not out socializing with people her own age.

On the other hand, at her professor's suggestion, she had joined a lunchtime Bible study group, so she was doing something with her peers. Olympia wished it was more, but she reminded herself that some just take longer than others.

At home in Brookfield, she was almost finished with the kitchen and was starting the great room which adjoined it. She had received three more letters from Frederick Watkins, and the restless soul that was sharing the old farmhouse with her was becoming more predictable in his or her activities—or possibly more amenable to Olympia's presence.

How do you make friends with a ghost, and is it a him or a her?

On the Monday after the long Columbus Day weekend, Olympia was sitting in her cluttered office with her grade book in her lap, her feet propped up on the edge of the

desk, and a stack of untouched papers in front of her.
There was a voice message from Jim asking her to give him
a call when she got a chance.

*Maybe he's turned up something on that Boston Fellowship
group,* she thought with a sigh of guilt and a glance at the
phone. Neither of them had had much time for
investigating anything since the start of classes, but to be
fair, nothing had happened to arouse any concern.

She opened the grade book and began doodling on the
inside cover, thinking about Bethany Ruth. The girl was a
terrific help in the classroom, but other than the weekly
Bible group, she wasn't really socially involved in the
student community. Olympia wasn't ready to be worried,
but she was concerned.

Olympia thought back to the dean's oblique warning
to the faculty at the beginning of the semester. He told the
faculty to be on the lookout for students with problems or
who might be at risk, but he never exactly said at risk for
what. Then she recalled Sonya Wilson, the girl who joined
the religious cult and starved herself to death. *Bethany Ruth
is nothing like Sonya,* thought Olympia, *she's just shy and
homesick. She'll get over it. They eventually do.*

Olympia eyed the phone and twirled a yellow pencil
between her fingers. She could hear the clicking and
clanking of the steam radiators coming on and warming
up the drafty old building. There was already a chill in the
air outside, and forecasters were predicting an early
winter. She would call Jim later.

Olympia's thoughtful solitude ended with the bubbly
chatter of students returning from their first long weekend
away. She sighed and dropped the pencil back in the

marmalade jar at the back of her desk. *Time to go to work.*

After class, Olympia and Bethany Ruth were putting away the rulers and scissors they had used in that day's lesson. Bethany Ruth was chattering on, as she did, about her family, her church in Oklahoma, and her beloved dog Betsy, but she said little about anything here and now in Cambridge, Massachusetts. Olympia understood that talking about home seemed to help with her continuing homesickness. *At least she's still here,* thought Olympia. *The really bad ones drop out by now.*

"Where do these go, Professor Brown?" Bethany Ruth stood with an armload of scissors.

Olympia was reminded that the girl never used her given name. "Over there somewhere. Anywhere you can find an empty space."

"Professor," said Bethany Ruth, with a broad grin, "in this place, there's no such thing."

"Well, then, put them somewhere where they won't cascade all over the next class, and let's go get a coffee. All this cleaning makes me weary, and in the middle of the afternoon I need a jolt of something serious to keep me going."

Olympia had grown quite fond of Bethany Ruth. Their coffee visits were a way to befriend the lonely young woman without appearing to be making too much of a fuss over her.

In the office they collected sweaters and backpacks and walked out to the chilly vestibule. The heavily carved front door of the old building always stuck, and Olympia had to give it a kick to get it open. Once outside, they were rewarded with an October day that was bright and crisp and picture-book lovely. The hundred-year-old oaks and maples along the streets were splashed with color in dramatic contrast to the dark green pines growing next to them. It was fall in New England, and Victorian Cambridge was dressed to kill.

The two walked side-by-side across the postage stamp quadrangle toward the snack bar. Bethany Ruth was scuffling through the crackly leaves that were already beginning to collect along the brick pathways, and she was calling out and waving to other students along the way.

"Looks like you've made some friends," said Olympia as they reached the door of the snack bar and collided, each trying to hold the door for the other.

"I'm getting to know a couple of girls by name, if that's what you mean. They're from that Bible group you told me about. They're nice."

Olympia laid claim to a table and then made for the counter. She ordered her much-needed coffee and for Bethany Ruth, orange juice and a chocolate chip cookie. Early on Olympia asked if she wanted coffee or tea. She knew that as a Nazarene, Bethany Ruth didn't drink alcohol or anything containing caffeine, but sweets and more specifically, chocolate chip cookies, were not on the forbidden list. Homesickness had not diminished her appetite, and while the few extra pounds she carried might not be fashionable in the current decade of broom-handle-thin models, a hundred years earlier her rounded curves would have been an artist's delight.

Over the weeks, sitting elbow to elbow across from one another, Olympia learned the details of Bethany Ruth's life, about the family's modest circumstances, their religious and social conservatism, and her parents' fierce resistance to their lovely, innocent daughter going to college so far away from home. Although it was still months away, she was already talking about Christmas. The previous day she had confided that going home for Thanksgiving would be too expensive, so she planned to stay in Cambridge and help out at a homeless shelter with her Bible study friends.

Olympia's first reaction was to ask the girl to spend the holiday weekend with her and her family in Brookfield, but in the interest of Bethany's connecting with people her own age, she decided to hold off and see if maybe her roommate or one of the other students might extend an invitation. *Best to let her sort it out on her own and not intervene.*

"Christmas Eve is the best," Bethany Ruth was smiling and talking through a mouthful of cookie. "It's just the family. We have supper, and then we all go to church. But Christmas day, all the aunts and the uncles and the cousins come to our house. My mom cooks for weeks."

"It sounds wonderful," said Olympia, catching the girl's infectious enthusiasm.

"This year, my twin nephews will be there. They were born on Christmas Eve last year. They might even be walking. I haven't seen them since …"

She couldn't go on. In the space of an instant, her exuberance for Christmas became a wrenching longing for home, and huge tears welled up in her deep-set, green-brown eyes. Olympia patted her arm and held out a paper napkin. Bethany Ruth wiped her eyes, blew her nose and whispered, "I'm sorry, Professor."

Olympia waved her hand in a universal never-mind-it's-okay gesture and handed over her second cookie.

"Here," she said, "take this and call me in the morning. Chocolate chips cure anything from colds to hemorrhoids. Might as well try it on homesickness."

At that, Bethany Ruth managed a feeble grin and accepted the cookie. Olympia swallowed the last of her coffee and looked up at the clock on the wall. They each had a class in ten minutes.

Olympia walked back to her office inhaling the sharp scent of dried leaves and the yellow chrysanthemums planted in bright clusters around the campus. She loved the colors and the smells of autumn, but she was puzzling about Bethany Ruth. The girl was a walking dichotomy with a midwestern drawl. She was bright and sincere with an impish sense of humor, and all of it was wrapped up in the modestly dressed, eyes-downcast demeanor of a devout Nazarene Christian woman.

Olympia wondered how much of a burden all of this might be. *I worry too much,* she thought, shaking her head and yanking open the cranky door to her building. *She's homesick, and she's a late bloomer, but she's definitely making progress, no doubt about that.*

Nine

"I think we might have a serious prospect, Brother David." Sister Miriam smiled, then lowered her eyes and began smoothing her skirt over her knees.

She and Brother Joshua were sitting side by side on an oversized sofa in the spacious living room of the Brighton residence. Brother David, personal assistant to the leader of the Fellowship, stood over them, leaning on the wide, painted mantel surrounding the fireplace. Sister Sarah was sitting off by herself nearer the window.

Over the years the one-time formal sitting room in the grand old house had been furnished with chairs and sofas collected and donated by various members. These had been uniformly covered with off-white canvas slipcovers. The walls and molded ceiling were painted the color of beach sand and the woodwork a shade lighter. The overall effect was a communal space that was open, clean, and functional with no hint of personal warmth. There were no pictures or mirrors on the walls, not even a plant in a window—nothing to distract the minds of brothers and sisters who interpreted the Bible, and more specifically, the second commandment, literally.

Thou shalt not make unto thee any graven image, or any likeness of any thing that is in heaven above, or that is in the earth beneath, or that is in the water under the earth: Thou shalt not bow down thyself to them, nor serve them: for I the Lord thy God am a jealous God, visiting the iniquity of the fathers upon the children unto the third and fourth generation of them that hate me; And showing mercy unto thousands of them that love me, and keep my commandments. (Exodus 20:4-6)

Brother David moved to a chair nearer to Sister Sarah. "How did this new one learn about us?"

"It's a young woman. She's been going to the Bible study group at Meriwether College. Then she went to one of the Sunday rock concerts on the Common. That's what got her interested."

"These lunchtime Bible groups seem to be a good idea, Sister Sarah. This is the second one this year that is showing interest. I think we should continue them for the foreseeable future."

Sister Sarah seemed to be both pleased and flustered at the unaccustomed praise. She flashed a half-smile in David's direction and then, like Miriam, lowered her eyes.

Ten

October 7, 1859
Father left his earthly life today. I was at his side until the
end. I had so many plans, but this changes everything, and I
am truly alone. On the one hand, no one can stop me from
doing whatever I wish to do – but no one can help me, either.
More anon ... LFW

After two hours on the phone with the Yellow Pages in her lap, Olympia finally located a chimney person who agreed to take a look at her fireplace flue. The weather was getting colder, and there was no way in heaven or hell she had been able to get her new woodstove to draw properly and stay lighted. The man who installed it assured her there was more than enough circulation in a drafty old house like this to maintain a steady fire, and the chimney, old as it was, was up to the task.

"So why can't I keep a fire going?" she asked the man with the name Archie embroidered on the pocket of his shirt. He was standing, hands in his back pockets, between her and the recalcitrant stove, looking around the room.

"Nice brickwork around the fireplace, Reverend Brown," he replied, not addressing her question. "Looks like the original. It's a shame somebody painted over it with that beige crap. I love old houses. I'll bet there's a lot of history in these walls."

"I'm going to strip off that god-awful paint and expose the brick." Olympia pointed to a spot under the mantel overhang. "See, I scraped some off. It's beautiful underneath. It's going to take me a while, but I'm going to bring this house back to as much of its original design and structure as I can."

"You'll have your hands full," said the man, grunting heavily as he knelt beside the stove and angled himself so he could peer up the chimney.

"See anything?" asked Olympia.

He wiggled the damper, opening and closing it a couple of times. "Nope, damper's okay. Let's try lighting it again. Maybe you don't know how to set a fire."

Olympia gritted her teeth and growled under her breath. She'd been a wilderness camper before this guy was out of short pants and had probably set more fires than he'd had peanut butter sandwiches, but she smiled sweetly and said, "Oh, yes, please show me."

To her surprise and delight, the fire blazed and soon spread its cozy warmth throughout the room.

"May have been the wind when you tried it before," he said, "These things back-puff like crazy on an east wind. Right off the ocean, you know."

I know.

"Plays hell with the draft. If it acts up again, I'll come back and put a cowl on the chimney."

Olympia stepped back as Archie stood and dusted off his knees. He reached up and ran his fingers around the wide-cut paneling above the mantel.

"You know, I think this place is old enough. Mid-1700s, right? I'll bet you've got a parson's cupboard in here. Hey, look at that, son of a gun, you do."

Before Olympia had time to ask what a parson's cupboard was, he slipped his fingers behind a raised bead on the wall and lifted out a square panel to reveal a dusty interior filled with yet more clutter for her to clean out.

"Why is it called a parson's cupboard?"

Archie winked and placed his index finger against his nose. "That's where they hid the booze when the parson came to call."

Olympia giggled. "How appropriate, me being a minister and all." Olympia stood on her toes trying to see inside. All she could see were rags and bits of paper that looked and smelled really old.

"Well that's a good project for a rainy day," said Olympia, thanking the man and getting out her check book. "Who do I make this out to?"

"Spencer Archibald, but everyone calls me Archie." The man lingered, looking up at the opening. "I'll bet the stuff hasn't seen the light of day in years."

It was obvious that he was positively itching to start exploring right there and then, but for reasons she couldn't begin to explain, she knew this was something she needed to do by herself.

"I'm afraid it's going to be a while before I can get to it." She held out the check. "I've got all I can handle right now getting the house ready for winter, and I can't take on another sorting project. There's so much I don't know about this place. I discover something new almost every day."

"If that's the case, you might try nosing around town hall and the historical society. They have family records and stuff from these old houses going back to the 1600s. This one was built by a Mayflower Winslow, I know that much. I'm a bit of a local historian. Say, if you come up with something interesting or you have any questions, give me a call. Maybe I can help you research it."

Olympia pocketed her pen and assured him she would. She wondered for a fleeting moment if the man was interested in more than just historical research.

Eleven

By late October Bethany Ruth was definitely settling into college life. Her Bible stayed inside her backpack now, and their coffee conversations were beginning to include stories about her roommate Wanda and a couple of other students.

On the Thursday before Halloween, Bethany Ruth said she and her roommate and a couple of other girls from the dorm were going to a free rock concert in Boston on that weekend. The mother in Olympia rose to the surface, and she automatically cautioned the girl to be careful when going into the city, put emergency telephone money in her shoe, and not talk to strangers.

"Geeez, Professor," said Bethany Ruth, "I'm going with a bunch of people from here, what can happen? The girl who leads the Bible study group told me about it. It sounds like fun."

"I still want you to be careful," said Olympia, bending down to pick up a scrap of paper on the floor. "You're still new to city life, and Boston is even bigger and faster than Cambridge. Just keep your eyes and ears open, and be careful what you say to people you don't know."

Olympia remembered having this same conversation with her own sons the first time they had gone into Boston alone. *They didn't listen either.*

"I'll be fine, Professor," said Bethany Ruth. "We've gone before."

By mid-November Bethany Ruth still didn't have any plans for Thanksgiving, and Olympia decided to take action. The two were standing elbow-to-elbow at the sink, chatting and cleaning paint brushes, when she found the opportunity.

"Bethany Ruth," Olympia began, shaking the water off her hands and reaching for a towel, "do you have any plans for Thanksgiving? If you don't, I'd like ..."

"Oh, Professor Brown, wait till you hear. Remember I told you I've been going to those rock concerts in Boston? They have one every Sunday on Boston Common, and the people who run them invited me to stay with them over Thanksgiving. They're a Christian Fellowship, and they have a place in Allston."

Olympia's internal warning signals were going off like air horns on an eighteen-wheeler, but she willed her face and voice into neutral and handed Bethany Ruth a wet paper towel.

"Here," she said, "get the paint off your hands, and let's go have a coffee. You can tell me all about them."

Olympia swished out the sink one last time and set the tattered sponge on the side to dry. "My son Malcolm plays in a rock group. I wonder if he's heard of them. I'll have to ask him when I see him on Thanksgiving." She hoped to heaven she was sounding curious and not horrified. "Come on, you," she said, taking Bethany Ruth's two damp hands in hers. "I need caffeine."

Olympia hunched her shoulders against the deepening chill of the late November afternoon and wished she'd remembered her hat. By the feel of it, it was going to be an early winter. Bethany Ruth fished a pair of bright red mittens out of her pocket and tucked her scarf tighter around her neck. As they talked, their words made white puffs in the dusky cold.

Inside the coffee shop, Bethany Ruth made a dash to their favorite table while Olympia went to pick up their usual order — coffee, orange juice, and two oversized chocolate chip cookies. Thinking she might need fortification, she added a third.

Once they were seated with the assorted goodies spread out between them, Olympia looked across the table at the lovely, wide-eyed girl and silently prayed for guidance. She stirred, then tasted, her coffee, stalling for time. "Before you tell me about your new friends, I have a question for you."

Bethany Ruth looked up, "Yes, Professor?"

"Back in the sink room I started to ask you about Thanksgiving, and you told me you'd been invited to stay with these Christian Fellowship people. Well, I was going to ask you to come home with me for the holiday — you know, traditional New England Thanksgiving with all the trimmings. You can still come if you want to."

Bethany Ruth's initial response was a sudden intake of breath and the most beautiful smile Olympia had ever seen, which was instantly replaced by a polite and more distant look.

"Oh, gosh, Professor Brown," she said, hesitating as though she didn't know how to say what she was about to say. "That's so nice of you, but I'll be okay. She looked around the room before leaning closer to tell Olympia that she had been invited to spend the long weekend at The

Boston Christian Common Fellowship Renewal Center in Brighton. "Instead of eating a big piggy meal," she ran her fingers through her hair in excitement, "we'll spend the weekend in prayer and Bible study. On Thanksgiving Day we'll go out into the streets and work with the homeless, you know, bringing them food and blankets. It's our Christian commitment to the poor and needy in the world. We did the same thing with my church back in Oklahoma." Bethany Ruth looked up at the woman sitting across from her and grinned. "Only we ate Thanksgiving dinner first."

Olympia picked up her hot coffee and blew on it out of habit. She spoke carefully. "I know you've been looking for a Christian group to socialize with," said Olympia, reaching for a cookie. "Sounds like you might have found it. What else do you know about them? I'm interested in anything to do with religion."

Bethany Ruth leaned back in her chair and smiled. Whatever her involvement might be, it hadn't dimmed her enthusiasm for the sound of her own voice.

"Oh, Professor, they're so loving, you can't imagine, and if you hadn't told me about the lunchtime Bible study group, I might never have met them. The girl who leads it is called Sarah, but I don't know her last name. I think she's Jewish. She told me about the concerts. She said I might like them, and so I went with my roommate. Remember me telling you? So I guess I have you to thank you for that."

Olympia nodded slowly, taking in every breathless word. *Oh child,* she lamented in her heart, *what in God's name have I done?* There was so much she wanted to say — to scream really, but she bit her lip and listened.

"I met a woman named Sister Miriam and a man named Brother Joshua. Last Sunday they invited me to go back to their Christian Renewal Center in Brighton." In her enthusiasm, Bethany Ruth almost knocked over her orange juice. "They were so nice to me, Professor. They even dress like me."

"How so?" asked Olympia. *Keep her talking.*

Bethany Ruth jumped up and twirled around. "See," she said, pointing to herself. "Nazarene women dress modestly. I think most of the women there have long hair, but they cover it, so I couldn't really tell."

Olympia knew if she said one word in opposition, she would lose Bethany Ruth's confidence.

"So," Olympia drained the last of her coffee and considered a second cookie. When she was nervous or upset, food was her tranquilizer, and she didn't need a prescription. She reached for the cookie.

"When do they meet, and what do they do when they're all together?"

"We meet …"

Olympia's heart sank at hearing the change in pronouns from *they* to *we*.

"… after the concert on Sundays. We go back to the Renewal Center." Bethany Ruth was warming to her subject. "We invite anybody who comes to the concerts to come and have supper with us. Afterwards, we sit around a fire in the living room and have Bible study."

All Olympia dared do was nod encouragement.

"Oh, Professor Brown," said Bethany Ruth. "I've been so lonely here, and I'm not anymore. Someday I hope you meet Joshua and Miriam. Some of them take Biblical names when they join."

The excited girl pushed a flyaway curl behind her ear. "They've already asked me to think about joining them, but I haven't told them I will, yet. I love my church in Oklahua, but they all want me to, especially Miriam and Joshua. They'll be my guardian angels, once I become an aspirant," she bubbled, "you know, watch over me and help me learn things."

"Think carefully," said Olympia, keeping her voice level. "It's a big step. You know some religious groups ..." She caught herself and changed direction. "Tell me what happens in the training period?"

Olympia couldn't tell Bethany Ruth that the Boston Christian Common Fellowship was the religious cult specifically banned from recruiting new members at Meriwether. *What about the Bible study group? Is that just a coincidence, or is there a connection?* She could feel her heart hammering in her chest and hoped it wasn't audible across the table.

"Have you told your parents?" Olympia chose her words. If the girl shut down, there might be no hope of intervention.

"I haven't told them everything yet." She was folding and refolding her napkin. "Sister Miriam and Brother Joshua told me all I needed to say was that I found some Christians to witness and fellowship with. So that's what I told them."

"And they were okay with that?"

"They were more than okay, Professor. They said that they could stop worrying about me. Mama said I finally sounded happy."

"Well, then," said Olympia, holding tightly to a delicate strand of hope, "that explains where you'll be for

Thanksgiving, but what about Christmas? I'll bet you're counting the days. It'll be great for you to be home with your family and your dog after all this time."

Bethany Ruth hesitated, and Olympia watched as a glass wall slipped down between them.

"I'm not going," she said, looking down at the table and squashing a cookie crumb with her fingertip. "Miriam and Joshua said that if I liked it there, I could move in over the holidays. If I do everything right, they'll let me enter the First Circle right after Christmas. We don't do gifts or trees or anything. That's pagan devil worship."

Olympia didn't know what do with her hands or the expression on her face and prayed that her mounting horror was not apparent.

"We'll honor the birth and life of Jeshua, that's what we call Jesus, by tending His beloved poor."

"But Bethany Ruth," Olympia's voice was rising, "you worked so hard to get the bus fare. You already have your ticket."

"I got a refund. I'm giving the money to the Fellowship for part of my tithe." Bethany Ruth reached for her coat. "I have to go, Professor."

"Your parents will be heartbroken," said Olympia, grasping in vain at vanishing straws.

"I don't think you can understand how much this means to me. They didn't want me to tell you."

Olympia's eyebrows went up of their own accord.

Bethany Ruth stood up and began to wind her scarf around her neck. "They said you'd try and stop me, but I told you anyway because I wanted you to be happy for me." For a fleeting second, her guard was down, and the innocent freshman she first met looked into her professor's eyes.

Into that tiny window Olympia whispered, "I want the best for you, Bethie. Just keep in touch, and let me know how you're doing?"

"I'll try, but ..." Bethany Ruth was looking away and twisting her fingers. "Sister Miriam said I'm only supposed to talk to you about school stuff. I wasn't even supposed to tell you this much, but I didn't want you to think I was mad at you or anything. You've been so nice to me."

"But Beth—"

"I hope you have a nice Thanksgiving, Professor, and thank you for inviting me." She was almost to the door.

There were so many things Olympia wanted to say, but she settled for, "Remember, keep in touch."

Bethany Ruth smiled in response, then turned and let the door swing shut behind her.

Olympia was stunned. She looked around the nearly deserted room and started to pick up the empty cups and napkins from the table when she realized the orange juice and cookies she'd gotten for Bethany Ruth were still on the table.

Twelve

"There's no doubt she's interested," said Brother Joshua, leaning back and stretching his feet towards the fire. "She's coming for Thanksgiving."

The elite Third Circle members of the Boston Christian Common Fellowship were sitting together digesting the evening meal and discussing the progress of their new recruit.

"How long have you been working on this one?" asked David. "Less than a month, isn't it? It usually takes them longer than that to stay overnight. Well done, Brother Joshua, but don't let her go too fast. After what happened last spring, we can't take any chances."

Joshua flushed with pleasure. "Thank you, Brother David," he said, turning to the woman beside him, "but it was mostly Sister Miriam. She did all the talking."

"She was so lonely," said Miriam. "God picked her out of the crowd and led her right to us. Once she began talking," Miriam smiled at the memory, "there was no stopping her."

"It might be easy at first," said David, getting to his feet and beginning to pace up and down the long room, "but the next part may not be. Take your time, and make sure she understands the requirements. We can't have any more awkward situations."

"I've been watching her," said Sarah, tucking a stray curl into place under her headscarf. "She's in my Bible study group at Meriwether. She's anxious to please — too anxious, maybe, but once we get her in here, we give her lots of support while she's learning the discipline. That's what everybody's looking for, isn't it? Love, security, and a good meal? You know," Sarah grinned and then sang," "who could ask for anything more?"

David stiffened and shot her a dark look. "Sister Sarah," he spoke in a flat voice. "We are a Christian fellowship trying to follow in the footsteps of our Lord and Master Jeshua. We are not performers in a cabaret. We are the hands and heart of God on earth." He paused, "You do believe that, don't you?"

Sarah looked up at the man without changing her expression.

"I believe what I am expected to believe, Brother David. Otherwise, I wouldn't be here, would I?"

Thirteen

Olympia had stopped by the faculty mailroom and was now trying to hang onto a slippery pile of envelopes and manila folders. She was badly shaken by what Bethany Ruth told her and hoped it wasn't already too late to intervene. Much as she didn't want to, she had to talk to the Dean.

In the gathering gloom of the late November afternoon, she had something else to think about as well, something with almost as many question marks surrounding it as Bethany Ruth, but they were question marks of an infinitely more pleasurable nature. Somewhere in the pile in her arms was a letter from Frederick. She wondered why he sent it to her college address instead of her home but assumed all would be made clear when she read it.

The arrival of this particular letter lightened Olympia's bleak mood considerably but not completely. Along with the Bethany Ruth situation, the looming specter of exams, final projects, and the inevitable end-of-year crises brought on by procrastinating students left little time in her schedule for a gentleman of interest.

"Shit!" The Reverend Doctor Olympia spat the word aloud into the cold, late afternoon air and felt better for doing it. Ministers weren't supposed to use four-letter words, but some things "just take cussin'", a southern lady friend of her mother's used to say. She walked on, trying to stabilize the clutter in her arms with her chin. The clutter in her mind was going to need more than that. *I need a human salvage project like a fish needs a bicycle,* she thought, *and where the hell do I begin?*

Olympia climbed the steps of the Arts Building, shifted her armload, and yanked open the door with more force than usual. At that hour of the day, the building was empty and silent. In the sink room outside her office, she reached up to the overhead shelf where she kept the door key and finally located it under a coffee can. *That's strange. I'm sure I left it under the brush jar. Maybe Bethany Ruth moved it when she was cleaning up.*

Olympia unlocked her door, added the mail to the heap of clutter on the desk, and fished out the blue envelope. Then, with a long sigh, she set it back down. Anything Frederick might have written would be entirely wasted in her present preoccupation with Bethany Ruth. She looked at the jumble on the desk in front of her and turned away. She needed time to think. The papers could wait. They were used to it.

She thought back to when she had met the quirky Englishman with the light blue eyes and wonderful accent. They'd been writing since the end of August. She reached for the phone and dialed her elder son Malcolm, and by an auspicious mischance, the boy picked up on the second ring.

"Hi, Malcolm, it's me. I didn't expect you to be in."

"I live here?" Malcolm had an irritating habit of turning declarative sentences into questions. "What's up?" He was chewing something.

"Any chance you could come over here for lunch tomorrow? I've got something I need to ask you in person."

"I'd rather have a new guitar, but lunch is okay. Actually, I'm playing a gig there in a couple of weeks, and I need to check out the sound system. I can do it while I'm there and save a trip."

"Whatever works, but do me a favor, will you? Don't say anything about this to anyone, not even to your girlfriend."

"What's this all about, Ma? You're not usually so secretive."

"I'll tell you everything when I see you."

Olympia broke the connection, cast a longing glance at Frederick's letter, and then dialed Father Jim's college number and left a message on his voice mail. "Jim, its Olympia. Call me back as soon as you can, here or tonight at home."

The message was urgent but deliberately vague. There was no way of telling who might be in the room when he listened to his messages. Then she called his number at the rectory and repeated it.

Olympia picked up the letter and looked up at the calendar on the wall over her desk. It was almost December. She'd known Frederick Watkins four months and was trying not to get too enthusiastic about him. The fact that he lived three thousand miles away made him geographically inconvenient, to say the very least. *On the other hand …*

Olympia considered all that empty space in her queen-sized bed. Maybe a trip across the pond on spring break would be worth thinking about.

She remembered on the drive from Maine to Boston, telling him about her antique house, minus any reference to the ghost, and her plans for restoring it. By the time they reached the Massachusetts border, they had learned a lot more about each other and agreed to keep in touch, never really expecting the other to make good on the offer.

Olympia sat listening to the intermittent hiss of the radiator under the window and turning Frederick's most recent communication over in her hand. Since his first letter, the two had kept up an erratic and almost entirely proper correspondence. He chatted about his mid-life career-change studies, and she talked about her teaching, her thoughts about Meriwether and her uncertain future. She told him things she wasn't ready to share with anyone other than a man so far away from Cambridge and Brookfield that she felt safe in doing so.

When she couldn't stand it any longer, Olympia stuck her finger under the flap, unfolded the letter and began to read.

It was a typical Frederick letter, newsy and with just the right amount of flirtatious innuendo in the repeat invitation to spend the Christmas holiday with him in England. He also said that he'd recently cleaned off his desk and in so doing had misplaced her home address and could only remember the name of her college.

Olympia was grinning foolishly when Margie, her long-time friend and colleague, burst through the door.

"So what's that?" asked Margie, standing in the doorway and looking at the letter in Olympia's hand, "a sonnet from a secret lover or something from an irate parent complaining because his little princess only got an A minus in your course?"

"You must be psychic," said Olympia looking at a spot somewhere beyond Margie's left shoulder. "How could you know it was from a parent?"

Margie favored Olympia with a long look, "It was the goofy look on your face," she said flipping a pencil into the air and catching it. "You always look that way when you're thinking about a guy you like."

"You know me too well." Olympia folded the letter in half and tucked it into her pocket. "Actually, I was just about to get started grading these papers."

"So, who is he?" Margie persisted.

"Just someone I met last summer." Olympia was trying to sound nonchalant. "He's from England. We're … pen pals."

"And I'm Napoleon," wisecracked Margie, throwing a wad of scrunched-up paper at Olympia and scoring a direct hit.

"Don't you have a class?"

"In half an hour," said Margie. "I came in to see if you wanted to go have a coffee?"

"I'm coffeed out," said Olympia. "I just had one with a student. I'm going to stay and straighten up the office before I leave."

"Well, I need something. Hey, did you see that notice about office break-ins?"

Olympia shook her head.

"It came in today's mail. Someone's breaking into faculty offices and going through desk drawers and files and taking things."

"I've been here over twenty-five years, and that's never happened before."

"The times, they are a-changing, my dear Olympia. You need to be more careful. I know you're a reverend, but you're way too trusting."

Olympia considered asking Margie if she'd moved the office key as she turned and started out the door, but she thought better of it and said nothing.

"If I don't see you, have a nice Thanksgiving."

"Thanks, Margie, same to you."

Olympia waited to hear the outside door click shut before she pulled the letter back out of her pocket and carefully re-read every lovely handwritten word.

Fourteen

Brother David and The Abba were seated in the Abba's private, third floor apartment. The deep claret and gold tones of the Oriental carpet on the floor, the soft, upholstered furniture and original watercolors on the walls were a startling contrast to the austere furnishings on the lower levels.

"You wanted to speak with me about something?" said David.

The Abba was leaning back in his chair with his hands clasped behind his head. There was a half-full glass of Merlot on the desk beside him.

"Tell me about Sister Sarah."

"Is there a problem?"

Brother David didn't like problems, especially if they reflected negatively on his management of the Brighton Renewal Center. Even on the best of days, Sister Sarah, intense, bright, and passionate about everything she did, took managing.

"Not at all, David," said the man in charge of everything. "She intrigues me, that's all."

Father Jim closed the door of his bedroom at St. Brendan's rectory in Dorchester and slipped a C.D. of Schubert's "Trout" quintet into the machine on the bookshelf. Then he lowered himself onto his reading chair and sat with his eyes shut, tapping out the piano part on the edge of the armrest.

The chair had been his last birthday gift to Paul.

He'd had a long day and needed to unwind before going back to the parish house for the weekly confirmation class. Balancing his job as a chaplain with his duties at the church was work enough for two men. With the growing shortage of priests, he managed as best he could under the circumstances, but it was beginning to take its toll, and Jim couldn't afford to take chances with his health.

It was only when he got up to change into more casual clothing that he noticed the message light on his answering machine winking at him. He poked at it without enthusiasm.

"Jim, it's Olympia. Call me back as soon as you can, here or at home."

Jim rubbed his chin. He would need to shave before he went out. By the sound of her voice, something was wrong. He checked the time. She would have left Cambridge by now, so he dialed her home number and left a message saying she could call him on his private line at the rectory any time after nine.

After shaving and brushing his teeth, he changed into jeans and buttoned a light grey cardigan over his clerical shirt. Out of habit, he smoothed the top of the bed before going out and across the street to the church.

Bethany Ruth McAllister was hurrying back to the dormitory and thinking about what Professor Brown had said about her joining the Fellowship. She shook her head in the chill November dark. *Miriam and Joshua said she wouldn't understand, and they were right.*

She pulled back her sleeve and looked at her watch. She needed to call her parents and tell them she wasn't coming home for Christmas. With the time difference, her mother would be just starting dinner. *I wonder what they're having.*

Bethany Ruth bit down on a trembling lip and quickened her pace.

Fifteen

Olympia was deep into think-mode when she finally left the office and climbed onto the front seat of her beloved VW van, and the thinking had nothing at all to do with Meriwether College or the approaching Thanksgiving weekend. On the best of days, the commute from Cambridge to her home in Brookfield, some thirty miles south of Boston, was a nightmare, but the drive also gave her time to think without interruption.

She backed out of her coveted faculty parking space and nosed the boxy old vehicle into the street. She wondered if tonight would be one of those relatively easy commutes, the normal hour-plus of *sturm and drang*, or a two- to three-hour period of mind-numbing, leg-cramping, knee-jerk shifting between first and second gear all the way from the Massachusetts Avenue entrance to the infamous Braintree split.

As she inched along the slip road toward the highway, Olympia went over her most recent conversation with Bethany Ruth. There was no doubt these people were actively recruiting her, and she was going right along with it. *Damn. And what about that Bible study group?*

Olympia signaled for a left and eased into the middle and most predictable lane of traffic as she considered an entirely different approach to the problem.

"As a parent, I'd want to know if my child was involved with one of these groups." Olympia spoke the words aloud as she straightened out the wheel. "But then, if Bethany Ruth ever found out that I called them, she'd never trust me again."

She knew families who had lost their children to groups like the Unification Church, The Moonies, or Heaven's Gate in California. Bethany Ruth was so vulnerable, so eager to please, and still so terribly homesick.

Olympia reached down between the seats and fumbled in her backpack for the apple she had saved from lunch. It was her defense against the weariness that descended at that time of day. She held the fruit in one hand and gripped the steering wheel with the other.

All she could do right now was to keep the girl's trust and keep her talking, but would that be possible? Olympia bit down hard into the apple. There was another aspect to all of this. She needed to talk to Dean Wilbur Jackson, but how and when, and how much should she tell him? She and the dean had a prickly relationship, at best, and this was not going to help. What did he know about the Bible study Group? *Too many questions.*

Keeping her eyes on the road, Olympia set the sticky apple core in the unused ashtray as she slipped into the left hand lane and headed toward home. *Then there's Frederick.* Olympia could feel the Bethany Ruth tension in her neck and shoulders diminishing as she pictured the man. *We have any number of interests in common. He's my age, and he's single. Double bonus.*

Traffic was easing. Olympia moved through the gears and was tearing along in fifth. Despite the distance issue, she could see distinct long-distance possibilities.

"Well," she said, again addressing her words to the taillights in front of her, "I've always loved England, but Christmas is way too soon. Maybe a spring fling, or a little March madness?"

Olympia was rapidly coming to the realization, as she flew past her exit at one hell of a clip, that despite the geographical inconvenience and the improbability of the whole thing, she really was interested in this gentleman and feeling far more like an infatuated sixteen-year-old than a menopausal pre-crone with two grown sons. Olympia giggled in the darkness as she checked in the rearview mirror and signaled for the next exit.

Sixteen

November 23, 1859

The days are so much colder now. This morning, there was a hoar frost on the corn stalks in the field across the road. So many things to be repaired and tended to.

Everything went adrift when father became ill. Mrs. Stetson from the church suggested that I find myself a husband to put things right around here. I know she meant her words kindly, but I can swing a hammer and dig a trench as well as any man.

This is my house, and I will do this myself. If I ever decide on having a husband, it will be because I want one, not because I need one.

More anon ... LFW

Olympia crunched to a stop on the gravel driveway leading to the house. In the dark, she shouldered her backpack, slammed the car door, and felt her way up the worn granite slabs that had served as the front steps, probably since the house had been built. *I really need to fix the light out here before I kill myself.* As she fumbled for her key, she could hear her cats, Thunderfoot and Whitefoot, making hungry squalls from inside the house.

Following her nightly routine, she dropped her school things on the pine trestle table in the center of the kitchen, got the cat food out of the back pantry, and poured herself a glass of chilled Chardonnay. She completed the circuit by smacking the playback button on the answering machine. She was simultaneously pulling off her coat, filling the cat dish, and lowering the level in her glass. The first two calls were telemarketers. She growled, hit delete, and topped up her wine.

The last blinking light on the machine was not a message but a long silence followed by a hang-up, the third one that week. Olympia shivered and hoped she wasn't being watched by some creep planning to break in when she wasn't home. *Time to start being more careful about locking the doors here, as well.*

Olympia was almost out of the kitchen when the phone rang. She picked it up and propped the handset under her ear so she could slosh off a few dishes while she talked.

"Hello? Yes this is Olympia speaking, who's calling?" Olympia turned off the water. "Can you speak up, please? The connection's fuzzy."

"Hello to you, American lady. Frederick Watkins here."

Olympia looked up at the clock and was mentally calculating the time difference as she greeted him. "Frederick! What a lovely surprise, how nice to hear your voice. What time is it over there?" Her heart suddenly seemed to be playing hopscotch with itself.

Frederick responded, saying that it was coming up on midnight, that he'd had a couple of pints at the 'local,' and now, emboldened by same, he had decided to call and see if she'd gotten his most recent letter. It had been too long since he'd heard the sound of her voice, and might she do him the honor of joining him at the Christmas holidays?

"I did get your letter," said Olympia, trying to take a quiet sip of her wine and not gulp or slurp in the man's ear. "Not for Christmas, Frederick, it's too short notice."

He made a woeful noise that came through loud and clear all the way from England.

"But I'd be delighted to accept for early spring or in June when I'm finished with my teaching. I've not been there in years, and I'm long overdue."

As the two chatted on, Olympia soon relaxed into the comfortable banter she remembered so clearly from their ride to Boston. He was easy to talk to and a good listener. Close to an hour later, as Olympia elected not to think about his escalating phone bill, they agreed that she would fly to England in February when Meriwether scheduled a winter break. If she could get the right connections, she would be able to stay with him for almost nine days *and eight nights.*

Frederick said he would arrange accommodations but declined to be specific, and a smirking Olympia elected not to press him. When she finally hung up the phone, her wine glass was empty, and she had absolutely no desire for another.

She looked at the wall clock and considered calling the dean of Meriwether but realized she was seriously preoccupied and would do a better job of it if she rang him in the morning. Despite the urgency of the Bethany Ruth situation, Frederick's call seemed to have altered her powers of concentration, and certainly twelve hours one way or the other wasn't going to make a difference.

This left supper and student papers to occupy her time. Olympia heated up a can of soup, changed the cats' water, and wrote herself a note to get a new bulb and an electric timer for the outside light. Then she locked and chained the front door, dead-bolted the kitchen door, and finally dragged herself to the pile of papers waiting patiently on the table beside her chair in the great room.

By way of further procrastination, she considered lighting the woodstove when she realized that ever since the chimney man had done nothing more than wiggle the damper, the obstinate thing was working perfectly. *Now what's that all about?*

It was yet another curiosity about this place in what was becoming a rather long list, but Olympia was getting used to them. No doubt, the house had character or *had a character*, but who was it? *Is it? Does one refer to a ghost in the past or present tense?*

The thought of a spirited housemate was no longer a question, it was a given, and she wondered when or if or what she might tell Frederick.

Olympia sat down and surveyed her surroundings with as much of an unvarnished eye as she could manage. It would be some time before work on the house would be finished. She was taking her time because she wanted to restore the ambience of the place as well as the structure. It wasn't a grand home. In fact, it was just the opposite. It was a farmhouse, a functional structure that reflected the character of the hardworking people who had built it and lived in it. The house had a personality all its own, and Olympia was coming to know it intimately.

Get to the goddamned papers, Olympia.

Two hours later, she awoke with a single ungraded paper in her lap and a crick in her neck. Bleary-eyed, she summoned the cats, checked the locks one more time, and went to bed.

Her bedroom, like most of the other rooms in the house, had a working fireplace. With a delicious grin, Olympia surveyed her queen-sized bed and wondered, with the holidays approaching, if it would be too forward of her to send Frederick a small Christmas gift, something thoughtful like a leather-bound collection of American short stories or perhaps a pair of black silk boxer shorts.

Seventeen

Before she left the following morning, Olympia caught Jim at the rectory and gave him a quick run-down of her conversation with Bethany Ruth and said she would call again after she'd spoken with the dean.

Two hours after that, she was seated in one of Dean Wilbur Jackson's latest acquisitions, a massive oak rocking chair with a lion's face carved into the headrest, sipping the gourmet coffee he had prepared. She planned to tell him only enough to get his attention and then see what he had to say in response.

As Dean of the college, he needed to know that another Meriwether student was being approached by the Boston Christian Common Fellowship. That being said, she didn't trust the man. He was not above turning a situation to his own benefit when he got the chance.

"Damn," said Will after Olympia described her conversation with Bethany Ruth. "It certainly sounds like the same group, but I don't want you saying anything to anyone until I check into it further. Not eating a cookie or finishing a glass of juice could mean she just wasn't hungry that day."

Will paused and then added, "I'm glad you told me. We certainly can't chance losing another student, but we can't tip our hand either. Word gets around fast here. The college can't risk its reputation on an unsubstantiated charge of enticement or anything else, for that matter. Think of what the newspapers could do with something like this. It could seriously affect our enrollment."

Olympia didn't like what she was hearing but knew better than to confront the man directly. She had done that once, and she'd been playing cat and mouse with him ever since.

"I hear you, Will. At the beginning of the semester you told us to report any unusual student behavior to you, and I just did, but I have another, possibly related, question."

"What's that?" Will set down his coffee cup.

Olympia sipped her own coffee, enjoying its warmth in her cupped hands. "This Bible study group that meets in the cafeteria, how much do you know about it?"

"You're not suggesting there's a connection, are you?"

"I hardly think so. In fact, I've recommended it to several students. I'm asking what you know about it?"

Will uncrossed his legs and sat forward. "The girl who offered to lead it is an extension student, you know, a part-timer, Jewish girl, Sarah something or other. She came to me for permission, and I granted it. I liked the idea that it's open to all religions and that it's student run. Actually, she made a point of saying having faculty present might inhibit open exchange between the students. I happen to agree."

Will got up and topped up his coffee, then closed the door to his office.

"I want to talk to you about Sonya Wilson."

"I'd appreciate that," said Olympia.

"Her death certificate lists the cause as complications due to anorexia nervosa, but over the summer, the parents found her diary and started reading about her involvement with a group she referred to as The Fellowship." Will held up his index finger. "That's when they hired the lawyer. Now they're saying we could have done more to protect their daughter, even making noises about a wrongful death suit."

"Do you think they'll want to talk to me?" said Olympia. "I knew her as well as anyone, and that's not saying much."

Will nodded. "If that happens, I'll tell you exactly what to say. It's important our stories agree."

The hell you will. Olympia reared back against the back of the elegant chair.

Will continued. "I want to get back to Bethany Ruth. What else can you tell me?"

"The girl is a long way from home," Olympia said, choosing her words with care. "She's been slow to settle in. I only became concerned yesterday when we were chatting in the snack bar. There was absolutely nothing before then, I swear it. I invited her for Thanksgiving, and that's when she told me she's been attending those Christian rock concerts on Boston Common since the end of October. She was all excited, because she's met some new friends there, and then she told me she's planning to spend the holidays with them and stay at their residence."

Olympia paused before continuing. "But it gets worse. They've asked her to become a member, and she told me she's all for it."

"You were right to come in here, Olympia. I'm sure it's the same group."

"Can you tell me what really happened to Sonya?" asked Olympia.

"She was one of the quiet ones, you know that." Will was turning a pencil over and over in his long, manicured fingers.

"There was something in the diary about purging herself of impurities. It was vague. I'm told she had a history of anorexia, so I'm guessing it was easy for her to stop eating as part of the purge. She lost weight so fast that she passed out one night during exams. The residence director went with her to the hospital, but the minute they left her alone, she slipped back out. I understand these fellowship people have a place across the river in Brighton. We think she might have been trying to get there."

Olympia elected not to tell Will what she knew about the group and where they lived. If he was playing it close to the chest, so could she.

Will shook his head. "She must have been sneaking through the back streets and collapsed again. A trash collector found her the next morning, sprawled on the pavement like a starved kitten."

"I noticed the changes," said Olympia. "I tried talking to her about the weight loss, but she shut me off. I can only imagine how the parents feel." She shook her head. "I have two kids, Will, it must have been awful for them."

"It still is, Olympia," said Will, his voice taking on a cautionary tone. "Now the mother and father are looking for someone to blame."

Olympia stopped rocking and began twisting her hands. "Oh God, Will, you don't suppose ..."

"From what little we know, the group is very well organized. They blend in and work the system, and they're not about to give up a good prospect without a fight. If they have a new recruit here, you can be assured they're keeping an eye on her."

"Do you think she's in any immediate danger? I mean, shouldn't we be doing something?"

"Not yet." Will looked down at his hands and then back up at Olympia.

"All you can do right now is keep her trust and watch her like a hawk. We might be able to learn more about this fellowship if she keeps talking to you, but leave the heavy-duty action to the experts, okay? There's a lot I can't tell you."

Will looked directly into her eyes, and Olympia wanted to believe him. Maybe he did care. Maybe this was bigger than a personal power trip.

"I know you want to help," he continued, his voice softer now, "and really, the fact that she's still talking to you is the only thing we have going for us. It's our only avenue into that organization. You're in a key position, Olympia. If anyone can keep her confidence, you can."

"Thank you for saying that, Will, I appreciate it."

"Keep your eyes and ears open, and for God's sake, don't tip your hand."

Olympia nodded. *No problem there, my friend.*

Will drew a long breath. "Another thing, Olympia. I think you need to be careful, as well. From what I understand, these people can be unpleasant."

Eighteen

When Olympia returned to her office, her son Malcolm was on her phone. "Hang on, I believe she's approaching the loading dock as we speak. Would you care to talk with her?"

"Dammit, Malcolm!"

Olympia yanked the phone out of his hand. "This is Professor Brown speaking. I apologize for the answering service. My son thinks he has a sense of humor." She stood, listening and tapping her foot. "No, you may not have an extension."

Malcolm rolled his eyes.

"I explained this on the first day of class. Do the best you ..." Olympia made a face and hung up the phone.

"Hey there, Malkie," she said, dragging him out of her chair by his rumpled collar and claiming her space. "How did you get in here?"

"The key was in the door. I thought you left it there for me."

No, I didn't.

"So, Ma, what's this super secret stuff you were talking about?"

"Let me just check my phone messages, and I'll tell you over lunch."

When the two were seated, Olympia got right to the point. She told her son she feared that one of her students was being recruited by a religious group and asked if he might be willing to do some investigating and see if he could find out more about them.

"Is this really any of your business?" asked Malcolm laying down his fork and leaning closer to his mother.

"Maybe not," said Olympia, "but the girl was pretty homesick at first, and I took her under my wing. I actually invited her home for Thanksgiving with us, but when I did, she told me she'd be staying with her new friends. The more she said about them, the more suspicious I got."

"What do you mean?" said Malcolm.

Olympia dropped her voice. "I have reason to think this particular group might not be as saintly or as piously Christian as they pretend to be."

Malcolm was looking interested.

"They attract young people with free rock concerts on the Boston Common. The members come on all friendly and loving, and for a college student who's lonely or confused, it feels like a safe oasis in a hostile world."

"So what's so bad about that?" he asked.

"It's not like you'd be in any danger or anything. Just go over to Boston Common some Sunday with your guitar on your back, and see if you can get them talking to you. Whatever you do, don't tell them you're my son. It's a good thing I took back my birth name when we divorced. Malcolm Patterson sure doesn't sound like Olympia Brown."

"I don't understand. Aren't religious groups supposed to help people?"

"Religious organizations offer community and security in a chaotic world, Malcolm. I'm in the business, remember? Some of these newer groups use everyday language and contemporary music to appeal to a younger crowd."

"I could get into something like that."

Olympia caught him eyeing her unfinished dessert and handed it over.

"Believe me, Son, not this one. This is a cult. They don't always play nice."

He paused midway through the second dessert and held up his spoon. "You don't really think they're going to tell me anything just because I walk up and ask, do you?"

Olympia shook her head. She finished off the dregs of her coffee and immediately wished she hadn't. It was cold and tasted awful.

"I don't know, but you're in a position to find out more than I ever could. You fit their profile."

"So, what exactly do you want me to do?" He was drumming his fingers on the table. "That is, if I agree."

Olympia smiled. *The musician in him is never still.*

"Information only, my boy. There's certainly no risk in that." Olympia could only hope she was right. "Just go over there and look interested. Ask about the music. If they actually do come on to you, start talking to them and find out whatever you can. Like I said, there's no way they'll connect us."

Olympia crumpled her coffee cup and reached back for her coat. "I think they may already see me as some kind of a threat. The student I'm concerned about told them she works for me and that she likes to talk to me. That means they know who I am."

Olympia started to get up, then dropped back into her seat and leaned in close to her son. "Malcolm, last year a freshman in one of my classes got involved with these same people and ended up dead. It happened last spring. I tried to help her, too, but it was too late. Now they're winding their tentacles around another of my students, and it looks like she's taking the bait."

"Jesus, Ma," said Malcolm pushing aside his plate. "This is serious."

"It's deadly serious, Son." Olympia tossed her napkin and cup into the trash. "So for God's sake, if you decide to go, be careful."

"If I'm only asking questions, what can happen?"

Olympia dropped her chin and looked at him over her glasses.

"Okay, Ma." He reached over and patted her hand. "I'll go after Thanksgiving." He looked down at his watch. "I've got to meet that guy about the sound system."

Mother and son walked out of the cafeteria into the deepening cold. As the two were saying their goodbyes in front of her building, a young man wearing a thick woolly hat pulled low over his eyes rushed out of the door and hurried past them down the street.

Must be somebody's boyfriend, thought Olympia, giving her son a quick hug and then placing her hand on his arm. "Remember, about that rock concert, don't say anything to anyone, even your girlfriend."

"Ma-a-a-a-a." Malcolm gave his mother a reassuring pat on the shoulder and turned into the moving tide of students, many already on their way home for the holiday weekend.

When she called Jim back later that afternoon, he suggested they meet for dinner at La Paloma in Boston's upscale and predominantly gay South End. They could do whatever talking they needed over a good meal. She needed no convincing. Cooking and eating by herself was a lonely fact of Olympia's life. Dinner out with a friend was a treat, and as her free-form waistline would attest, eating was one of her preferred activities.

Seated across from her, Jim held his glass of pinot noir up to the light and twirled it, watching the ruby liquid cling to the inside of the glass. "Good legs." Jim was a wine snob.

Olympia shook her head in amused resignation. They couldn't get down to business until the officious waiter stopped pirouetting around them long enough to take their order. He eyed her empty glass of house white, and the waiter asked if she'd like another.

She made a sad face. "I'd probably like three more, but since I'm driving, I'll have a diet soda, no ice, and a slice of lime, please."

Jim winced.

Olympia waited until they were alone before continuing. She wanted to tell Jim, now swirling and sniffing his wine, about her conversation with Malcolm.

"Oh, for God's sake, Jim, drink the stuff."

Jim ignored her, inhaled the bouquet, and took a slow, appreciative sip.

"You've got that look on your face, Olympia. What are you up to now?"

After she described her plan, Jim agreed that it could indeed add something to the meager scattering of information they'd managed to collect. She also told him she hadn't told the dean about it and that she'd sworn Malcolm to secrecy.

"I think that was wise," said Jim. "And now that we've got that sorted, we might as well enjoy our meal, because I see it approaching."

Over dinner, he offered to contact some of the other deans and chaplains in the area and see if they had had any experience with the Fellowship or knew of any students who had gotten involved with the group.

Jim paused, holding up his fork. "You know, Olympia, I think there might be more so-called freak or tragic accidents involving people connected to this group that have never been investigated. I'm on pretty good terms with the Police Captain in Brighton. He might be able to do some checking for me that the average person couldn't tap into."

"It's because you're a priest, isn't it?" said Olympia. She pointed to his collar. "With that thing on, you can walk through walls."

"You can borrow it any time you need it," said Jim, "but as long as it works, I might as well use it, right? I may be a Polish kid from the old West End, but Irish Catholic Boston doesn't check our ancestry. All they see is a priest, and the world is my oyster, at least sometimes."

Jim fell silent and looked off into the distance.

Olympia reached across the table and took her friend's hand. "Are you sure you wouldn't like to come down for Thanksgiving this year, Jim, just for the meal? You wouldn't have to stay long."

He shook his head, and Olympia knew better than to press the issue.

Nineteen

Father Jim sat and stared at the wall in front of him. One day he would tell Olympia the whole story. She knew most of it already, and she, of all people, would understand and not pass judgment. But even seven years after Paul's death, a wave of raw grief could still blindside him, and now was one of those times.

Every Thanksgiving since Paul died, Jim took off his collar and went down to Provincetown, an artists' colony and safe haven for gay and lesbian people at the tip of Cape Cod. There he put yellow roses on Paul's grave and spent time being who and what he was with no one watching him. Dressed in casual clothes, he served hundreds of Thanksgiving dinners to people, old and young, gay and straight, in the basement of the church where he and Paul had been married in a ceremony of Holy Union. Six months later, Paul had died of AIDS. He remembered sitting numb and hollow-eyed through the memorial service. This was a personal pilgrimage to another place and time forever gone from him.

A year after Paul's death, Jim returned to the seminary, took a vow of celibacy, and resumed the studies he had set aside when he'd fallen in love. Three years later, he was ordained to the priesthood.

He met Olympia while he was still in seminary, and the two were taking a course in systematic theology at

Harvard Divinity School. Over that semester and in the years that followed, the two formed a curious sort of owl-and-pussycat friendship which was based as much on what they didn't say to one another as on what they did.

Eventually, Jim told Olympia about Paul, and Olympia told Jim about her lost daughter. Both understood the unspeakable anguish of irretrievable loss, and each in their own way would be driven to be advocates for those who would otherwise fall by the wayside. Olympia was a minister working as a chaplain in a women's college and taking in strays on the side, and Jim was a fragile, dedicated, celibate, priest, both of them servants of a God they understood in their own way.

Jim turned his head and stared out over the rooftops of Dorchester into the mist hanging over the bay. He had a few more parish details to clear up that evening so he could leave early the next morning and avoid the worst of the holiday traffic.

After a few minutes, he got up, stretched, and went over to his closet and took out a small black suitcase. There was time to pack before Mrs. Haggerty, the housekeeper, called him in for dinner. He smiled at the thought of her. He was one of her boys, and she fussed over him as any mother would.

Tonight she had made one of her famous, whiskey-laced Irish stews. Jim could smell the robust aroma, but from the bangs and crashes coming from the kitchen, he wondered if she might have been sampling the main ingredient a little too enthusiastically.

Twenty

Sister Sarah was standing at the kitchen sink, peeling onions and wiping away stinging tears with the back of her wrist. She and Sister Miriam were chatting in the way of women in kitchens as they prepared the evening meal.

"So how did it go with Bethany Ruth?" Sarah looked up from her onions. "I'll tell you one thing. She did a double-take when she saw me here."

"What did you tell her?" Miriam asked.

Sarah chuckled. "I just said it was part of our street mission. I told her that one day she might even get to do it, but she wasn't supposed to talk about it when she was back at Meriwether. We don't talk about our good works in public."

"And she believed you?"

"I think she did," said Sarah.

Ordinarily, members of the elite Third Circle didn't have housekeeping or cooking duties, but Sarah wanted to know how the new prospect was doing. She knew that conversation flowed more easily, and more privately, in the big old-fashioned kitchen where male members were rarely seen. There were times when 'women's work' had its advantages. Sarah leaned back and away from the pungent onion fumes. "Do you think she liked spending the weekend with us?"

"Seemed to," said Miriam, looking up from the great sticky wad of dough she was alternately turning and pushing on the wooden table in front of her. "She kept saying how happy she was to be here. She did everything we asked and more. She's eager to please, almost too much so."

"That can be good and bad." Sarah was now trying to peel the onions with her head turned to the side and not cut herself. "You have to ask yourself if she wants to make points with us or do the work of Lord Jeshua?"

"Probably a little of both," said Miriam, giving a final whack to the mixture in front of her. "She kept saying how lonely she's been. She got weepy every so often, but the new ones do."

"What about the food thing?" asked Sarah. "How did she handle that?"

"Seemed okay with it." Miriam had started slapping the beige blobs into loaves and was arranging them on baking sheets. "Brother David said we should wait until this coming weekend before starting up the full regimen with her. She was hungry, but she managed."

"Ah, yes," said Sarah, rinsing her hands and wiping them on her apron, "Brother David knows all, sees all, and tells us all what to do. What is this food thing with him? I think it's downright sadistic, if you ask me, just another one of his little power things with women."

"Don't let him hear you say that," admonished a wide-eyed Miriam. "You don't want to get on his bad side."

"Too late for that," said Sarah looking in the refrigerator. "Where's the fish?"

"Bottom shelf, left-hand side, and what do you mean, too late?" asked Miriam, dropping her voice. "Too late for what?"

"In case you haven't noticed," said Sarah, unwrapping a large, whole codfish and running it under cold water, "David doesn't miss an opportunity to pick on me. He's constantly looking over my shoulder, waiting for me to do something wrong so he can correct me, preferably in public."

"Don't cut yourself with that fillet knife," said Miriam with a sly grin. "I just sharpened it. No blood in the chowder, please. And in case *you* hadn't noticed, my dear, obtuse Sister Sarah, it's my belief that our prickly Brother David is in love with you."

Twenty-One

November 23, 1859

It will be the first Thanksgiving without father. Sweet Mrs. Stetson from the church asked me to join her family. I accepted and offered to bake some bread and an apple pie. She said the bountiful food and companionship would cheer me, and no doubt it will.

I had no idea how quiet an empty house could be. I'm sure I will become accustomed to it in time. I miss my father more than I thought possible, but I'm not afraid to live alone. I suspect that some of the local women think that I should marry, but marriage to a man looking only for a house and land is not what I envision for myself.

More anon…LFW

Over the course of the Thanksgiving weekend, Olympia Brown marked forward progress on three fronts. In a quiet moment between the turkey and the frontal attack on the array of homemade pies, she grabbed a few minutes with Malcolm and went over what he would and would not do when he went into Boston.

On Friday, after putting away the last of the dishes and finishing the remainder of the squash pie, she called Frederick and confirmed her intent to travel to England in February, exact dates to be determined.

On Sunday, Olympia climbed up on a footstool and slipped out the wooden panel concealing the parson's cupboard. Sputtering and coughing from the layers of dust, she began to lift out pieces of old crockery, rags, and layers of brown, crumbling newspapers from the1800s. *So far, so good, no dead mice or live spiders.*

The cupboard was deeper than she thought, and Olympia needed to climb on a higher chair in order to reach all the way to the back. As she stretched up and in, she wished she had remembered to buy flashlight batteries. With her right hand in as far back as it would go, she could feel something. She traced the shape with her fingers. It was rounded on top and felt as though it was made of wood. Next to it was something flat, wrapped in fabric.

Careful not to get stuck with a splinter, Olympia eased her fingers around the curiously shaped object and slowly drew it out into the light. It was an old mantel clock, and it felt warm. Surprising, she thought, running her fingers over and around its planes and curves, since the fireplace and parson's cupboard were on an outside wall, and the interior was deathly cold.

The glass over the painted face was missing, but the gold-filigreed hour and minute hands were intact and very beautiful. Olympia couldn't determine what kind of wood it was. When she turned it over to look at the back, it chimed, a beautiful silvery sound, and for no earthly reason she would be able to explain, she found it comforting.

She fetched a damp rag from the kitchen and gently wiped its face and hands and cleaned the grime off the wooden case, then gave it pride of place, front and center on the mantel over the fireplace.

Olympia climbed on the chair a second time and reached back for the second mystery treasure. It was wrapped in a linen table napkin, yellow and dusty with age. Slowly and carefully she lifted a corner of the fabric to discover a leather-bound diary. Surely it must have belonged to someone who lived in the house — but who, and how long had it been there? She carried it out into the kitchen and flicked on the overhead light. There, seated at her kitchen table, she lifted the smooth, leather cover and read the words, *The diary of Leanna Faith Winslow, The year of our lord, January 1, 1859 – December 31, 1859.*

Have I finally found met my ghost? Olympia looked at the handwritten name a second time. *And her middle name is Faith.*

Olympia eased the diary open to the date exactly one hundred and fifty years ago. She caught her breath when she realized that the day noted on the page in front of her was the same day of the week as today, the Sunday after Thanksgiving of the year 1999.

She could feel a bubble of excitement at the top of her chest as she began reading the words written by a woman she knew nothing about, a woman who most likely wrapped that diary in linen and placed it at the far back of a deep cupboard, knowing one day someone would find it. *And what about the clock? Is there a connection?*

Sunday, November 28, 1859
    We had a hard frost last night. The weeds in the field across from the house look like shards of broken crystal in the morning sun. It was wise to gather in the last of the harvest.

Even the pumpkins, bulky as they are and difficult to store, will last me the winter.

They were the last things he planted. Plan and plant ahead, he always told me. I feel as though he is still caring for me, but how long will it continue?

"You think as well as any man," he used to say, and I would scowl and stamp my feet and say, "No, Papa, I think as good as any woman." It was our little joke. We had so many of those between us with mother gone so long.

The almanac predicts a long hard winter. I must bring in more wood.

More anon…LFW

On Monday morning Olympia was back in her office, still feeing the after-effects of the overindulgent weekend and the mysterious wonder and coincidence of finding the diary and worrying about Bethany Ruth. She knew Jim would call when he had something to report. As much as she hated admitting it, the dean was right. Whatever it took, she had to keep Bethany Ruth's confidence. Right now, hers was the only window into the cult, and if she could manage to keep it open, they might learn something.

Even though she tried, she wasn't able to help Sonya Wilson. *Now there's a very fine line between Bethany Ruth being an informant and a sacrificial lamb, and I'm straddling it,* thought Olympia.

She felt restless and agitated with so much on her mind. *Tea! Just the thing for an over-full stomach and an uneasy mind.*

She got up from her chair, plugged in the electric kettle, and rummaged around in the tea basket she kept on the shelf beside the door. She selected a packet of something called Wintergreen Spring and sniffed the lemony-mint contents. *It must be one of the student's contributions.*

Tea mug in hand, Olympia leaned back in her chair. She sipped the hot, pale green liquid and thought about the clock and the diary. *Who was, or is, Leanna Faith Winslow, and what would their relationship be now that she had a window into her life?*

In the next room she could hear the incoming students twittering like sparrows after the long weekend. Olympia turned to get up and found Bethany Ruth standing in the doorway. Her cheeks were flushed from the cold, and her eyes were bright but wary.

"Hey," said Olympia waving with both hands. "Look what the cat dragged in. Was it a good weekend? What's the place like?" She was babbling. Gone was any resolve to watch and wait in silence, and she had a class about to begin.

"Bethany Ruth," said Olympia getting up and giving the girl a quick hug before she could escape, "I have a class right now, but could we go for a coffee this afternoon?"

"I can't," said the girl, looking away, "I shouldn't even be here now. I'm starting my Aspirant Training tonight. There won't be time for anything else." Bethany Ruth dropped her voice, "It's going to be hard with finals and everything, but I did so well this weekend, they said I could start early. I … I just wanted to come and tell you." Bethany Ruth ducked her head, trying to hide her pleasure.

"Well, that's wonderful," said Olympia, with a smile she didn't feel, "Maybe later in the week?"

"I'm not sure."

"Anytime," said Olympia. "You tell me."

"I have to go, Professor."

She sat for a moment in the troubling emptiness Bethany Ruth left behind her and wondered if it was the lack of make-up, but the girl looked as if she had lost weight. There was something else. Moments before, when Olympia picked up her grade book, she noticed the papers on her desk were not arranged the way she had left them.

Someone's been in my office, and what about Malcolm finding the key in the door last week? Maybe Bethany Ruth came in earlier looking for something. She knows where we keep the key, or maybe it was Billy from campus maintenance. Stop it! I'll deal with this after class.

Between classes she dashed back to her office to check her voice mail and reconfirmed her uneasy feelings. Something was out of place, but what?

When she returned to the classroom, Bethany Ruth was seated and working on her final project, an image of Jesus surrounded with glued-on bits of tissue paper. The effect was a sticky, stained glass window.

Olympia walked across the room and peered over her shoulder.

"It's Jeshua." She looked up at her teacher. "I'm trying to make it look like one of the windows in my old church back home in Oklahoma."

"Are you going to hang it in your room when it's finished?"

The young woman turned and spoke in a low voice, "I can't. I shouldn't even be making it. We don't believe in graven images or holding on to earthly possessions. Would you like it?"

She was so earnest and so vulnerable. Olympia bit her lip.

"Tell you what, I'll keep it in my office. Then if you ever …"

"Thank you, Professor," she whispered and bent again to her cutting and pasting. The conversation was at an end.

Olympia moved on, checking the other students as they worked their projects. She caught snippets of conversations about Christmas presents and boyfriends and bus tickets home. Bethany Ruth slipped out while Olympia was in the bathroom.

Not much to report today, she thought, looking at the empty chair. *But what about 'no graven images' and 'letting go of earthly possessions'?*

Rather than braving the loathsome tide of irritable Boston commuters, Olympia decided to stay and work on her grading. With some trepidation she walked back into her office, put down her papers, and stood looking around the dusty, cluttered room. *Something's been moved, but what in hell is it?*

In one last futile attempt at procrastination, Olympia considered sharpening all of her pencils, but duty prevailed. She reached for the top paper on the stack and froze. Underneath was a torn scrap of blue-lined notebook paper with the name and numbers of a Bible verse, *Matthew 13: 41-42*, printed in green crayon.

Olympia felt the hairs at the back of her neck lifting. When the first spasm of fear subsided, she swiveled in her chair and looked at her bookcase. She shook her head at the complete absurdity of a college chaplain not having a Bible ready to hand.

It has to be from Bethany Ruth. She's not supposed to talk to me, and she's trying to tell me something. She knows where I hide the key. Now it all makes sense, but what's she trying to say? Is it a plea for help, or is it something else?

The empty building was deathly quiet now, good for pondering things and fearing the worst. Olympia picked up the phone and dialed the Dean's extension.

"Will, its Olympia. I need to talk to you."

He told her to come right over. Olympia pushed the Bible verse into the pocket of her denim skirt and pulled on her coat. In the early darkness of approaching winter, she hurried across the parking lot and up the wooden steps to his office.

Once inside, Olympia held out the paper. "Somebody left this in my office. Do you have a Bible here?"

Will looked down at the scrap of paper and said, "Don't need one. Matthew, Chapter Thirteen, verses forty-one and forty-two are, 'The Son of Man shall send forth his angel, and they shall gather out of his kingdom all things that offend, and them which do iniquity; and shall cast them into a furnace of fire; there shall be wailing and gnashing of teeth.'"

"I'm impressed." Olympia dropped her coat and went directly for the rocking chair.

"When I was ten I memorized all four gospels. I got myself a big gold star, a picture of Jesus, and a gold-embossed leather bookmark for my efforts." Will's voice went serious. "This could be a warning, Olympia. Somebody wants to throw *those that do iniquity* into a fiery furnace. Somebody might be telling you to stay away from Bethany Ruth. On the other hand, maybe it's a prank in very poor taste. You teach an Arts and Religion class." Will handed back the scrap of paper. "Was Bethany Ruth in today?"

Olympia nodded. "She stopped by my office this morning, but she was uncomfortable." Olympia stopped and looked hard at her dean. "I could be imagining it, but I think she's lost weight. We can't wait, Will, we have to do something."

He shook his head. "We are, but I can't say what."
He looked directly at her. "Please trust me." For once, there seemed to be no artifice or personal agenda in his words.

Olympia looked at the man and nodded a silent yes.

He continued. "Keep her talking, and don't do anything to scare her off."

The last thing Olympia would ever do was betray the fragile bond between her and Bethany Ruth. Everything she believed in as an ordained minister and a mother was about trust and keeping confidence. On the other hand, she was allowed to reveal a confidence in case of mortal danger However she looked at it, this was a tall order.

"Okay, Will, I'll do what I can, but I should get going."

Will stood up and held out her coat.

"Changing the subject completely," said Olympia sliding into it and pulling the bulky garment up over her shoulders, "do you think we'll get that snowstorm they're predicting?"

"Too early to tell," said Will, "but it sure would mess up exams if we do."

Olympia thanked him for his help and walked out into the dark toward her car. There was no getting around it. If Will was correct in his interpretation of the Bible verse, this whole thing could be getting nasty, very nasty. The sharp chill in the air helped to focus her thinking. *Maybe it's from Bethany Ruth, and if so, what is she trying to tell me?*

In the dimly lit parking lot, Olympia unlocked the door of her van and pulled herself into the front seat. She tossed her things onto the floor and started the engine. As she began back out of her space, she saw something move behind her and slammed on the brakes.

A man wearing a hat pulled low over his eyes walked past the driver's side of the van, paused, and then walked off into the darkness.

Olympia knew she'd seen him before.

Twenty-Two

Brother David closed the door and sat down next to Sarah. "We can't take any chances with Bethany Ruth. She's from the same college as the one who died last spring, and she has the same professor. What's your take on her? You're doing the Bible study over there."

Sarah folded her arms across her chest.

"There was no way I could have known Sonya Wilson was anorexic. I should have picked up on that. It won't happen again." She shook her head. "Can you believe it, they think I'm Jewish."

David and Sarah were alone in the drafty upstairs room that served as office and general meeting room for the Brighton Renewal Center. On Monday afternoons the two reviewed the numbers and set up the street-mission schedule for the coming week.

"I've told Miriam and Joshua to be extra careful with her," said Sarah, "but it's hard to curb their enthusiasm."

Sarah reached up to check her headscarf and remembered what Miriam said about David being in love with her. *Not this, and not now. I've come too far.*

"I'll talk to them," said David.

"Good thinking," said Sarah, busying herself with the papers in front of her and not looking at the man sitting too close to her. "They'll listen to you."

"I saw you shiver." David started to reach out his hand but stopped when she pulled back. "Is it always this cold in here? I can have an extra heater installed."

"It's only like this when the wind is out of the north," said Sarah. "I keep a sweater behind the door."
She held out a manila folder. "I've done the numbers, but you need to check them and sign off before I can record them."

David reached for the papers, touching the back of her hand with his fingertips.

"Well done, Sister. You're always thinking, aren't you?"

Twenty-Three

On Wednesday, Bethany Ruth was absent from class. Olympia considered picking up the phone to see if she was ill but remembered Will's sharp hands-off warning and stayed her hand.

Jim called on Thursday to tell her he had some information on the matter they'd been discussing and to ask when they could get together. Then he added that he hoped the predicted monster snowstorm would miss them, because it would really mess up the Advent schedule at St. Brendan's.

Olympia reassured him, saying they'd never had a full-blown blizzard as early as this, and weather or not, Malcolm was going to the Fellowship concert on Boston Common that Sunday. She suggested they meet after that, because maybe she would have something to report, as well.

Friday morning, Olympia found a plastic grocery sack full of papers hanging from the doorknob outside her office. There was an envelope stuck to the front with Olympia's name written in green crayon.

Olympia dropped her things on the floor and pulled opened the envelope.

Dear Professor Brown,

Here is my final project. You told us that we didn't have to come back if we finished all our work. Thank you for a wonderful class.

Love, Bethany Ruth

P.S. You can keep the picture of Jesus if you want it.

"Damn!" said Olympia out loud, "Now what do I do?"

By Saturday evening, some of the local forecasters were predicting a snowstorm of major proportions, but none would say exactly how major. Ordinarily, Olympia would be rooting for the big one, but this time she wasn't so sure. She called Malcolm to suggest that maybe he should wait a week, but he wasn't home, so she left a message.

By then it was too late to call Frederick but not too late to light a cozy fire in the woodstove, enjoy a solitary glass of wine, or two, with her cats and think about what she might say to the man across the sea when next they spoke. As she set about laying the fire, the cats arranged themselves on the mat, rumbling in anticipation. Olympia bent low and blew the sparks from the flaming paper curls into the kindling. She could hear the wind pushing at the oak tree branches that arched low over the shingled roof.

Watching the fire and listening to her contented animals, she realized she was no longer an intruder in this curious old house of hers. She was home. *Where was home for her daughter Faith, and would she ever know? Please God, one day…*

By the next morning all the local forecasters were predicting a blizzard but were vague on specifics. Since it was not expected to hit full force until later in the afternoon, Malcolm Patterson, Olympia's firstborn, set off from his student apartment in Somerville under an ominous green-grey sky with only the odd sleety flake skittering across the urban landscape. He could easily check out that group his mother was so interested in and be back before supper.

By the time he had climbed the long flight of stairs out of Park Street station, only a fine mist of snow was sifting through the trees and along the walkways. Malcolm looked up at the pewter sky and shrugged his shoulders. *This is nothing.*

The golden dome of the Boston State House loomed high in front of him, and God only knows what waited on the Common itself. He turned and started toward the bandstand. The snow was coming faster now, but it was still little more than a dusty white powder that swirled and eddied in wave patterns on the pavement. He hiked his guitar higher up on his shoulder and sidestepped a panhandler wrapped in a ragged sleeping bag who called out to him from a park bench. He could see a small crowd gathered off to his left.

The air temperature was dropping, and Malcolm was glad he had remembered his hat and gloves. He wondered how the musicians were managing, but when he joined the people listening to the music, he saw the guitarists had cut the fingertips off the ends of their gloves, and the drummer was wearing big, fuzzy mittens. *These people must be really dedicated,* thought Malcolm, *or crazy.*

Snow was sifting down the back of Malcolm's neck and collecting on his eyelashes, and the wind seemed to be picking up. The musicians were out of the worst of it, but they, too, were starting to brush away the icy grit as it hissed around them. The music and the words were about someone named Jeshua and his all-welcoming love and how anyone could come near and find welcome and refuge from the storm.

The song ended with the people in the band repeating the refrain, "Just look around you, He is near, just look around you, He is here." Malcolm looked around, and right on cue, he saw a bearded man walking toward him, smiling and extending a mittened hand.

"Welcome, brother," said the man. "You must be a musician. Would you like to sit in? It will probably be the last number, what with the weather and all." He looked up at the sky. "It seems to be getting worse."

Malcolm was not prepared for such a direct approach. He planned to be an observer and ask the first question himself. He was momentarily thrown off guard but recovered quickly. "I'll probably just stay for this set and then head back. It's getting bad."

The young man held out his hand a second time and introduced himself as Brother Ezra. He began an easy conversation about music, asking what kind of a guitar he was carrying, and was he in a band, and what kind of music did he play? All were subjects Malcolm could easily warm to—and immediately did.

So far so good, thought Malcolm pulling up his collar against the wind and stamping his feet to keep warm. *The guy just wants to talk about music. No problem with that.*

"Are you doing anything tonight?" The man named Ezra rested a snowy paw on Malcolm's shoulder. "On Sunday nights after the concert we go back home for supper—nothing fancy, just homemade bread and soup. After that we hang out and talk and play music." He removed his hand and wiped the snow off his eyeglasses. "If it gets really bad, you can stay the night. Welcoming people in out of the cold is what we do best."

If Malcolm smelled a sweet Christian rat, he didn't let on. This was a major bonus. What better way to find out about these people than to get inside where they live? He wasn't driving, so he could leave when he wanted and get a train back to Somerville.

"Why not?" said Malcolm. "If you want, I can help the guys break down the band. I've had practice."

"Have you found Jeshua?" asked Ezra. "We call him by his ancient name."

"I didn't know he was lost," quipped Malcolm, not missing a beat.

Ezra made a hollow laughing sound that neither one of them believed.

"Uh, sorry about that, Ez," said Malcolm. "Don't take it personally or anything. Sometimes my mouth doesn't know what its doing. Hope I didn't offend."

"It's an old joke, my friend, and I've heard it many times, but Jeshua isn't lost. It's the rest of us who are until we find him."

Here it comes, thought Malcolm, not losing hold of his smile.

"We'll talk about that tonight," continued Ezra, pulling up his collar so it covered his ears. "It's not like church or anything. It's what we do on Sunday nights. Do you still want to come?"

The engaging grin was back. *The man could sell cars,* thought Malcolm. "Sure," he said. "Good musicians and good food, that's a no brainer."

When the equipment was packed and secured, a beat-up Dodge passenger van materialized out of the swirling snow. Malcolm and Ezra, the musicians and a couple of women, plus two others whose faces he couldn't really see, stamped the snow off their feet and brushed each other's shoulders before climbing into the van.

When everyone was squeezed in, Ezra apologized for the malfunctioning heater but assured them that their body heat would help. Squashed in among the piled-up passengers, Malcolm couldn't see faces or even determine the genders of the people pressed against him and wondered if he would ever regain the feeling in his toes. The fogged-up windows of the van were caked with road salt, the snow was making the driving treacherous, and the visibility was next to zero.

"Where is this place?" asked Malcolm after Ezra had done a round of introductions which Malcolm knew he'd never remember.

"Not far," said Ezra. "It's a big old house on the Allston-Brighton line. "We bought it from the Hare Krishnas when their numbers dropped. Surely it was the hand of God encouraging our mission."

Confident that no one could see him, Malcolm mentally rolled his eyes. He could smell wet wool and feel his empty stomach grumbling. He was not having second thoughts as they slid along, bumping against each other in the chilly darkness. He was having seventh and eighth thoughts. Included in these were some very unforgiving thoughts towards his must-save-the-world-mother and a few more for his own stupidity in saying yes to this latest of her crazy schemes.

After an hour and a half of crawling, sliding, and cautious braking, they arrived, hungry and desperately cold, at The Boston Christian Common Center for Fellowship and Renewal, Brighton, Massachusetts.

Everyone pitched in getting the bulky band equipment through the mounting snow and stacking it in the far corner of a huge, old-fashioned kitchen. Malcolm and two other guests, a young man named Raymond who looked to be near his own age and a pale, thin woman whose name he'd forgotten, were ushered into a large living room to warm up by the fire. Malcolm asked Ezra if there was a telephone he could use to call his girlfriend, but Ezra shook his head, saying there was no phone in the building.

That's odd, thought Malcolm. *I wonder what that's all about?* Before he could think more about it, he and the others were called to supper.

Within minutes all were seated at a long oval table, everyone except a hollow-eyed woman standing in the doorway. She was dressed in a loose-fitting garment that fell to her ankles, and like the women at the table, her hair was concealed beneath a knotted scarf.

At a signal from a man sitting at the head of the table, they bowed their heads and joined hands as an intense-looking man stood and introduced himself as Brother David. He began an interminable grace and eventually ended his oration by thanking God for delivering everyone safely through the fury of the storm and for the gift of their three guests and for the many blessings of their holy mission—all in Jeshua's holy, merciful and gracious name. Amen.

Malcolm looked at the somber-faced woman standing just beyond the door and turned to the man sitting beside him. "Isn't she going to eat?"

"We take turns serving the table, Brother Malcolm. Here, have a piece of this bread. It's just now come out of the oven."

Twenty-Four

The snowstorm wasn't predicted to begin in Brookfield until later in the day, so Olympia had plenty of time to make an end-run to the grocery store for wine, extra cookies, cat food, and milk. *First things first.*

She was worried about Malcolm and tried calling him to suggest he make it another time. She got his girlfriend, who told her he'd gone off to see some rock group on Boston Common but said he'd cut out early if the weather got bad. She told Olympia not to worry. He could take care of himself.

Malcolm's mother hoped she was right.

From the look of the slate grey sky and the penetrating damp of the air, Olympia decided she had better drag in some more logs. She had never used the woodstove as the sole source of heat before and figured if they lost power, she had better have an ample supply of dry wood. As the snow began to fall, she congratulated herself on her Yankee prudence and ingenuity. Out of habit, she caught a few flakes on her tongue. They tasted even better than they did when she was seven.

Experience told her to leave the shovel inside the front door and move the car to the end of the driveway facing the street. After that, she filled a number of containers with fresh water, just in case, and put an extra layer of litter in the cat box. Neither cat was fond of squatting in deep snow. *Can't say as I blame them.*

By the time she completed her preparations and lighted a fire, Olympia was ready to think about food. She dug around in the freezer and located an undated iceberg of minestrone soup, which she pried loose with a screwdriver and set in a pot over the fire to melt. Before long, the earthy aroma of tomato, garlic, oregano, and God knew what else she threw in when she made it, was spreading throughout the house. The scene was set, and Olympia was ready to enjoy the oncoming storm. She snuggled into her wonderful old house and let it wrap itself around her like one of her grandmother's quilts.

With the cats purring in a heap by the stove and Miss Winslow's diary on the table beside her, Olympia breathed a long sigh of contentment. Whoever might be trying to send her a warning was back in the wilds of Boston and Cambridge, surely as immobile as she. For now, at least, with the wind mounting and the snow already blowing horizontally, Olympia was safe from harm.

She'd try calling Malcolm again later, but now all she wanted to do was to open the precious diary and learn more about Leanna Faith Winslow. The only information she had gleaned thus far was that Miss Winslow was the great-great-granddaughter and last descendent of Mr. Otis Winslow, the man who built the place, and that she lived her entire ninety-four years in the house Olympia Brown had more recently claimed as her own.

Twenty-Five

When Brother David finished the prayer, he directed the woman in the doorway to bring in the rest of the meal. Malcolm was careful not to stare as she walked in, carrying an enormous pot of thick, steaming soup.

"I think it's best if you wait in the kitchen, Sister." Brother David began filing the bowls and passing them left and right. "I'll call you if we need anything."

"In God's name," said the woman, bowing her head and leaving the room. Malcolm looked around and noted that the other two guests were, like him, seated between two members who were plying them with hearty food and friendly conversation. Ezra, on Malcolm's immediate right, passed him the butter, and the smiling woman on his left, Sister Miriam, asked for the salt but invited him to take some first. The food was delicious, and this was not a casual seating.

Malcolm tried to take in as much as he could without being obvious. *They're a little quirky,* he thought, reaching for a third piece of bread, *with the old-fashioned clothes and the brother and sister stuff, but other than that, I think my dear mother is overreacting, as usual. They're not so bad, they're just different. Surely they mean well.*

Outside the storm was gathering strength, but he was warm, dry, and full. He leaned back in his chair and liberated a gentle burp as the silent woman with the big eyes and a single, chestnut-colored curl visible from under her headscarf returned from the kitchen to clear the table. Brother David rose and directed them into the living room where they could enjoy the fire and get to know one another. *It's a good thing my last name isn't the same as my mother's,* thought Malcolm lowering himself onto the oversized, off-white sofa and stretching his feet toward the fire. *There's no way they'll connect us.*

Ezra asked them to go around the room and introduce themselves and say where they lived and what they did and if or where they went to church. When it was his turn, Malcolm told them he was a rock musician and a sometime college student, that he had worked his musical way up from a neighborhood garage band to the point where his group played in some local places around Boston, and they were almost ready to record their first C.D. He told them that he didn't attend any particular church but went if one of his girlfriends did.

"Tell us about your family," said Ezra. "Do you have brothers and sisters?"

"I don't talk about my family," said Malcolm, shaking his head and looking at a blank space on the wall opposite him.

"Hey, man," said Ezra raising both hands, "I didn't mean to pry—it's okay."

"No problem," said Malcolm.

Ezra took the hint, turned in his chair, and directed his attention to the next guest, a raggedy-looking waif who kept pushing back her lank, waist-length hair and wiping her nose as she told them that her adopted Native American name was Yellow Bee Pollen, and she thought she might be pregnant, and she also thought was going to be sick, so please could she be excused? With her hand clamped over her mouth, the girl made a desperate dash for the door that led to the bathrooms. In an instant, sisters

Miriam and Sarah were out of their chairs and running to help her.

Brother Ezra looked in the direction of the empty doorway and directed his next question to Raymond, the other male guest who had joined them after the concert.

Over Raymond's extended recitation of his personal history, Malcolm heard the wind rising and noted that the light overhead was beginning to flicker. He listened to the sharp clatter of dishwashing coming from the kitchen and wondered as he gazed into the dying fire what, if anything, he might learn about these curious people as the night wore on.

The storm was building, blowing and drifting snow piling in graceful swirls along the windowpanes and against the doors, shrouding the world outside in clouds of whirling white. Brother David got up and added another log to the fire. Taking a place beside the mantel, he opened his Bible and began to read aloud.   Just   beyond the doorway to the kitchen, Bethany Ruth could hear their voices as she finished the dishes and put away the leftover food. She reached up to her headscarf and tucked in the wisp of hair that escaped when she was serving dinner. Modesty and obedience in women was expected, and so was self-denial. Prospective members were expected to cleanse their bodies of impurities. On weekends, new aspirants were restricted to a diet of clear liquids, juices, broth and lots and lots of water. During the week they were allowed to eat normally but sparingly. They said it was to help her focus on Jeshua's love.

Bethany Ruth believed what they told her, but standing there alone in the kitchen, she was so hungry she thought she might faint.

"Drink lots of water," they said. "That way, you'll rid yourself of impurities and stop the stomach growls for a little while."

Not for long, thought Bethany Ruth miserably as she stacked the dishes back in the cupboard. *All it makes me do is have to run to the bathroom twenty times a day.* Mealtimes were torture, smelling all that food and serving it to the others, but after dinner when she was doing the dishes, she would run her fingers around the dirty plates and lick the greasy leavings before she put them into the sink. Later, alone in the bathroom, filled with remorse and praying for forgiveness, she would force herself to vomit. She ran the water and flushed the toilet so the brothers and sisters in the Fellowship would not hear the awful gagging and retching.

As she wiped down the surface of the work table in the kitchen and listened to the voices coming from the next room, she recalled the first night she had stayed here and done those very things they were doing now, talking and getting to know one another. These people were so wonderful.

She could hear Sister Miriam talking about love and family and belonging. Next, Brother David would talk about deliverance from evil. The guests would then be invited to ask questions, and before they left, Brother Aaron would take addresses and phone numbers.

Within a few days, a Fellowship member would call each guest and see how they were doing and invite them back for another visit. But the storm outside was now a full-blown nor'easter, and it was unlikely that anyone would be going anywhere.

She could hear Brother David saying that public transportation had been cancelled, and a city-wide snow emergency was in effect until further notice.

Bethany Ruth leaned against the sink and looked out the kitchen window. The snow was already halfway up the railing on the back porch and blowing into wavelike sculptures around the base of the evergreen in the back yard. She shivered and tried pouring herself another glass of water, but instead of drinking it, she set it on the counter beside the sink, covered her face with her hands, and prayed for strength.

Twenty-Six

In the cozy warmth of the living room, Brother David invited the three guests to stay the night. Yellow Bee Pollen was back, still looking very much the color of her name. Raymond, the other first-timer, looked vaguely uncomfortable and made some noises about being a nuisance, but Brother David reassured him, saying it was their duty and greatest pleasure to offer food and hospitality to anyone who came to their door.

Malcolm accepted the invitation at once and marveled at his good fortune. He couldn't have planned this if he'd tried. He had already figured out that Bother David and a woman named Sister Sarah appeared to be in command. He also could feel an electric tension sparking between them and wondered what that was all about.

He stretched his arms up and out in front of him until his shoulders creaked and cracked and then stood up. The sofa was low, and he was stiff from sitting so long.

"What do you need? Is there something we can get for you?" Brother Ezra was standing beside him, effectively blocking him.

"Mind if I get a glass of water?"

I'll get it," said Ezra, not moving.

"No no," said Malcolm, moving towards the door. "My foot is cramping, and I need to move around."

"I'll get you a glass," said Ezra, turning towards the kitchen.

It was clear to Malcolm they did not want him walking around unescorted. He followed Ezra into the kitchen and was drinking his water when he saw the silent woman again. She was standing in the corner looking like a guilty child with her hands behind her back, looking away from them.

Malcolm was totally thrown off guard. Everything inside him said something was wrong here, but caution told him to shut up and get the hell out of the kitchen. He followed caution and turned to leave but not before Miriam came into the kitchen.

"Sister," said Miriam, rushing toward the girl in the corner. "Are you tired? Perhaps you need to rest."

The girl in the corner said nothing as the older woman shielded her from Malcolm's view and hurried her out of the kitchen. Malcolm wondered if this was the person his mother was so worried about, but he said nothing and followed Ezra back to the living room where Fellowship members were discussing sleeping arrangements. Because of her condition, Yellow Bee Pollen would be staying upstairs with the women, and he and Raymond were assigned to the two sofas in the living room.

The Sisters were already handing out pillows and blankets. Malcolm and Raymond each appropriated the sofa nearest to where they were standing and began to set up camp. They made awkward small talk and took turns in the bathroom where Malcolm, out of habit, cleaned his teeth the best he could by rubbing them with his fingers and rinsing his mouth out with cold water.

As they were settling down, Ezra came in to wish them a blessed good night and thanked God again for bringing them all in out of the storm. As he left, he pressed the light switch by the door, and the room dissolved into the eerie half-light of a snowy night in New England, not bright enough to read by and not dark enough to sleep easily.

Malcolm wiggled himself into a comfortable position on the sofa cushions and lay there, staring at the dying fire and trying to make sense of what he'd seen and heard. It wasn't long before the insistent, rhythmic hiss of the snow against the windows and the buffeting of the wind against the old house did its work, and Olympia Brown's elder son slipped into a light, uneasy doze.

Twenty-Seven

The power went out at seven minutes after six, and Olympia reached for the matches and the squat, four-hour plumber candles she had prudently left on the table beside her chair. Cupping the flame with her hand, she lighted two more candles and placed one on either side of the mantel clock, letting the mirror behind them reflect and double the light. After adding another log to the fire, she sat alone in the flickering candlelight and thought about the people who had lived in this house before her—and more specifically, about Miss Leanna Faith Winslow.

The cats were skittish, but at least they weren't freaking out the way they did when she first moved in. Before the lights went out, she had checked in with Randall, her younger son, but Malcolm still wasn't home. *He's savvy,* she kept telling herself, trying to stem a tidal wave of anxiety with white-knuckle positive thinking. *Why the hell did I involve him? What if something happens?* Olympia was working herself into a panic, and she knew it.

"Okay, Girl," she said out loud, "stop this foolishness, and get hold of yourself. Have another glass of wine. You're not going anywhere tonight." *But where in God's name is my son?*

Olympia went out to the kitchen and poured herself a second glass of her most recent *vin ordinaire,* an inoffensive little chardonnay without one single fruity overtone, the kind of wine that didn't need room or time to breathe. Then she arranged a plateful of cookies to wash down with it. *I'll have the soup for dessert,* she told herself, trying to be funny and not succeeding.

The scent of the bayberry candle flickering on the kitchen table, the hot metal smell of the glowing stove in the great room, and the pervasive smell of old house wood were all familiar now and gave her comfort.

Back in the great room, Olympia set down her glass and reached for the diary. In the two weeks since she had discovered it, she'd done little more than glance at it, but now the night and the diary were hers.

It was a small volume and surprisingly intact, considering its age. Olympia loved the warm feel of the soft leather in her hand and took great care as she looked for the entry for that exact day one hundred and fifty years ago.

December 11, 1859

The freezing rain has turned to snow, and depending on the length and nature of this storm, I could be confined for days. The root cellar is still half full, and I have ample stores to keep me fed, but it's the others I worry about. I will occupy my time with baking and reading and this, my long neglected diary.

It's been five months since Father died, and I still think I can hear his footsteps coming through the kitchen door. I promised him before he died I would not sell the house, but the farm is far too much for me to keep, and in truth, I have no interest in it. Books and learning are my passion, and teaching school here in Brookfield might suit me very well.

Mr. Jackson from the parish church approached me in respect of purchasing the acreage across the road, and I am giving it some favorable thought. The money from the land and what I earn from my teaching will keep me well enough.

I am predisposed to think that Mr. Jackson may have another offer to make as well, but as I am not inclined to farming, so am I similarly disinclined to marriage. I may be a mere woman (oh how I loathe the term, "the weaker sex"), but I am not called to wife and motherhood, blessed states they may be, and have no wish to be constrained within the bonds of so-called holy matrimony.

More anon...LFW

Olympia was interrupted in her reading by the simultaneous ring of the telephone and the musical chime of the mantel clock. Olympia looked over at the clock. *The hands haven't moved, the clock doesn't work, but the clock just chimed. What's that about?*

The phone rang a second time, and she reluctantly set down the diary and picked up the receiver. The connection was crackly, but despite the storm static, she instantly recognized the voice.

"Frederick—of course I know who it is." She could feel herself grinning like a Cheshire cat with a face full of canaries. "I don't get many charming Englishmen calling me in the middle of howling snowstorms."

Frederick ended his introductory pleasantries by saying that he'd seen on the 'telly' there was a history-making snowstorm blasting coastal New England and wondered how she was faring.

"How kind of you to call," said Olympia. "It really is wild. It's beautiful, though, especially when you're home next to a cozy fire. We've lost power, but I've plenty of wood and candles. There must be half a foot outside already, and it isn't supposed to stop until sometime tomorrow."

Olympia shifted and reached for her wine. She looked at the clock on the mantel and wondered if she had imagined hearing the chime. *No, I heard it.*

"Tell me what's happening in Merry-Old?"

But Frederick was far more interested to hear how she was keeping in the storm.

"I have a very efficient woodstove," said Olympia, "and enough food for a week. The only thing that could improve the situation would be to have an Englishman to share it all with."

Frederick took the opportunity to ask if she might consider coming over a bit sooner.

"I only wish I could," she said, smiling into the receiver. "What are you doing for the holidays?"

He told her he might be in the Home Counties visiting family, or maybe not, that he hadn't decided yet, and would she please send him a photograph of herself, and her voice sounded strained, was there something bothering her?

Without intending to, Olympia found herself pouring out the whole story of Bethany Ruth and how she had asked her son Malcolm to do a little investigating, and now she couldn't reach him, and it was snowing like hell outside, and he might be in trouble, and she'd never forgive herself if anything happened to him, and …

Olympia stopped for breath, realizing it was the first time she had articulated all of her fears and the enormity of what she had gotten herself inextricably tangled in against the express orders of the Dean of Meriwether College.

Frederick's usual witty repartee changed instantly to words of genuine and helpful concern. She knew then that she was talking to a man who not only listened but asked for her to tell him more.

This one is different.

Fearing if she hung up she might not be able to call back out, Olympia excused herself for an expensive long distance moment to lay another log on the fire. She noted she might have to get more wood in before she went to bed if she wanted to keep the ancient pipes from freezing.

When she picked up the phone again, Olympia looked down at her watch. "Jesus, Frederick," she said. "This is costing you a fortune."

"Nothing I wouldn't do for Her Majesty the Queen," said Frederick.

Olympia was charmed by his Briticisms and touched by his attempt to lighten her mood without being dismissive of her concerns.

"You've helped me enormously. Just being able to say all of this out loud gives me a much clearer sense of the situation and what I may or may not be able to do to help."

"Be careful, Olympia," said Frederick, his voice serious. "I don't know anything about these people other than what you've told me, but I have the sense there's a lot they don't want the general public to know about how they do business, and it appears they could get very unpleasant if someone, like you, for example, were to try and find out."

"I'll be careful," said Olympia, noting the concern in his voice. "Actually, there is someone over here who is working on this with me. His name is Jim Sawicki. He's a chaplain at a college nearby. We're good friends, and we've worked together before. I'll call him tomorrow."

"How good friends?" came the instant response.

"He's a priest, Frederick." Despite her concerns, Olympia could not keep from smiling.

"Oh, all right then, in which case let me change the subject. I'd like to get you a little something for Christmas. What size do you wear?"

"What size what?" said Olympia with a look on her face that Frederick couldn't possibly see. "A lady never divulges her dress size to a gentleman." *And this lady never will until I lose a few pounds.* "Tell you what. Let's plan to have our Christmas when I get there. Then I can have a few surprises for you, as well."

Olympia could hear some merry muttering and sputtering on the other end of the line, but she chose to ignore them. When they finally said their goodnights, she arched her back, stretched her arms high over her head, and wondered why she felt as though she'd been transfused with champagne.

Yes, there definitely is something worth looking into with this one.

Frederick was a good listener, and talking to him helped Olympia put the Bethany Ruth situation into some sort of perspective. From that enlightened vantage point, it was bad and getting worse. Meanwhile, she really did need to get in some more wood before going to bed.

Olympia could hear the wind whipping around the back of the house and knew it was blowing the snow against the kitchen door. The sound of it made her shiver. She'd have to ram the door through it to get out to the woodpile.

When she was fully geared up to brave the weather, she eased the door open, pushed hard against the accumulating drift, and stepped out into the wildness of the storm. It was cold and heart-stoppingly beautiful. She loved the feel of the icy snow stinging her face and the sibilant hiss of it falling in the darkness around her, especially with such a nice warm home to go back into.

I wonder how much snow they get in England, she thought as she plowed her way back toward the house, staggering under the load of three big logs and extra kindling. She was still worried about Malcolm. Instinctively, she knew he was someplace warm, but the same instinct said nothing about safe. Back inside, Olympia brushed the snow off the wood and piled it near the stove to dry. There would be puddles in the morning.

She had collapsed back into her chair when the phone rang again. Hoping it was her son, Olympia reached for the receiver and held it to close to her ear.

"Professor Brown?"

"This is she." Olympia was instantly on alert.

"Malcolm is staying the night with us.

Olympia gripped the receiver. "Who are you?"

"We here are doing the work of Yahweh, Professor Brown. The Bible tells us of the evil which befalls those who oppose Him. You, as an ordained minister, should be aware of that."

"Let me talk to him." Olympia tried to keep her voice from shaking.

"I'm afraid that isn't possible," said the man on the other end of the line. "As God has commanded us to befriend the stranger, we have taken him in out of the cold and given him food and lodging. He doesn't know that we know who he is, and it will be safer for all concerned if he never finds out."

The speaker paused and then whispered, "Professor Brown, it is in everyone's best interest that you stop prying into other people's business. It will only cause pain and suffering if you continue."

And then the line went dead.

Twenty-Eight

Sister Sarah and Brothers David, Joshua, and Aaron were closeted upstairs away from the others. The sound of the storm was muted now, the wind more a groan than a shriek as the accumulating snow softened the edges of the world beyond their walls. Sarah could feel the old house creak and shudder beneath her feet. Storms made her uneasy.

"Did you get through, Brother Joshua?" asked David.

"I did. At least the phones are still working, but I expect the lights to go any minute. They've been flickering for the past hour." Joshua looked up at the yellowish ceiling light as if to make his point. "I told her in so many words it could be unhealthy for her and her son if she continued to involve herself in other people's affairs, and then I hung up. She heard me."

"I had a feeling this one was going to be a problem," said David, getting out of his chair and starting to pace, "but what can she do? If she calls the police, they'll just think she's some sort of delusional nut case hearing messages in a snowstorm."

"We can never be too careful," said Aaron, scribbling on the note pad he carried with him. "We had a serious slip-up with that other one from Meriwether. I'm sure that's why the professor is nosing around. We were lucky when it happened that the parents wanted to keep it quiet."

"Nobody came to us directly," said David, correcting him, "but I heard that the Meriwether dean was asking questions. The drowning incident at Allston was unfortunate. That could have raised suspicion, being so close to the other one, but an accident is an accident, an unfortunate happenstance. We're reviewing our policies, of course, but only as a general precaution." He paused, "Enough about that. What's the new one's name again?"

"Bethany Ruth," said Sarah.

"She told Sister Miriam who Malcolm was," said Joshua. "She said he looked familiar, that she remembered seeing him at the college sometime back. She was really upset that her trusted professor friend would do something sneaky like that."

"That's a good sign," said David with a thin smile. "She'll stay."

"Don't be too harsh with her, David," said Sarah. "She's so naïve, and she's trying so hard."

There was so much more that Sarah wanted to say about the new one. Something in Bethany Ruth had gone straight to Sarah's heart and awakened something she had buried years ago.

"You are supposed to call me Brother, *Sister* Sarah," said David, interrupting her private thoughts. "We can't relax the rules even in the privacy of the third Circle."

"Yes, of course, Brother David." Sarah lifted her chin and looked directly into the eyes of the man castigating her. "How very careless of me."

Twenty-Nine

Malcolm hadn't been asleep for long when something awakened him. It wasn't a specific sound so much as the lack of it. He opened his eyes, pushed himself up on one elbow, and listened. Raymond was a blanketed mound snoring softly across the room, but that was the only sound he could hear.

He pushed the button on his watch, illuminating the dial. It was a few minutes after midnight. He'd been asleep for a less than an hour. Listening again, he realized there were no house sounds—no refrigerator hum, no sound of clocks ticking. Then he turned and looked out the window and saw that the streetlights were out. They had lost power, and already the house was starting to cool down.

Malcolm wanted a drink and remembered there was a bathroom just off the living room, but when he slipped out from under his blanket and tried to open the door, it wouldn't move. It was locked from the other side. He twisted the doorknob back and forth, thinking it might be stuck. Not wanting to wake his roommate, he gave up and went back to the sofa. *I don't like this,* he thought, *something weird is going on, but what is it?*

Malcolm wondered if they had locked the door to the kitchen as well. He got up again and slipped his feet along the wooden floor through the dining room toward the kitchen and pushed open the door. Even with the power off, the pale snow light made it possible for Malcolm to see his way into the kitchen without tripping or crashing into something.

He located some drinking glasses beside the sink and filled one with water from the tap. As he drank, he looked around, noting the location of the now silent fridge, a large worktable, and a door that likely led to a pantry. He was surprised he could be hungry after all he'd eaten earlier. He began looking around for something to eat when he heard the sound of a mewing kitten.

Jesus, some poor animal is outside in this weather. He was sliding his now freezing feet across the linoleum toward the back door when he heard it again and realized it was not coming from the outside but from behind the door he thought was the pantry. He crossed the kitchen, put his hand on the doorknob, and eased it open.

In the half-light he could see someone wearing a long-sleeved nightgown sitting on the edge of a bed. It was the same woman he had seen in the kitchen at dinnertime. As he inched the door open a little farther, the girl looked up and put her hand over her mouth, trying to stifle the sound of her crying.

Here's my lost kitten, thought Malcolm, wondering why she was in here and not upstairs with the other women in the Fellowship. He tiptoed across the room and sat down on the bed beside her. He wanted to put his arm around her to comfort her but instantly thought better of it.

"Shhh," whispered Malcolm. "Everyone's asleep. What the hell is going on?"

Bethany Ruth looked at him and shook her head, but he persisted.

"Who are you? What are they doing to you?

The miserable girl edged away from Malcolm and clamped her other hand over her mouth. Finally, she lowered her hands and whispered to Malcolm that she was really all right, and he shouldn't be here, because if they caught her with a man in her room, she would be in big trouble. Sitting up a little straighter, she explained between sniffs and gulps that she wasn't sick or anything. She couldn't sleep because she was hungry. She was going to get up and get a glass of water, and he needed to go back into the living room. The members of the Fellowship didn't like strangers wandering around the house.

"But they seem so friendly," whispered Malcolm, not mentioning the locked door in the living room.

"They are until you break a rule," whispered Bethany Ruth. "There are strict rules for initiates, and being here means too much to me to do anything wrong — anything." She turned to him, pleading in the cooling grey light. "I know you mean well, but just go back, and whatever you do," she placed a cold hand on his arm, "don't say anything about coming in here tonight."

But Malcolm would not be put off. "If you're hungry, why don't you get something to eat? You're sleeping right next to the kitchen."

"I'm only allowed liquids on weekends," whispered the girl. "It's a mind-body purification process that ... never mind, I'll be okay."

"That's crazy," said Malcolm. "No wonder you can't sleep." He got up and started toward the kitchen. "I'm going to get you some food, and no one's going to know unless you tell them."

"Please don't," she begged, but Malcolm was out of the room, feeling his way around on the cold, slick floor. He located two bananas and a half-loaf of bread on the table and carried them back into her room.

"Come on," he said, breaking the bread in two pieces, "eat this. If anyone asks, I'll say I ate it. I'll even put both banana peels on the floor beside my shoes so they'll believe it was me."

As much as she may have wanted to refuse, Bethany Ruth took the offered banana and the bread in her two hands and looked up at Malcolm.

"A banana and a hunk of bread are not going to kill you," he said turning to leave the room, "but not eating sure as hell will."

Bethany Ruth didn't respond, but when he closed the door behind him, she began wolfing down the forbidden food, wishing between bites and gulps that she hadn't told Sister Miriam who he was.

Back in the kitchen, Malcolm finished off his own banana and the smaller piece of bread and then went back into the living room. In less than an hour the house had gone from chilly to cold. He placed the two banana skins on the floor next to his shoes. If anyone asked about them in the morning, he'd say that he didn't want to make any noise searching around for a trash bin. Malcolm shivered and rolled himself tighter in his blanket and tried to burrow deeper into the cushions on the sofa.

As he was drifting back to sleep, he heard a toilet flush somewhere in the house. Then he heard it flush again and then again. He pulled the scratchy blanket more tightly around his shoulders, turned onto his side, and let his breathing grow deep and soft and even.

Outside, the wind-driven snow continued, shrouding the house, covering the secrets and making it all so white and soft and so very, terribly, pure.

Thirty

Olympia surprised herself by sleeping until after eight. She had been dreaming strange, disconnected images in brilliant color, but they had been too fleeting for her to remember. The cats had already gone off into the kitchen, and she could hear the old one, Whitefoot, complaining.

The power was still off, and the house was cold. From her bedroom window she could see that over two feet of snow had fallen during the night. The sky was clearing, but her son Malcolm was still in the dubious company of the Boston Christian Common Fellowship. She shivered. *Please, God, protect him.*

Trees and fences in the neighborhood were little more than rounded elevations in a surreal landscape. She could see only a depression in the road where a snowplow must have gone by in the night, but already the blowing snow was reshaping the scrapings. Later on, an army of avaricious neighborhood children would show up on her doorstep, shovels on shoulders and mittened palms outstretched, demanding hugely inflated prices for shoddy work. She would welcome them and pay their fees. It was an earned privilege of her middle age.

When she was dressed in as many layers as she could manage and still move, Olympia, the former Girl Scout, poked a few bits of kindling into the embers, delivered a few well-aimed puffs at the crumbly ashen pile, and in minutes, the fire was blazing up and warming the silent room.

With that accomplished and a cold knot of fear in her stomach, she called Malcolm's apartment. His girlfriend said he still wasn't back but not to worry. It wasn't the first time he'd lost track of time when he was out jamming with a bunch of musicians.

Easy for you to say, Buttercup. You didn't teach him to blow his nose and tie his shoes.

Olympia thanked her and asked that he call the minute he got home. After that, she went into the kitchen to round up something for breakfast. The food in the refrigerator was still cold enough, but if the power stayed off for too long, she might have to pack the food and the frozen things into a handy snow bank.

She got out her camping coffee percolator, a frying pan, a couple of eggs, butter, and two slices of bread. Comfort food, lots of it, cooked on a woodstove after a big, bad snowstorm was going to be pure bliss. When Olympia was worried or upset, food was a great comfort. In fact, food was great any time of the day, even when she didn't need comforting.

After breakfast, Olympia poured herself another cup of coffee. It was sludgy, but by God, it was hot. Thus fortified, she picked up the phone and dialed Jim's rectory number.

"Hey, Jim, it's me. How are you managing in the storm?"

"Snowed in like everyone else, Olympia, but I've known you too long to think you're calling me about the weather. What's going on?"

"I got a phone call from someone in the Fellowship last night. He told me my son was there, and then in so many words, he told me to butt out of their business, or there would be consequences."

Jim's voice went flat. "Tell me everything you can remember."

"Malcolm went into the Boston Common yesterday, storm and all, to check out these people and ended up at their place. I don't know the details. "

"This is bad," said Jim, "and I'm about to make it worse. How much time do you have?"

Olympia told Jim she had all the time he needed but to hang on until she grabbed something to write with. Over the next hour, he told her that since they had last spoken, he had been in touch with some of his colleagues. From what he could gather, it appeared that at least three more students with connections to the Fellowship had died in unusual circumstances, but no one had been able to make a direct link between the cause of death and the Fellowship itself.

Olympia was writing as fast as she could. She asked if anyone had actually contacted the police in any of these incidents.

"Other than filing an accident report, no. There's still not enough hard data to warrant it," said Jim. "I don't think anybody's actually thought about investigating the deaths. The details are vague. When the students died, their deaths were recorded as accidental or unexplained like your anorexic student at Meriwether last year. We know of a girl at Massachusetts College of Art who died in a freak car accident last year and a young man at Harvard who supposedly contracted a rogue virus that killed him in less than twenty-four hours. Then there was my student, the one who vomited, choked on it, and drowned in the university swimming pool."

"That's a horrible way to die," said Olympia.

"It is, indeed, and therein might be the link in the chain of events which might be the key. I learned that three of them died because they choked on their own vomit, as well. Your Sonya Wilson didn't, but she was anorexic. If there's a pattern here, she was different. Her death most likely *was* accidental, but no one has ever looked into why the other three victims were vomiting just before they died. I may be way out there, Olympia, but I'm thinking that may be the connection."

Jim paused to catch his breath. "The other thing is, these fatal, so-called accidents occurred when the students were trying to get out of the Fellowship. Your student was in the process of joining. That could be significant as well, but I don't see how yet."

Olympia set her coffee cup on the edge of the stove to reheat and shifted to a more comfortable position. Her neck and shoulders were beginning to cramp.

"What about Bethany Ruth?" Olympia was still taking notes as fast as she could.

"She's still a recruit, so she can't know very much. I think she's safe for now. As long as she stays in contact with you, we have a link, and as of right now, Olympia, she's our only one. The Fellowship's public face is superbly constructed. Nobody's been able to get behind it. It will be interesting to find out what your son has to say when he calls."

Olympia shivered and reached for her coffee. Just as she did so, the electricity came back on.

"It's not against the law to be a religious group or to join one," said Jim, "and it's not a crime to get so malnourished and exhausted that you're easy prey to any wandering virus or bacterial infection. If you get sick and die alone in your room or start throwing up and drive under a truck or drown in a swimming pool, it's a terrible, unfortunate accident, but to the casual observer, it's still an accident. All four deaths would appear to be tragic twists of fate, only I don't think for a minute that they are."

Olympia could hear him take a deep breath.

"They're murderers," Jim's voice was tight with emotion, "and they're getting away with it. It's the worst kind of con game, Olympia. These bastards are offering salvation and security in the name of God. The price is total submission and mindless obedience, or suffer the consequences."

It was not like Jim to swear. These tragic accidents were not savage twists of fate but the results of a deadly aberration of human behavior perpetrated under the guise of religious practice. It was the antithesis of everything that she and Jim, theologically different as they were, held sacred in their lives.

Olympia looked down at her watch. Because of the power outage, she needed to reset the clocks.

"Jim, let me think about all of this. I'll call you back after I've talked with Malcolm. We've got to find a way to get inside that operation. The snowstorm was too convenient for words, but I doubt if we can arrange another one."

"I'm not going anywhere, Olympia. Meanwhile, I'll see what else I can dig up, snow pun intended."

Jim never let an opportunity pass, no matter how grave the circumstances. Olympia groaned appropriately and rang off. Then she switched on the television and heard the forecaster announce that the fast-moving storm was over earlier than expected, but the high winds might not die down until the next day. Local newscasters reported that driving was hazardous, and only public transport and emergency vehicles were allowed on the streets until further notice. This meant she had at least two days at home without interruptions before she would have to go back to the college.

She reached down beside her chair, dug around in the basket of miscellany she kept there for a second piece of paper, and began to outline her thoughts.

It would appear that this group was directly or indirectly responsible for the deaths of as many as four college students. Now they had explicitly threatened her and her elder son, but if she said anything to anyone right now, would anyone believe her?

Olympia spent the rest of the morning going over what Jim had told her, making notes, and trying to find more connections and similarities. By lunchtime, she thought she might be on the outermost edge of a plan, and that, in Olympia's way of thinking, meant it was time to eat.

She cast a longing look at the diary, closed and sitting on the table beside her. She hoped she would be able to get back to it tonight. There was so much more she wanted to know about Miss Leanna Faith Winslow. She was finding connections and similarities here, as well, and it was not only the dates and days of the week.

What about my own Faith? Is she safe and out of the cold?

Thirty-One

Malcolm rubbed a porthole in the frosty window next to the sofa. The incandescent whiteness of the snow was blinding in the brilliant morning sun. He could see cars and buses inching along the rutted streets, transforming the pristine beauty of the record-breaking snowfall into an amorphous slushy hash.

The familiar sounds of meal preparation coming from the kitchen made Malcolm and Raymond more than ready for breakfast. The two dressed quickly, then folded and stacked their blankets and pillows on an empty chair. Malcolm really wanted to ask Raymond what he thought of all of this but prudently opted for more general conversation about the weather and the anticipated meal.

"Food for the body and food for the soul," intoned Raymond. "I like it here."

Malcolm bit back the wisecrack that was doing its best to escape when the living room door opened. Miriam, leading a less bilious Yellow Bee Pollen, came in and invited them all to breakfast.

"We'll give you both a nice warm start before you set out. It looks like a beautiful day, but it's dangerously cold out there. We've got extra clothes, if you need anything."

Raymond and Malcolm walked into the next room and took their places at the table.

"We never did get to hear you play your guitar, Malcolm," said Joshua. "Maybe some other time?"

Joshua said the words with his mouth but not with his eyes. Malcolm continued the polite charade, wondering if maybe they did know who he was. *Nah, how could they? There's no way.*

"I'd love to come back and do a little noodling around with you guys sometime," he said. "The snow cancelled everything yesterday, but maybe I'll come by again some Sunday."

Malcolm didn't see Joshua glance at David, but Bethany Ruth, who was standing attendance in the doorway, couldn't miss it.

After the blessing, Malcolm maintained an easy, friendly chatter through another bountiful and delicious meal. He deliberately avoided making eye contact with the serving girl, fearing any hint of recognition might get them both in trouble. She had to be the one his mother was worried about. *Poor kid,* he thought, *mopping up the last of his egg with a still warm piece of bread. She looks like a scared, hungry rabbit.*

After breakfast, Malcolm wasted no time collecting his jacket and guitar. Yellow Bee Pollen had gratefully accepted an invitation to stay and went off with Sister Miriam. As Malcolm looked around the room doing a final check, Raymond turned to Joshua and asked if he could stay for a while and talk to him about the Fellowship's mission.

Even though he had told Joshua that he might like to come and play with them sometime, Malcolm knew he was never coming anywhere near this bunch of weirdoes again, and the sooner he got his coat and was out of there, the better. The night before, Malcolm had stuffed his hat, scarf, and gloves into his sleeve the way his mother taught him when he was in kindergarten. He smiled at the memory. *Man, is she going to get an earful when I get back.*

It was evident that sooner was better for all concerned, because no one wasted any time seeing him out and locking the heavy oak door firmly behind him. Bitter and windy as it was, Malcolm was glad to be breathing the cold, clean air and on his way home.

Standing at the bus stop and stamping his feet on the snowy sidewalk, he and a few other hardy souls shared storm stories as they waited. *This is better,* he thought, *cold as hell maybe, but at least these people are normal.*

When the bus finally lumbered up the snowy street and grunted to a stop, they all piled on board, kicking the snow off their feet and filling in the empty seats. Malcolm pushed through to the back. He was going all the way to Harvard Square, and as much as it was even remotely possible on a packed commuter bus, Malcolm needed to be alone with his thoughts.

He sat down on an ice-cold orange plastic seat, winced at the shock to his nether parts, wedged his guitar case between his knees, and loosened his scarf. As the heat began to come up, Malcolm took off his gloves and was pushing them into his pocket when he felt a folded piece of paper. He drew it out and unfolded a hastily scrawled message: *I know you meant well, but don't ever come back and try to help me. I want to be here. If you come back it will be bad for both of us. I told them who you are.*

Malcolm read it a second time, refolded it, and wondered what kind of a fit his mother was going to have when he showed it to her.

When he finally did call her, it was just past one in the afternoon. He said that he would have called earlier, but they said they had no phone.

"I'm just glad you're all right," said Olympia, trying not to let her relief sound too obvious, "I was worried, but you're okay—so tell me what happened."

For the next fifteen minutes, Malcolm related the entire curious saga. As much as she wanted to, Olympia knew not to interrupt. She could ask questions later.

He told his mother about the concert, the ride back to the residence in the van, and having dinner with them and then staying the night because of the storm. He told her about the door to the front hallway being locked and finding the hungry girl. He described going into her room and getting her some food and promising not to tell any of the other brothers or sisters. He finished by telling her about the note in his pocket

"Do you want me to read it to you?" he asked.

Olympia said she did and got up out of her chair, phone in hand, and began pacing out a tight, nervous circle circumscribed by the length of the phone cord.

When he finished, Olympia said, "Let me ask you a couple of specific questions." She returned to her chair and picked up the pen out of habit. There was still a little space left on her crumpled scratch sheet.

"I'm almost certain the girl you described is Bethany Ruth. Tell me how they were treating her and more importantly, how she was reacting."

"Mostly they were telling her what to do," said Malcolm. "They weren't mean to her or anything."

"What about the food thing?"

"Now that was weird," said Malcolm. "She told me she doesn't eat food on weekends, only liquids. She said it was, what did she call it, some sort of cleansing required of new members. She used another word, but I can't remember it. What the hell is that all about?"

"Purification? Did she use that word? Bethany Ruth is a lonely, homesick, Bible-based Christian, Malcolm, and she believes this is what she wants. She's eighteen, and nobody can stop her. She's not breaking the law."

"Is there anything anyone can do?" Concern was evident in her son's voice. "You want me to try and get back in there?"

"Don't even think about it," Olympia snapped. "This is my mess you've stepped into, Malcolm, and I don't want it sticking to your shoe. Do you understand? I'm sorry for getting you involved at all."

"Hey, Ma-a-a-a," he said, trying to reassure her. "Lighten up, okay? Nothing bad happened. I had a good meal and met a bunch of crazy people I never want to see again, and I didn't find out very much, but at least I tried. I wish I could have done better."

"You did far more than I could have hoped for," said Olympia. "Don't worry about not being able to get anything else out of them. They've had plenty of experience guarding their secrets. Hang on, I'm going to switch phones."

Olympia went out to the kitchen, picked up the wall phone, and began to smear a peanut butter and jelly sandwich for herself.

"Look," she said, gesticulating with the sticky knife, "just stay out of it from now on, okay? Like I said, it's my problem, and I'll find a way to deal with it or I won't. End of story."

"Ma-a-a-a," said Malcolm again. "I know you too well, and you won't leave it alone, so now I'm telling *you* to be careful — and let me know if there is anything else I can do, okay?"

He does know me, thought Olympia with a fond smile, *damn it.* She took a bite of her sandwich and immediately wished she had chosen something easier to talk through.

"Actually," she said around a mouthful of peanut butter, "now that I think about it, there is something you might be able to do that won't put you in any direct danger but might help. Ask around, and see if any of your friends have heard anything about this so-called Fellowship. I need information, and I don't want them to know who's looking for it. Do it without being obvious or using specific names or places. See if anyone you know has heard of anyone who's gotten involved with them." Olympia didn't bother to add *and lived to tell the tale.*

Malcolm said he would, but he had to go and would call her back later.

"Hey, Malkie," said Olympia, "I love you madly, and be careful."

After she hung up the phone, Olympia realized that Malcolm had not given her his customary hell for using his childhood name.

Maybe he's feeling vulnerable, as well.

Thirty-Two

Olympia's plan for the rest of the afternoon was to find out all she could about the Fellowship's belief system and social structure. With her half-finished sandwich in hand, she walked over to the kitchen window and wiped away the icy condensation with a paper towel. Then she leaned against the sill and let the beauty of the curving rhythms and undulating whiteness of the still drifting snow ease her mind and calm her racing thoughts.

Step one would be to call the Harvard Divinity School Library and see what information they might have on religious cults, and in particular, the Boston Christian Common Fellowship. When she and Jim went there the previous summer, they didn't really know what they were looking for and came away with little more than references to a few scholarly articles and chapters in obscure books.

So when Olympia dialed The Div School, as it was called by those in the know, she could not believe her good fortune when the woman who answered said she knew a post-doctoral scholar there, Dr. Melissa Ericassen, who taught a course on religious cults in America, and would she like the extension?

Olympia allowed herself a sliver of hope.

After writing down the number, she swallowed the last of a glass of warm diet soda, burped loudly enough to spook the cats, and tossed the empty can into the recycle bag. Then, with malice aforethought and nobody watching, she opened the pantry door and took out all of the cookies.

After he hung up the phone, Malcolm sat thinking about his mother. Clearly, she was upset, but when she was on one of her crusades, she often got upset. She could make the most superb mountains out of molehills. *On the other hand,* thought Malcolm, giving his mother the benefit of doubt, *that girl in the fellowship place last night was weird – and scared. And what about the note in my pocket?*

The more he thought about it, the more he was thinking himself back into a more active role in his mother's mission. He would certainly do the casual information gathering his mother requested, but if she could take matters into her own hands, so could he.

I'll ask questions all right, he thought, getting up and heading out to the kitchen. *I'm going back next Sunday and ask that unholy bunch of rock and rollers a bunch of my own questions. I just won't say anything to Mummy.* Malcolm smiled. *What she doesn't know won't hurt her.*

Because of the storm, their outside street mission work was temporarily impossible, so Fellowship members turned their collective efforts to catching up on neglected housekeeping. Sister Miriam organized a cooking project with the women, making extra bread and soup they could bring to the needy as soon as the streets were passable. Brother Joshua set the men to shoveling out the residence, and then the brothers went plodding up and down the streets, knocking on doors and offering assistance to anyone needing help.

David was looking for Sister Sarah. With everyone busy, he thought they might use the time alone to organize and review the business accounts … without interruption. He finally found her hidden away in a little-used room, sorting blankets and clothing donations with Bethany Ruth. As part of the Third Circle, Sarah was no longer involved with day-to-day operations such as this.

David was pleased to see her taking a sisterly interest in the new recruit. She had a tendency to hold herself apart from people more than he would have liked.

Thirty-Three

Bethany Ruth was in a cheerful state. For the first time since the previous Friday, she was neither hungry nor exhausted. No one mentioned Malcolm's midnight visit. Her liquid-only fast was over until the following weekend, Sister Sarah had asked her to help clean out the donations closet, and best of all, Joshua and Miriam suggested she leave the college dormitory and move into the Renewal Center.

Why waste all that time going back and forth to the dorm, they said when they suggested it. As long as she was over eighteen, she didn't need her parents' permission and could live wherever she wished. That way, she would have more time to prepare for her initiation to the First Circle and more time to be surrounded and protected by her Fellowship family who loved her so much.

Nobody added that she would also be away from a certain professor who was a little too nosey for her own good.

Bethany Ruth continued to sort, fold, and stack blankets. She told herself that she was safe and happy here. Well, almost happy. What she couldn't and wouldn't admit to anyone was that she couldn't stop thinking about her family back in Oklahoma, but Jeshua had said to his followers, "Leave your wives and your children and follow me." She didn't have wives and children like the Bible verse said, but she had a mother and a father and brothers and sisters. She reached into the pile for another blanket. Keeping busy prevented her from thinking too much, and it pleased Sister Sarah.

When she had met Sarah at the Meriwether Bible study, Bethany Ruth had no idea she was a member of the Fellowship, and look what happened. Sister Sarah was being so good to her. Even Sister Miriam noticed it.

Later in the afternoon, when she had finished her kitchen chores, she was going to read her Bible and memorize the passages assigned for the week, plus she had one more book report to finish for her English class. Maybe she would go find Professor Brown and wish her a Merry Christmas when she dropped it off.

She felt bad that Miriam and Joshua were so down on Professor Brown. They had made it very clear that the less time she spent at the college, the better, especially during her training period.

Later that afternoon, alone in the kitchen, Bethany Ruth finished chopping the vegetables and started them sautéing in some oil. The smell was heavenly, but it made her almost faint with hunger. Out of habit, she poured herself a glass of water and then realized she could eat. She peeled a carrot, and then a second, and ate them both.

With the food preparation finished, Bethany Ruth washed her hands and spread the damp dishtowel on the edge of the sink to dry. She looked at the clock and wondered what her mother was cooking for supper. She blinked a few times and went into the living room. There, she took a small piece of wood from the basket beside the grate and pushed it into the glowing embers.

Sitting alone on the oversized sofa, she allowed herself the luxury of staring into the fire for a few minutes. She was finding it hard to concentrate. Her thoughts kept going back to Olympia's son and the night of the storm. *Like mother, like son,* she thought. *I'm sure he meant well.*

When she'd realized who Malcolm was, she told Miriam as soon as she could catch her alone. Later that evening, carrying the guest bedding downstairs, she overheard Brother David telling Aaron that they needed to be really careful of what they said, and under no circumstances was he to be left alone with Bethany Ruth. She smiled. They were so protective of her.

She knew she had taken a terrible risk putting that note in his coat pocket, but she made absolutely sure no one saw her. Olympia needed to know this was her choice, and she intended to stay.

Sitting in front of the fire, she thought about life here and about the circles above the First Circle. She knew there were two more, but that was all she was allowed to know until she was a full member. It was another one of the rules. There was never any question about what was right and what was wrong here. She was safe from the ever-present, greedy hands of the devil and from evil thinkers and evil doers. She might be hungry and tired sometimes, but all the while she was walking in Jeshua's way. Surely this was worth more than what she was leaving behind.

Upstairs in the private conference room, Miriam and Joshua, along with the three other Third Circle Fellowship Members, were seated at the table. The scratched plastic surface of the Formica table was a sharp contrast to the Victorian architecture of the room itself. The molded ceilings and mahogany-paneled doors were fragments of remembered elegance in a room which now held only the table, a few folding chairs, and a half-empty bookcase. The elite five were in deep discussion about Olympia, Malcolm, Bethany Ruth and Fellowship security.

"I can't believe he actually got in here," said Ezra. "That was a major slip on my part."

"Look," said Aaron lifting his head from his notepad, "it happened, things happen. You couldn't have known what he looks like. Don't worry. He won't get near us again."

"But what if he comes back?" Sarah leaned forward and adjusted her headscarf, tucking in a few stray curls that were constantly resisting arrest. "Do we just tell him to shove off, or our Fellowship equivalent of that?"

She couldn't see David behind her frowning at her use of street language, but she could feel it, and it pleased her. *Two can play his little game.*

"What I mean is," she continued, "we know there's no doubt that he came here to get information, and we were really friendly like we always are, but we made sure he didn't learn anything more than any other guest might learn on a first night. If he comes back, and we act differently, won't that make him suspicious?"

"Frankly, I don't care," said David, beginning to pace back and forth along the wall of the long, narrow room. He was hunched forward as though he were ready to break into a sprint at any moment, his tension palpable. "It's the mother we have to worry about." David turned and looked down at Sarah. "That Olympia woman is too nosy for her own good, and she appears to have connections. I found out she's friends with the chaplain at Allston College."

"That's bad news," said Aaron. "That telephone call the night of the blizzard might not be enough of a warning."

"Both deaths, the Meriwether girl and the one from Allston, are recorded as accidental," said David. "The only connection, if anyone makes it, is they were both members of the Fellowship. There's no law against following the path of Jeshua."

David was almost marching now, emphasizing his words with his footsteps, fists clenched against his chest, his head half bowed.

"Sit down, David," said Sarah and immediately wished she hadn't. She'd gone too far again.

David lifted his head and glared at her. "Sister Sarah, even in times of duress, a woman does not tell a man what to do. 'As in all the churches of the saints, the women should keep silence. For they are not permitted to speak, but should be subordinate, as even the law says. If there is anything they desire to know, let them ask their husbands at home.'"

"Corinthians chapter fourteen, verse thirty-four," droned Aaron.

"Sister Sarah," David continued, "why must I continually remind you that women are expected to keep silent until asked to speak?"

Sarah bowed her head. Hot tears of humiliation welled up in her eyes, but sheer determination kept them there. It was another slip of the will, and she would likely be disciplined. Even though she had risen to the innermost rank of the Fellowship, the elite Third Circle, she still had her headstrong moments. Not so often these days, but like her unruly hair, her strong personality, intellect, and passionate nature struggled against the submissive demeanor expected of women. It had been an ongoing battle from the day she entered.

"Perhaps I should leave," she said, starting to push back her chair."

"Sit down, Sister." David looked down at her from across the room."

Sarah swallowed and did as she was told.

"The Abba has a little project for you," said David, "and when you have accomplished it, we should hear no more from Professor Olympia Brown."

Two floors below, Bethany Ruth sat alone by the low fire trying not to think about her old dog Betsy and how her beloved pet would always sneak up on the sofa when she thought no one was looking. Then her mother would come into the living room and make a big show of being surprised and shoo her back off. It was a game they'd played every night right after supper.

Thirty-Four

December 13, 1859

The weather remains cold, and little snow has melted. The roads are passable, but walking is difficult, especially for the elders. We women at the church are tending to them, bringing food, extra firewood and other comforts however we can.

I've been asked to speak on Christian charity at one of the Sunday services in the New Year. Dare I tell them that the words Christian and Charity are not synonymous? That Jews and Mohammedans practice charity as well. Will they see me as some kind of heretic? And, if that's the case, so must I be.

More anon...LFW

Olympia needed a stretch-break from her investigations and went out to clear more snow off the back steps and widen the path to the wood pile. Even though the snow had stopped falling, the blowing wind was still rearranging the contours of her holdings. Before returning to the house, Olympia allowed herself the frivolity of making a couple of snow angels.

Back in the house with dry socks and shoes on her feet, she was ready to call Harvard Divinity School and try and connect with Dr. Melissa Ericassen, the religious cult expert. She dialed the number, planning to leave a message, when Dr. Ericassen picked up the phone.

Once she introduced herself, Olympia explained the situation with her student and asked what Dr. Ericassen might be able to tell her about this particular group. Beyond that, might she suggest a way to help Bethany Ruth? For the time being, Olympia thought it better to say nothing about the questionable deaths of the other students.

Dr. Ericassen began by describing her own research into the theological and social structure of cults and what it is in particular which makes them so attractive and successful. "Conversely," she added, "I'm also exploring the psychological profile of a person most likely to fall victim to cult propaganda."

"I had no idea this was so complex," said Olympia. "I'm a Unitarian Universalist minister and college chaplain. You'd think I'd know more about this kind of thing."

"The average person, even the average minister, has very little knowledge of cult behavior, Olympia."

"It sounds pretty scary."

"It goes way beyond scary. Groups like the Fellowship have destroyed the lives of individuals and families. People have no idea how insidiously destructive some religious cults can be. It's the subject of my research," said Dr. Ericassen, "but this is more than an academic exercise." She waited a fraction of a second before continuing. "I lost my only daughter to a religious cult, Olympia. I can only hope that one day my work will make a difference to another confused young person or a distraught parent, maybe even save someone's life."

Olympia could hear a long intake of breath on the other end of the line. Now was not the time to tell her that she, too, had lost a daughter.

After she regained her composure, Dr. Ericassen told Olympia to please call her Melissa and then went on to tell her all she knew about the Boston Christian Common Fellowship.

"It's definitely a cult, and we hear of suspicious goings-on behind all their sanctimonious posturing, but no one has been able to prove anything. They're very secretive, and getting any detailed information about them is nearly impossible."

Olympia nodded. This much she knew but didn't want to influence or sidetrack anything the woman might say.

"We do know," the researcher continued, "that there's a network of these Fellowships across the United States and possibly in Canada, and we're pretty sure that more is changing hands than money. But ... was there something specific you wanted to ask me?"

Olympia took along breath. "This may take a while."

"I have the time," said Melissa Ericassen. "I have a vested interest, remember?"

After Olympia outlined the situation in as much detail as she could, Dr. Ericassen responded with the equivalent of a mini-course on contemporary cult structure, psychology and pathology. When she finished, Olympia thanked her and offered to take her to lunch and express her appreciation in person.

"Olympia," Melissa said before ending the conversation, "I think you can understand why this is so important to me. You have children, and you're a religious professional. These people are dangerous. Please stay in contact with me, and let me know what you come up with. I think we can help each other."

Olympia said she would, thanked her a second time, and hung up the phone. It had just gone four in the afternoon, and it was getting dark. She looked over her pages of notes. She had a great deal of information, and all of it was disturbing.

What she now knew was that this was much bigger than Bethany Ruth and Sonya Wilson and Gary Vanderloop at Allston. She also knew that following this through would be dangerous.

There's still so much more to be done, she thought, *so many more questions to ask and a whole group of people determined to see that I don't accomplish any of it. At least I have Jim. Among other things, we have to find a way to gain access to college and police records.*

Olympia drummed her fingers on the arm of the chair. She knew they should try and talk with the parents of the dead students, but would they be willing? And how could she do it and not tell the Dean, or if she did and he found out, without losing her job?

She thought about exactly what she might say to Dean Wilbur Jackson. Considering the fact that he undoubtedly had his own agenda, Olympia decided to keep her own counsel and continue to say nothing. Her mother always used to say, "Least said, soonest mended." *Right again, Mother, dear.*

Having sorted that much out, she needed to stand up and move around again before she called Jim. She had been sitting for over two hours. Her shoulders ached, and her fingers were stiff. She got up and walked to the kitchen window. A silver dusk was settling over the snow-hushed landscape.

Olympia turned and cast an eye towards the refrigerator where a fresh bottle of her Vin Familiar was chilling. *Surely the sun will have slipped over a yardarm somewhere on the planet.*

Thirty-Five

"After we've finished with our meeting," said David, inclining his head towards the woman seated on his left, "the Abba will explain to Sister Sarah what will be required. But before that happens, I need to speak with you all about the importance of her mission." David was standing with his back to the door.

Sarah was twisting her fingers under the table and wondering what the Abba could possibly want with her. The very thought of it gave her an uncomfortable feeling in her gut. She knew their leader did not usually entrust important Fellowship business to women.

As a member of the Third Circle, her tasks were mostly administrative. She directed their public street ministry, kept records of membership, and dealt with day-to-day communications with the other Fellowship centers across the country. She also started the highly successful Student Centered Bible Study groups at local colleges and Universities, but it was in the course of her administrative duties that Sarah first began to suspect there was another layer of Fellowship activity that even she didn't have access to. She knew there were locked files labeled with code names that only David and Aaron were allowed to open. Until recently, she had no reason to ask about them and never questioned what they were, but something she had overheard a few days earlier, plus the discovery of some alterations in the figures in one of her own files, had started her thinking.

She shifted in her seat and fussed at the knot of her headscarf. *I know it's probably about a new surplus food contact, and they want me to approach him or her in person.* Because of her rank and trusted position, she regularly went out to negotiate directly with some of their outside suppliers, which meant she got to go out alone. Sarah liked getting away from the rigid discipline of the Fellowship and David's constant watching and belittling her. It gave her a chance to breathe, and more importantly now, time to think.

"You see, Brothers and Sisters," said David, beginning to pace, "I believe that Olympia Brown's son coming to our residence was no accident. He came here for a reason. The Fellowship doesn't ever take direct action against an outside threat, but we do need to exercise every precaution to avoid even a hint of negative media attention that might detract from our charitable work with the hungry and the homeless on the streets of Boston."

David stopped and raised his hands. "Remember, Jeshua supped with the lepers and the outcasts, and so must we go and do likewise amongst his beloved poor."

Joshua and Miriam looked over at one another but said nothing.

"Jeshua praised men who did their good works quietly and did not make a public display of their charity." David turned on his heel and looked toward Aaron. "Are we not following the example of His life and work? Blessed are those who pray and do their good works in silence and out of the eyes of the unfaithful."

Aaron nodded.

David's voice was rising. "We need to keep the inner workings of our Fellowship hidden from public view and scrutiny," he continued. "It is Jeshua's way, and it is our way."

The Fellowship members seated at the table murmured their assent. One did not challenge or interrupt him when he was agitated. Brother David was the appointed leader of the Third Circle and the single trusted confidante and personal assistant to Abba Mordecai, the reclusive founder and absolute leader of the Fellowship.

Sarah knew that a breach of security or an information leak of the wrong kind to the wrong people could threaten the very life and good works of the Fellowship, as well as David's position of privileged authority. She also knew David would make sure that never happened.

David explained that the telephone call to Professor Olympia Brown was the first part of the warning to stay away from Bethany Ruth and the Fellowship. Once the second part had been accomplished, there would be no mistaking the message. David paused for dramatic effect, "Until she has been duly informed of this situation, and we have her affirmative response, Fellowship members must take extra care in guarding our privacy and sanctity, especially when we are out in public. We can have no casual talk on the streets or even among ourselves about Fellowship work that could be overheard and misinterpreted."

David stopped pacing and put his hand on the doorknob. "The meeting is adjourned. Sister Sarah, I believe the Abba is waiting for us."

Sarah stood without speaking and followed David out the door and along the dimly lighted hallway to the narrow stairwell leading to the private apartment and office reserved for the exclusive use of the Abba when he was in residence. As they ascended the stairs, Sarah traced the beautifully curved mahogany banister with her fingertips, wondering what it was this man was going to ask her to do.

She stopped on the landing and waited for David to unlock the door. She had never been inside the Abba's private quarters. Sarah heard the sharp click of the bolt as the door opened. All she could see was a dark shape silhouetted in the light behind him.

"Sister Sarah," said the man standing before her, "I am pleased to see you."

I had no choice, thought Sarah, "I am honored to be in your presence, Abba." She kept her eyes down, looking only at his feet. He was wearing sandals with thick wool socks. She wondered what his toes looked like.

"Sit down, Sister," said the Abba, indicating an upholstered arm chair. "Brother David, you sit there," he pointed to a matching chair, "and I'll sit in the middle."

There was a raspy quality to the man's voice. Sarah wondered if he had a sore throat.

"Please look at me, Sarah," said the Abba. "I like to look into the eyes of the person I'm speaking to."

Sarah did as she was told. He was a spare man, probably in his late forties, but it was hard to tell. He was wearing a loose-fitting, off-white tunic which fell almost to his knees over a pair of equally loose-fitting trousers of the same color. Like David, he had a short, well-trimmed beard. For a forbidden instant, Sarah was reminded of the austere Dominican monks of her Catholic childhood. She didn't trust them either.

"Sister Sarah," he said, crossing his legs and leaning back in his seat, "you have a trusted position in the Fellowship, and for that reason, I'm asking you to do something that I couldn't ask of anyone else. There is a person on the outside we feel might pose a danger to the efficacy of our good works. Her name is Olympia Brown. She's a professor of religion and the college chaplain at Meriwether College. We've already sent two messages telling her not to interfere with a new recruit by the name of Bethany Ruth McAllister, but it would appear that we need to convince her once and for all to stop prying into our affairs."

"I know who she is," said Sarah.

"Don't you think ..." David began.

"Not now, Brother David." The Abba dismissed his second in command with a quick gesture. Sarah saw the flash of anger in David's eyes.

I wonder how he likes being shut off?

For the next half-hour, the Abba explained to Sarah that the next time she went to Meriwether for the Bible study, she was to leave a tea packet in the basket she would find just inside Professor Brown's office door. If the key was not in its usual place over the sink, she was to locate a security guard and say she was a student and needed to leave an assignment in her office.

"What's in the packet?" asked Sarah.

"A message for Olympia Brown," said the Abba, "one she can't possibly misunderstand."

"Why not write a letter and have me leave it on her desk? What if she doesn't find it, and someone else gets it?"

"Women do not question." He was watching her with something that might have been a smile. "I assure you, whoever finds the teabag will get the message to Professor Brown. The surprise factor is part of the plan, but we can't have that surprise message traced back to us. We do our good works in secret, remember?"

"But ..."

"You intrigue me, Sarah," said the Abba. "I admire your spirit."

Sarah lowered her eyes and nodded. *None of this is making sense.*

"David, will you see that Sarah has the tea packet, and then I'd like you to stay on for a few minutes. There's a membership induction issue we need to address."

The Abba turned to Sarah. "Thank you, Sister. You may let yourself out."

Sarah was neither stupid nor naïve. The mysterious errand was entirely too circuitous and could leave far too much to chance. *What if someone else gets it? What if she never sees it?* It felt more like a Nancy Drew mystery of the 1930s than real life in the last year of the last decade of the millennium. *But what is real life? Do I even know any more?*

By choice, Sarah had locked herself away from herself and the life she was born to, and until recently, anyway, it had been working. Now she wasn't so sure.

Thirty-Six

By Wednesday morning the main roads were barely passable, and the giddy romance of the historic snowstorm was definitely over. Rather than risk driving, Olympia decided to take public transportation to work for the rest of the week.

When she called Jim to tell him about her conversation with Dr. Ericassen, he suggested they meet at the food court at South Station. It was one of the transfer points on her way to work and not too far from the rectory where Jim lived. They could indulge themselves in oversized muffins and gourmet coffee, while they compared notes. When Olympia questioned the choice of location, he said the terminal was a noisy public space where, courtesy of the chaotic din, they could speak privately. Olympia chided him on his paranoid thinking and then realized with an unpleasant shock that maybe it wasn't so paranoid after all. Someone was tracking her movements and now possibly Malcolm's, maybe even Jim's. Nothing like this had ever happened to her before.

When she reached the station, Olympia followed the lumpy tide of winter-bundled commuters up out of the depths of the earth and into the high-domed central rotunda. Her backpack was full to bursting with the papers she had finally finished grading, and she was muffled to the eyeballs in winter storm gear. *I feel like a pack mule,* thought Olympia, *and I probably look every bit as lovely.* She peered around and spotted Jim seated at one of the little wire tables scattered throughout the place for the convenience of waiting commuters.

She waved and then got herself a double cappuccino with extra cinnamon before joining him. He stood and gave her a quick hug. Then, ever the gentleman, he pulled out her chair. Once they were settled, Olympia leaned forward, "You first or me?"

"I'll go," said Jim "I think I may be onto something. I told you that Allston College is just up the street from the Fellowship residence?"

Olympia nodded, stirring her coffee.

"Yesterday, I went down to the local police station on the pretext of finding out something about the group for the college." Jim reached up and pointed to his clerical collar. "The duty officer read between the lines and looked the other way when I asked to go through some records." After that, I went into the Boston Public Library and looked up the newspaper coverage of the art student who had the automobile accident. It seems that before she lost control of the car and drove headlong under a tractor-trailer, she vomited with such force that it was all over the window glass and front seat. At first they thought she was drunk, but there was no alcohol in her blood. She was decapitated."

"Oh, my God, and you said your student choked on vomit and drowned." Olympia was leaning over the table so she could hear him over the cheery pre-holiday music and crowd chatter swirling around them.

"So did the student who died mysteriously at Harvard," said Jim, "the one reported as having a rogue virus."

"Don't tell me," said Olympia.

"Uh huh," said Jim, nodding. "He went to bed early because he thought had the flu, started throwing up, aspirated it, and suffocated."

Olympia blew on her coffee and started to take a sip, then changed her mind and put down the cup.

"I spoke to their respective deans and learned they were all involved with the Fellowship," said Jim. "It seems that when they wanted to get out of it that things turned bad, and it's also the point where there's no more information." Jim was tapping the tabletop with his index finger.

"So we find people who knew the victims — roommates, girlfriends or boyfriends. But with the winter break coming up, we might not be able to start until after they come back. The parents of Gary Vanderloop knew very little about his dealings with the Fellowship, but they told me what they could."

Just then, the station manager began announcing the incoming and outgoing trains, and Olympia had to lean closer to be heard over the loudspeaker. "Kids don't talk to their parents these days, Jim." She was almost yelling. "And I know from Bethany Ruth that once someone joins the Fellowship, they aren't supposed to have anything to do with friends or family."

Jim shouted back against the metallic din. "These three deaths may still be technically listed as accidental, Olympia, but I'm pretty certain that the circumstances leading up to them were orchestrated to result only in serious and messy discomfort. The fact that at least three of those so-called accidents turned out to be fatal may or may not have been part of the plan. That's what doesn't add up. From what little I do know about the group, they seem to be too well organized to make fatal mistakes."

Olympia grabbed hold of Jim's hands. "So we're talking about murder."

"Or second degree murder or manslaughter, but whatever we call it, we still have to prove it. When's your next class?"

Olympia dug through several layers of clothing to locate her watch and gasped, "Thirty-five minutes. I'll never make it, and I haven't told you what that woman from Harvard told me."

"I'll call you at home tonight. Meanwhile," Jim pointed to a booth near one of the exit doors, "you get going, and I'll call Meriwether and tell them you're going to be late and ask them to put a notice on your door. I've got the number. We can't do any more now."

Olympia yanked her backpack up over her shoulder. "Do you think it's time to call in the police?"

Jim shook his head. "Not yet, but we're getting close." He stood and pushed in his chair. "It's only Wednesday. Let me do some more checking around. See if you can find out anything more at Meriwether, you know, residence directors, roommates — on the Q.T., of course."

Olympia nodded, waved, and took off running in the direction of the down-escalator. She was in luck. A train was just pulling up to the platform. Minutes later, Olympia was rattling toward Cambridge lost in troubling thought. She and Jim were uncovering the tip of a very convoluted iceberg, and Jim still had no idea the Boston Christian Common Fellowship was part of a much larger and far more sinister operation than either one of them could have imagined. She never had time to tell him.

I haven't told him about Miss Winslow either, or that I've submitted the forms and given my permission allowing my daughter to contact me, should she ever want to.

Hanging onto the strap and resting her head on her arm, Olympia lurched and swayed with the crowd as the train hurtled down into the tunnel, deeper and deeper into the darkness that lay ahead.

Thirty-Seven

Olympia heard the quick steps of her colleague, Margie Westcott, approaching the office. Seconds later, her friend bounced through the door with a resounding "ta-da," but one look at Olympia's grim face suggested this was not a ta-da moment.

"Hi, Margie," said Olympia, forcing a smile.

"Jesus," said Margie, "what the hell is wrong? You look really upset."

"I am, and it's so convoluted, I don't know where to begin." She swiveled back and forth in her chair while Margie took off her coat and tossed it on top of her briefcase.

"Speak," said Margie, sitting down and turning towards her colleague.

"It's going to take a while."

"How long? Is it a one or two cups of tea story? You want one?"

"Make yourself some," said Olympia. "I had a huge cappuccino, and it hasn't run all the way through yet."

Margie got up and took down the electric teakettle, filled it with water and plugged it in. While it was gurgling, she began to rummage through their collective tea stash.

"Here's one I haven't tried," she said, holding up a packet of something called Heavenly Sunset. "One of yours?"

"Must be something one of the students left. They do that. They know I like different kinds of teas, and every so often they leave me some. It's sweet of them."

When Margie finished the tea-making ritual, she sat with one foot curled around the other ankle, blowing into her mug and waiting for it to cool.

Before she began, Olympia demanded absolute confidence and then told her about Bethany Ruth, the Fellowship, and the threatening phone calls. Margie listened and began to drink her tea, alternately sniffing and sipping the fragrant liquid. Olympia continued, telling her what she had learned about the Fellowship from Jim Sawicki and the woman at Harvard.

"How's the tea?" asked Olympia, taking a break from the grizzly narrative.

"Different."

"How so?"

"I don't know, sort of herby, maybe a little medicinal, licorice overtones." Margie smirked at her wine-reviewer's reference. "It's probably good for me. It's hot, and hot is what I want right now. Are you sure you don't want ..."

Margie never finished the sentence. With a horrified look, she dropped the mug, clapped both hands over her mouth, and started to run out of the office. Before she reached the door, she doubled over and began to vomit.

Olympia grabbed a wastebasket, shoved it under Margie's chin, and called 911.

The next few minutes were a blur. Margie was gagging and retching so badly that she was having difficulty breathing. Olympia held Margie's head over the wastebasket, trying to calm her and wiping her mouth between bursts.

The EMTs were there in minutes and with practiced authority took control of Margie and the situation. They lifted Margie onto the stretcher, turned her on her side with a gag bowl next to her mouth, covered her with a blanket, and strapped her in place. Olympia collected her own things while giving them what information she could. When Margie was secure, Olympia collected Margie's coat and purse. She started to follow the paramedics to the ambulance but stopped at the threshold.

"I'll be right there," she called after them. Olympia turned, picked the squashed teabag out of the sink, wrapped it in a paper towel, and tucked it into her purse.

Maybe there was no longer any point in locking the office door, but out of practice, Olympia clicked it shut and put the key in her pocket. Tomorrow, she would call maintenance. Right now, all she could think about was negotiating the icy snow piles outside the building and taking care of her friend.

Margie was still gagging when they reached the hospital, but the severity had lessened considerably, and her breathing sounded more normal. Olympia stayed at the admissions desk and gave them what information she could, then settled down with an ancient copy of *Time Magazine*. She was prepared to stay as long as needed and wondered, eyeing the coffee and snack machines, how long that might be.

In less than an hour. a nurse came out and told Olympia she could see her friend. Inside the curtained cubicle, Margie was half-sitting against a pile of pillows looking like something out of a Pre-Raphaelite painting. She was nibbling at a soda cracker and sipping a Coke.

"Good grief, Margie," said Olympia, trying to keep the quaver out of her voice. "What happened?"

"That's what the doctors are trying to find out," she said in a weak voice. "My throat really hurts from all the retching, so it's hard to talk."

"Take your time. It doesn't look like either one of us is going anywhere for a while."

Margie took another sip of her Coke and looked up at her friend. "I owe you," she said. "They're going to analyze the stuff I threw up and see if I ate something bad. I didn't have fever or anything. My blood pressure really dropped, but it's almost back to normal." She paused and leaned her head back on the pillow to catch her breath. "If I can keep this stuff down for another hour, I can leave, but I don't know how I'm going to get home. I'm shaky as hell. Could you take me home?"

"I took the train," said Olympia, tapping her lips with her index finger, "but give me a minute. I'll think of something."

Margie picked up another cracker and sipped some more of the Coke with no signs of it coming back up. Her color was returning to normal.

"I know," said Olympia, "I'll try Malcolm. He's only ten minutes away in Somerville. If his rust bucket of a car is moveable, I'll see if he'll bring it over and let me use it for the night."

Olympia went off in search of a pay phone and in a few minutes returned with good news that Malcolm would be there as soon as he could.

It was after eleven when Olympia eased and cajoled Malcolm's decrepit tank into the drive. Exhausted, she turned off the engine and made her slippery way toward the house. Once inside, she performed the coat, hat, cat, wine ritual and checked for phone messages. There were two.

Olympia made a face, fearing another threat or anonymous hang-up, and hit the playback button. She was gratified to hear Margie's voice.

"Olympia, its Margie. The hospital called right after you dropped me off. They found traces of ipecac in my vomit. I thought that tea tasted funny. Was that somebody's sick idea of a joke, or what? Call me tomorrow, okay? I'm going to bed."

The second call was a scratchy recording of a few lines from an old song Olympia remembered from her childhood tap dance lessons. "Just tea for two and two for tea, just me for you and you for me alone, Dear. Nobody near us to see us or hear us ..."

Then whoever was on the other end of the line broke the connection.

Thirty-Eight

December 15, 1859

The temperature went above freezing today and as a result, the roads are an unpleasant mixture of mud and slush.

I have accepted the invitation to speak on Christian Charity and when I do, I will cast out a few seeds of my (heretical) Unitarianism along with the loaves and the fishes. Let's see what the townsfolk think of that! Fortunately, it won't be until early March, so I have ample time to prepare.

I have accepted Mr. Jackson's offer to purchase the land across from the house, and to hear him talk, I'm inclined to think he has another offer in mind, but I'm having none of it.

More anon…LFW

Olympia padded into the kitchen wearing her ancient and honorable flannel nightgown and pink chenille bathrobe. Her first thoughts were for Margie and how she had fared through the night. She made her way slowly around the kitchen, stepping over the cats and making coffee. When the breakfast necessaries were accomplished, she called Jim at the rectory and told her trusted friend the whole grizzly story.

"By any chance, did you keep the teabag?" asked the ever-practical Jim.

"I did," said Olympia. "I stuffed it in my purse, but I was too upset at the time to even think of giving it to the doctors at the hospital. It's still there, but I already know it was laced with ipecac. Margie called after I got home and told me."

"Wrap it in plastic and stick it in the freezer anyway," said Jim. "You've still got the message on your answering machine?"

"I do," said Olympia.

"Good on that one, too. I think we're almost ready to go to the police. Give me a day or two. I've got a meeting this afternoon with a couple of the swim team kids. If that turns up anything concrete, I think we might be able to present our case."

"I know I should talk to the Dean."

"I know what you're thinking, Olympia, but Bethany Ruth is safe right now. She's still trying to get into the Fellowship, remember? From what I know, it's when they try and get out that it gets messy. Let's see what we can dig up between now and the end of the year. If we show up at police headquarters with nothing but a collection of assumptions and suspicions, they won't give us the time of day. From what you've said, your arrogant Dean could muddy the waters in his own way if we tell him too soon."

"I know you're right, Jim, but ..."

"And I know *you*, Olympia Brown. Patience is not one of your virtues."

"Speaking of virtues ..."

"Uh oh."

Olympia never failed to be amazed at the way the man could switch gears. She couldn't help smiling. It broke the tension.

"Just listen to me, okay? It's about something else."

"I'm listening, but I have to say Mass in twenty minutes."

Olympia took a deep breath. "I think I may have met somebody, a man, a nice man, and I think I may know who my ghost might be."

"Tell me in order given, gentleman of interest and then your ghost."

"The man lives in England. Ever since we met we've been writing and talking on the phone. I told him about this whole Fellowship-cult-Bethany Ruth thing last night. He's a good sounding board, and he has no connection with anyone here, so I felt okay about talking about it. I think you'll like him."

"Am I hearing possibilities in your voice, Olympia? I didn't ever think that would happen."

"We both know I don't have my Ph.D. in relationships, but I'll know more when I go over there in February."

"February? Over there? This does sound serious, my dear. Are his intentions honorable?"

Olympia grinned at herself in the reflection of the coffee pot. "I certainly hope not, Jim, but meanwhile, back to the holidays. You are coming for Christmas dinner?"

"Wouldn't miss it, Olympia. Even though they're almost all grown up, I consider myself your sons' Christmas and Easter uncle. As such, I have responsibilities."

Olympia laughed and told him to bring his usual several bottles of champagne and leave the Roman collar at home. They agreed to hold off going to the authorities until after the holidays, since tipping their hand at this stage could be dangerously premature.

"There is one awkward little detail, Jim," said Olympia, returning to an earlier thought. "At some point, I really do have to tell the Dean what we're doing."

Olympia shooed a cat off the kitchen table, poured herself a cup of coffee and inhaled the lovely rich scent before taking the first sip. The smell of freshly brewed coffee was one of life's supreme pleasures. Then she thought about visiting Frederick and moved fresh coffee a little lower on the list.

"Let's cross that bridge when we come to it," said Jim. "Involving him right now would be pointless. We'll talk to him after we go to the police, and we'll do it together. He won't dare fire you with me standing there."

"Don't be so sure about that. Go say Mass, and call me if you think of anything else. Oh, and I almost forgot. I'm pretty sure my ghost is a woman who lived in the house a hundred and fifty years ago. I found her diary in a secret cupboard, and I've been reading it in bits and pieces when I get the chance. She seems to be quite a character, and would you believe her middle name is Faith?"

Thirty-Nine

Before Bethany Ruth could change her status from resident to commuting student, she was required to have a residence exit interview with Dean Jackson. After that, she could clean out her room and take up residence at the Fellowship Center.

So it was that on the Thursday morning after the big storm, Bethany Ruth was hurrying across the snow-heaped campus quadrangle to the dean's office. As she slipped and slid along the frozen walkway, her long skirt, wet from the snow, slapped against her legs and wound around the tops of her boots. It got cold in Oklahoma but not this damp, penetrating kind of cold, and there was a whole winter left to go. She shivered and pushed on, once again trying not to think of home.

Her appointment was scheduled for nine. She stopped outside his office and peeled her wet skirt away from her legs, hoping it would dry a little in the indoor heat. She hadn't really figured out all the necessities for New England winter weather, and unfortunately for her chapped, raw legs, she was learning the hard way. *But isn't suffering of any kind a gift to God?*

As she waited to be called in, she wondered if Dean Jackson was married and what his house might be like and if he had any children. In the Fellowship, everyone married sooner or later. It was another one of the rules. Sister Miriam told her when the time came to be married, the Abba would choose someone for her, and they would be moved off to one of the family compounds where she and her husband would raise and home-school the children. Her family would be safe there, away from the outside world and the prying eyes of unbelievers. It was all so well thought out.

Bethany Ruth was so lost in her thoughts that she literally jumped when the door opened and the Dean beckoned her.

"I'm sorry. Did I startle you, Miss McAllister?"

"Oh, no," said Bethany Ruth, "I was just thinking. I guess I was a million miles away."

"Well, when you get back, come into my office, and leave the door open." He stepped back to allow her to pass in front of him through the door.

"This is really just a formality," he said, offering her a chair. "If you're self-supporting and over the age of eighteen, you can live anywhere you want. We just have to make sure that your decision was not made because you are unhappy with the college or dormitory life."

Dean Wilber Jackson did not sit behind his desk, but instead positioned himself in the rocking chair opposite Bethany Ruth. There was a plate of muffins on the table between them. She smelled them the minute she walked in and was trying not to stare.

The Dean leaned forward and picked up the plate and held it out to her. "Here," he said, "I can't possibly eat them all myself, but they looked so good in the bakery, I just had to have some." He smiled at her. "Here, take one. You look like you could use a few pounds on you."

Praise Jesus, thought Bethany Ruth, not daring to believe what she just heard, and before she had time for a second thought to stop her, she picked out the biggest blueberry muffin on the plate and took a huge bite.

Will sat easily in the chair, smiling at the girl as she demolished the sugary confection, oblivious to the crumbs sticking to the corners of her mouth.

"So, Miss McAllister, you are moving out of the dorm and into ... ?"

"The Boston Christian Common Fellowship Spiritual Life and Renewal Center in Brighton, Massachusetts," said Bethany Ruth through a face full of muffin. "It's a Christian group I've been involved with since the end of October. They've invited me to come and live with them until I become a member. I'm going to join officially over the winter break—that is, if I qualify."

The Dean leaned forward and selected a cranberry muffin for himself.

"Tell me about them." He broke the muffin into pieces before eating it.

Bethany Ruth wondered how much she should tell this man, but fortified by the food, her own enthusiasm, and the comfort of sitting near a hot radiator, she began to talk, and for the next twenty minutes she told him absolutely nothing he didn't already know.

"Do the members live there for free?" he asked, trying a different approach. "Do they give you room and board once you're a member?"

"Oh, no," she said licking her fingers and chasing down the crumbs which had fallen into her lap. "The money that I would have paid the college for room and board will go to the Fellowship as part of my tithe."

He was listening intently now.

"Tithe?" he said.

"Tithing. You know," she said, "giving ten percent of your income to the church. That's how the group supports itself. They get donations, too, I think. I really don't know all of it, because I'm not a real member. I suppose I'll find out more when I am. Trouble is," she continued, starting to reach for another pastry and then withdrawing her hand, "my education here is being paid through scholarships and student loans, and that money can only be used for tuition and room and board here, but not for anywhere else. I'll have to come up with the extra money for the tithe myself. I'll get a part-time job somewhere. That's what the other members do."

Will nodded, stood, and walked over to an oak file cabinet, another one of his antiques. He took out the folder containing the forms that would put her change of status into effect. When he turned back, Bethany Ruth was halfway through a second muffin.

Later that day, when she returned to the Renewal Center, Bethany Ruth was warmly greeted by Miriam and Joshua. She had taken the first big step by agreeing to move out of the college. She was now fully committed to living with them and learning their ways. Tomorrow she would go back to the dorm one last time with Miriam and Joshua and pack up those few things she would be allowed to take with her.

Tonight, she was content and warm in the Fellowship kitchen, and her only job was peeling and chopping potatoes. She tugged at the knot at the back of her headscarf, tied a long apron firmly behind her back, and picked up the paring knife. Reaching down into the basket for the first dusty potato, Bethany Ruth kept reminding herself that she'd never been so happy.

Forty

The day after the tea bag incident, Olympia called Will to talk about what happened. The last time they'd spoken he had been adamant that the college did not want a scandal attached to its name, but the events of yesterday changed everything. Still, Olympia knew she would need to choose her words carefully.

When she tapped lightly on the wall outside the open door, the Dean looked up and beckoned her into his office. She threw her coat on the loveseat and went directly to the rocking chair. Will had set a tray with a small ceramic teapot and two porcelain cups of green tea on the coffee table between them. Olympia eyed it warily.

"It's okay," he said, "I made it myself, and I've already had one cup. You can relax," and then added, "for the moment, at least."

Olympia picked up the one nearest her. It was so thin and delicate she could see the blurred shapes of her own fingers through its translucent wall. She held it carefully and wondered which dynasty it came from. "We need to talk about what happened to Margie Westcott, Will."

Will avoided her eyes. "Right now the college is treating it as a malicious prank and is threatening to expel the person who did it."

Olympia set down her teacup before she threw it against the wall.

"For God's sake, Will, you know that's bullshit! Are you going tell me what's going on behind the scenes, or do we wait for something even worse to happen?"

Will shook his head. "Sonya's Wilson's parents and their lawyer are threatening legal action. You have to understand I can't take any chances with a false lead or accusation. I need proof."

"This isn't proof?"

"It didn't happen to you, Olympia, and there's no discernable connection to Bethany Ruth or the Fellowship."

Olympia decided to say nothing about the "Tea for Two" phone call. If she needed to make her point later on, it would be useful. She cleared her throat.

"So even though it happened in my office, it's still a he said, she said situation as far as you're concerned?"

"I'm afraid so, Olympia. I know you're an action person, but right now I need you to be an observer. You'll have to take my word that we are doing all we can. As soon I can tell you more, I promise I will."

Olympia nodded in uneasy agreement, leaned forward, and retrieved her teacup. The thing was probably two hundred years old. The tea was pale green and tasted perfectly awful. *Where does he get this stuff?*

Will picked up his cup, swirled the contents in his hands, and changed the subject. "By the way, Bethany Ruth came in this morning for her exit interview."

"How'd it go?" Olympia sniffed her own tea and wrinkled her nose. "You actually drink this when nobody's looking?"

Will looked at her over his gold-rimmed glasses and nodded. "It's an acquired taste. If you're asking whether I learned anything new about that Fellowship group this morning, the answer is no." He shook his head. "She is totally committed to joining and can't wait to move in, but she's going to have to take some kind of work to pay her tithe."

Olympia winced and wondered what else besides money she would be required to give them?

"She's coming back tomorrow to clean out her room." Will held up the teapot, but Olympia waved away the offer.

"Will, do you think maybe I should talk to her?"

"Absolutely not." He dropped his voice. "Look, Olympia, I can't say this to anyone else, but there's no doubt in my mind that tea bag was intended for you. I just don't know what do about it yet."

Olympia shivered involuntarily. "You're probably right, Will, but it damn near killed Margie and scared the hell out of both of us. By the way, I forgot to tell you, there was nothing in any of the other teabags. That was the only one. The police came and took my whole tea stash and ran tests. Some guy called me this morning and told me, and he said he was going to call you, too. You're still telling everyone it's a student prank? Give me a break."

Olympia's stretched patience was growing even thinner.

"It could have been really serious, if either of you had been alone," said Will, semi-changing the subject. "It was lucky for Margie you were there."

By the tone of his voice, Olympia knew she had gotten as much out of the man as she was going to get.

"As long as that's the case, Will, let me get Christmas and New Year out of the way. We'll pick up after that."

Olympia got out of the chair and reached for her coat. She was thinking about her investigative plans with Jim and the tea bag sitting in her freezer. *Two can play this game,* she thought, *and as long as he thinks I'm following orders, he won't be breathing down my neck.*

Will nodded. "Is this your last day on campus?" he asked, walking her to the door of his office.

"I have one more day of classes," said Olympia, lingering in the doorway. "I usually stay late on my last day so I can finish my grades and get them in. That way, there's nothing hanging over me."

Nothing but threatening phone calls and a teabag laced with ipecac and a homesick kid from Oklahoma tangled up with a religious cult and a house-ghost with an attitude, nope, nothing at all. Merry Christmas, Professor Brown.

Olympia laughed inwardly at the grisly absurdity of it all and stepped out into the clear December cold.

"Olympia," said Will. There was a clear warning tone in his voice. "If you do stay late, lock your building and office doors and tell security you're there by yourself, okay?"

Olympia nodded but said nothing.

Forty-One

Miriam and Joshua accompanied Bethany Ruth to help clear out her room. They told her to take only appropriate clothes, her text books, papers, and writing supplies. When she hesitated over a book or a family picture, they assured her that she was leaving the material and evil world behind and that it needed to be a complete break.

After more than an hour of brutal sorting, Bethany Ruth stood and looked at the pile of boxes and bags in the middle of the room. There seemed to be so much and wondered where it all had come from.

"What are we going to do with these?" she asked, hoping they couldn't hear the quaver in her voice.

"We'll put them in the van with the other things," said Miriam. "Most of it will be distributed among the poor this weekend. It's easier that way. Don't think about it, just do it, and get it gone so you don't have to look at it."

"What do we do with the things we can't give away?" asked Bethany Ruth.

"Isn't there a dumpster somewhere on campus?" Miriam was closing, taping, and marking the specified boxes with the word *Donate*.

Bethany Ruth nodded.

"We'll drop them in before we leave," said Miriam with a sympathetic smile. "It was hard for me, too, but once you let it all go, you'll be free. I promise."

Bethany Ruth said nothing. Of course they were right. She had to leave the material world behind. The separation must be total. It was proof of her commitment to membership. She could hold nothing back.

"What about the pictures of my family?"

"Oh, just put them in the pile with the rest of the stuff you won't be taking," said Joshua. "They won't be of any use to anyone." He was already halfway out the door with a load of boxes.

"No," said Bethany Ruth, biting her lips against an unexpected flood of longing for her family and the hot, dusty streets of Oklahoma. "No, not any more."

Miriam smiled and looked at Joshua. The Abba would be pleased. They had done their work well.

When the three returned to the Fellowship Center that evening, it seemed that everyone was in the kitchen waiting to welcome her. She was almost one of them now. Joshua and Miriam carried her few possessions to the second floor room she would share with three other women. As a guest, she had been staying in the downstairs guestroom off the kitchen, but now she could live upstairs with the others, her sisters and brothers.

In the far corner of her room beside the window, there was a painted wooden dresser. Next to that was her bed, and beside that, a smaller chest with a reading lamp on it. On the opposite wall were four empty pegs for her clothes and a plastic tray on the floor for her shoes.

The walls of the room were painted white with off-white muslin tab curtains pulled together over the single window. In the waning light of the December afternoon, the austere room offered little in the way of warmth or personal comfort, but that's not why she came. Here she would be doing the work of God, of Yahweh and his blessed son Jeshua. He would be her love and her comfort.

After setting her things on the floor, Miriam and Joshua left her alone to unpack. With everyone busy elsewhere in the house, Bethany Ruth had a few precious moments to collect herself before she was expected in the kitchen to help with the evening meal. Alone in the stark, empty silence, she reached into her skirt pocket and pulled out a tattered envelope. Inside were two photographs. One was of her entire family with herself in the middle. The second was of her beloved, scruffy old dog Betsy.

Holding them in her hand, Bethany Ruth indulged in a few moments of sweet and forbidden reminiscence. Then she slipped them back into the envelope and tucked it under the bottom sheet and the mattress pad where the bedding would hide the telltale shape.

With her secret put away, she started down the back stairs to the kitchen and promised herself she would get rid of the pictures right after the beginning of the New Year.

Forty-Two

On the final day of the fall semester and less than two weeks before Christmas, Olympia was finishing up the last of the end-of-semester details still outstanding. One of those was informing the Fellowship that she would make no more attempts to contact Bethany Ruth. It was Jim's idea, and it was a good one. When she told him she had no idea how to contact them, he suggested that she try looking up the number and phoning them. If they believed her, she and Jim may have bought themselves some time without scrutiny as well a little casualty insurance against further events of the teabag nature.

After a few minutes of page flipping in the phone directory, she found it, complete with street address, an 800-number, and the words, *Leave Message*. Olympia was annoyed with herself for feeling nervous, but she didn't let it stop her. She took a deep breath, picked up the phone, and dialed. To calm her thumping heart, she reminded herself she was simply a professor delivering a message to a student. Despite the fact that these people had threatened her and her son and were actively recruiting another of her students under her nose, she had every right to do this.

After three rings, a recorded message announced she had reached the Study and Christian Life Renewal Center of the Boston Christian Common Fellowship and offered three choices: *street ministry, scripture for the day,* and *leave message.* Olympia poked number three and spoke carefully into the receiver.

"This is Professor Olympia Brown from Meriwether College. I have a message for," she gulped, "Bethany Ruth McAllister. Would you please let her know that I've received her final project and that she has earned an A for the course. Tell her I'll leave her papers in her mail box, and she can pick them up when she returns in January." Olympia paused, "Would you also let her know there's no need to return this call, and in the future I will not be contacting her."

There were so many more things she wanted to say, but she settled for, "Thank you."

With that out of the way, she dutifully finished recording the last of the grades, squashed everything into a special envelope marked *Confidential*, and hand-delivered it to the registrar's office.

Because of the road conditions, Olympia was still using public transport. Tonight, despite the frigid temperature and the slushy streets, she welcomed the opportunity to walk through the various courtyards and quadrangles of historic Harvard Yard. The cold, fresh air would help clear her head.

As she slip-slopped along the snowy pathways, Olympia veered to the left and detoured through the main hallway of the science building where students and professors were walking around, talking and drinking coffee—in other words, being normal. The noise and the clatter of crockery cheered and warmed her before she went back out into the cold.

Weaving her way along between snow piles and clusters of chattering students, Olympia looked up at the

Christmas lights and the occasional electric menorah flashing in dormitory windows. Scattered strings of tiny white lights were swinging crazily from bare old trees along the uneven brick walkways. As she drew closer to the square, she could hear the familiar sounds of the Salvation Army Band, playing outside the Harvard Coop, as they did every year. It all was working wonders on her bleak, mid-winter mood.

By the time she reached the corner of Massachusetts Avenue, her anguished concerns about Bethany Ruth would, by virtue of the holidays, be put on hold until January. This, in turn, allowed the more pleasant thoughts of a certain blue-eyed Englishman to float to the surface.

Olympia knew she needed to do some serious thinking about him, as well. A potential relationship with Frederick was one heck of a lot more pleasurable to consider than a tangled mess involving an unholy religious cult. *The man lives in England, and I seem to be relationally challenged. Who knows? Maybe distance is the answer.*

As Olympia waited for the light, the band started to play "It Came Upon the Midnight Clear." As the carol came to its end, Olympia's world hardly lay in solemn stillness, but the holiday spirit, which had been swirling just out of reach, suddenly enveloped her in an unexpected rush of comfort and joy.

The light changed, and Olympia joined the crowd and squished gratefully toward the entrance of the station. She stopped in the up-rush of warm air coming from the tunnel below. Fishing around in her pocket for a subway token, she started down the stairs and lustily joined in singing the fading refrain of "Joy to the World" … *and wonders of his love, and wonders of his love, and wonders and wo-o-on-ders of his love.* Olympia smiled and wondered if somebody else might be trying to send her a different kind of message.

Olympia caught the commuter bus to Brookfield out of South Station, and in less than five minutes of listening to the comforting rumble of the diesel motor overlaid with the soft chatter of the commuters, Olympia fell into a deep and much-needed sleep.

She came awake with a start when a kind-faced woman tapped her shoulder and asked if this was her stop. Befuddled and bleary-eyed, Olympia mumbled a sleepy thank you, collected her things, and made an inglorious, stumbling exit. She stood and waited on the sidewalk while the big blue and white bus drove off. After looking both ways, she crossed the snowy street and headed for home.

The night *was* midnight clear and beautiful, and she had a million stars to light the Christmas card path to her door. Once inside, Olympia eased her way through the ankle-twirling cats to where her answering machine was not blinking. *That's a bonus,* she thought.

The Salvation Army Christmas music high was holding, and some of the tension she had been carrying for the past several days began to ease. Feeling festive, she located some Christmas music on the radio and noted that she still needed to get a tree. Picking out a Christmas tree by oneself was a lonely operation, but her not-all-the-way-grown-up sons still expected one.

The microwave dinged, announcing her nondescript dinner, which in turn called for a glass of wine. Out of habit and self-indulgence, Olympia lighted a candle and carried her steaming food to the kitchen table. With her cats on the floor beside her, a hot meal in front of her, and the house taking shape around her, Olympia Brown was content.

Tomorrow morning she would call Jim, tell him she had left a message at the Fellowship Center, and remind him what time to come for Christmas dinner. Like Bethany Ruth, his family lived too far away for a one-day drive, and a parish rectory was a very lonely place over the holidays.

If there was another reason for his not going home, he didn't say, and she didn't ask.

Forty-Three

December 17, 1859
Cold and clear this morning, but I suspect a change in the
weather. The cat is always out of sorts before a storm.
I've been asked to help out with the annual Christmas
Eve service. We've managed to collect a small group for a
choir, but that pestilential Mr. Jackson insists on being part
of it. The man can't carry a tune in a potato basket, but I
suppose I must be civil to him until the land transaction is
completed.
More anon...LFW

Olympia was sitting in the kitchen, flipping the pages of
the newspaper and finishing a second cup of coffee.
Finally, she eased a reluctant cat off her lap and fished a
bare foot around the chilly floor in search of her slippers.
The To Do list said *buy and decorate Christmas tree, sort out
holiday logistics with kids and mother, and start Christmas
shopping.* These would consume most, if not all, of the day
and should serve to keep her from stewing about Bethany
Ruth, but she knew they wouldn't.

So it was that at 8:14 a.m. on a December Saturday
morning in Brookfield, Massachusetts, the thought crossed
Olympia's mind that in England it was early afternoon—
1:14, to be exact—and maybe Frederick was near a
telephone.

Olympia poured a third cup of coffee and picked up the phone. She dialed the endless string of numbers and was finally rewarded by the metallic *brrrp-brrrp* sound of a telephone ringing somewhere outside of London. She began to pace out her usual route around the kitchen as a telephone half a world away continued to ring. By the fifth ring, The Reverend Olympia Brown was having second thoughts.

"He's not home," she said aloud, almost relieved. "Why should he be? It's the middle of a Saturday. He's probably out with some elegant English duchess or playing cricket, or I'm interrupting something, uh, private. Oh, God, this is crazy. I don't own him."

An inexplicable shyness caught up with her. She turned at the edge of the table to go back and hang up when Frederick picked up the phone.

After a few garbled words of greeting and holiday wishes from both sides of the Atlantic, Frederick said he was absolutely delighted she had rung him and to what honor did he owe this call or perhaps to what lucky stars should he direct his gratitude?

Olympia told him she was delighted to hear his voice, as well, and found herself stammering as she began to talk.

"Uh, well, actually Frederick," she said hoping the mad thumping of her heart wasn't audible on the other side of the Atlantic, "I've called for two reasons. One is to wish you a pleasant holiday and discuss the logistics of my coming over there, and the other ..." She paused, not knowing where to begin.

"What is it?" he said, without a trace of his usual middle-class English banter. "Something's wrong, isn't it,

Olympia? Tell me what it is, and then let me know how I can help you."

Trusting he meant what he said, Olympia switched phones and ensconced herself in her chair opposite the woodstove. She recounted the entire unpleasant saga, starting with the questionable death of Sonya Wilson, to Bethany Ruth's decision to join the Fellowship and Malcolm's visit to the Renewal Center. Then she told him about the tea bag incident, the threatening phone calls, and the fact that there might be as many as four other students with connections to the Fellowship who died in suspicious circumstances. Finally, she poured out her own fear and frustration in wanting to learn the truth about Sonya Wilson's death but at the same time protect Bethany Ruth without getting caught in the crossfire or losing her job.

"Is that everything?" he asked when she had finished.

"Everything to date," said Olympia, grateful to have been able to get it all out. "I feel so helpless. The Fellowship is so secretive. They put on a public show of Christian charity and good works, but anything we've managed to find out about them points to a double standard with something very sinister behind the pious façade."

"Anything else?" asked Frederick, his voice flat and his concern evident.

"It would appear," said Olympia beginning to doodle hearts and circles on the phone pad, "that the circumstances surrounding the so-called accidental deaths of at least three students I mentioned may have started out as scare tactics intended as warnings not to leave the Fellowship. In these three particular cases, anyway, the warnings misfired, and the students died as a result."

"That's dreadful."

"It's murder, Frederick," said Olympia, "maybe not exactly premeditated, but murder nonetheless."

"You think it was deliberate?"

"If they had lived," Olympia dropped the pencil and paper back in the stuff-basket and began pacing again, "they might have told their stories and exposed the inner workings of the Fellowship. If this group is anywhere near as awful as I'm beginning to suspect they are, then the last thing they want is someone digging around their secret chambers."

"Then, my dear lady," said Frederick from his vantage point three thousand miles away, "that is exactly what we must do."

"Uh, what do you mean, we?"

"Olympia, if what you are telling me is true, then this so-called religious fellowship has got to be exposed for what they really are. With their doors and their books opened for all to see, they will shrivel like vampires in the dawn."

"That's the same thing my friend Jim told me," said Olympia, "but he didn't say it as eloquently as you just did. You remember me telling you about my priest friend, Jim Sawicki?"

Frederick said that he did.

"We are trying to investigate this on our own, but it's so slow, and now, after everything I've told you, I have to be really careful if I'm going to continue, which of course I am."

"Why is that?" asked Frederick.

"The Dean at Meriwether is ultra cautious about anything which might cause a fuss or attract negative media attention or make him look bad. Olympia couldn't stop her voice from rising in anger and frustration, "Meanwhile, a student of mine has moved out of the dormitory and gone to live with them, and the college has done fuck-all about it."

There was a long pause on the other end of the line before Frederick began speaking again, and Olympia wondered if she'd offended him by using the F-word.

"This may seem a bit premature, Reverend-Doctor-Professor, considering we don't know each other all that well, but what say I jump on a nice, shiny little airplane and come over there for Christmas? Have you any room on your dance card for a lonely Brit who would otherwise probably drink himself silly in an empty pub on Christmas day, for a knight in squeaky armor who would throw his tattered cloak across murky puddles and possibly trip over it, for a man who yearns to see your lovely face again?"

His voice took on a more serious tone. "For a man who doesn't want to see you or your family in danger and is prepared to defend, if not your virtue, at least your safety so he can perhaps address the matter of your virtue afterwards?"

Olympia couldn't keep from laughing.

"What say, Olympia, lady with all those titles and letters dangling off the end of your name, what say to the offer of another set of hands to help out in this muddle you seem to have gotten yourself into?"

"I honestly don't know what to say," said Olympia. "You're serious, aren't you?"

"I am," said Frederick, "but let's begin at the beginning. Would you like me to come for the holidays and," he paused for dramatic effect, "among other things, add my thinking to this situation?"

Olympia knew that however unexpected this all was, and despite what Jim, her children, and mother might say when he turned up at Christmas dinner, she could think of nothing she would like more.

"Yes, please, Frederick," she said, wondering at the sudden tightness she felt at the back of her throat. "I should like that very much."

"See that?" he said with a chuckle. "You're already beginning to sound a bit British."

"What do you mean?"

"I *should* like that," he said repeating her words. "A very British turn of phrase, that."

"You are serious," she repeated. "You'd really come over here and try to help us?"

"I am, indeed," he said, "I'll call you back in two shakes, right after I've booked the flight."

Within the hour Frederick called back to say he would be at Logan Airport's Terminal E on Monday at three forty-five in the afternoon, her time, and in real time, that was slightly more than forty-eight hours.

"I'll be there with bells on—jingle bells," said Olympia, who suddenly felt foolishly and deliriously happy. "For heaven's sake, Frederick, bring warm clothes. It's freezing here."

"I'm British. We laugh at freezing."

"You may be British," said Olympia through a totally ridiculous full-body grin, "but you might not be prepared for an all out, full-blown, New England winter."

"I'll be there before you know it," was the answer. "Please do carry a red balloon so I'll recognize you."

"Already thought of it," said Olympia. "Looks like I have two days to have a total body transplant and-or clean the house, whichever seems more within the realm of possibility."

"Don't you dare!"

"Dare which?"

"Neither of the choices you just described. I like you the way you are, at least what I remember, and I don't give a rat's arse about the quality of your housekeeping. You should see my flat. I'll see you in two days' time, Olympia."

"So much for Plan A," said Olympia crumpling up the discarded To Do list and tossing it in the direction of the cats sprawled in front of the woodstove. "I think Plan B is going to be one hell of a lot more fun."

"Plan B?" asked Frederick.

"I'll explain when you get here," said Olympia, winking lasciviously at the woodstove.

After she hung up the phone, Olympia stood in the middle of the great room and surveyed her holdings. *I don't have a guest room or even a guest bed,* she thought. *How very convenient.* But she did have the fold-out sofa that Jim had used the previous summer. For decorum sake she'd offer it to him. What happened after that was going to be either a delicious or a disastrous unknown.

With sleeping arrangements sorted out, at least temporarily, she walked around the room trying to decide where to begin tidying up.

What the hell?

Olympia stopped in front of the woodstove and stared at the clock on the mantel.

I'm sure I set the hands in the 1:50 position, but they seem to have moved to 3:45. What a curious coincidence that is.

Forty-Four

As an aspirant, Bethany Ruth was not allowed on street missions. So on this particular morning with everyone out and no one to see, Sarah held up two mugs of contraband cocoa and invited her to enjoy some quiet time by the fire. She said it was so they could get to know each other a little better. What she didn't say was, *and so I can keep an eye on you and protect you from the autocratic and judgmental Brother David.*

Later, with their cocoa mugs scrubbed clean of evidence, Bethany Ruth went to work in the laundry room, and Sarah slipped quietly upstairs. She was taking advantage of the alone time to do a little investigation on her own. Recently she had been privy to some discussions she had found troubling. The way David and the others talked about numbers and money and ratios made the Fellowship sound more like a business than a Christian Mission, and there was something else. Just yesterday, she found some changes in her records, changes she hadn't made.

Prudently, she left the door to the office wide open so she could hear if someone approached and started looking in file cabinets and cupboards she hadn't opened before. If someone did come in, she would say that she couldn't find one of her folders and wondered if someone might have misfiled it.

After an hour of hunting, taking care to reposition anything she moved to exactly where she had found it, the only things she could come up with was an occasional penciled *JME*, sometimes with a date scribbled beside it, and in another cabinet, what appeared to be a parallel set of records to the ones she kept. *Why two sets of records?* There wasn't enough time to compare them line for line right now, but Sister Sarah intended to come back when there was.

Also, Sonya Wilson's folder wasn't in the membership file. *Did someone move it after she died? Who would do that, and why not tell me?*

Sarah was in charge of the membership records, and as far as she knew, the Fellowship didn't keep a separate file for deceased members. When a brother or a sister died, they just wrote *Deceased* on the front.

She heard voices from below, which meant the brothers and sisters were back. Sarah knew from experience that within minutes, Brother David would be up there on some pretext or another. She smoothed her headscarf, tucked in her blouse, and checked one more time to see that nothing in the room was out of order.

By the time she got to the door, Brother David was standing there smiling.

Forty-Five

Fifty-two-year-old Olympia bounced into her bedroom for a long, critical look in the mirror. There she saw a relatively nice-looking, middle-aged lady wearing mismatched socks, a ratty pink chenille bathrobe feathered with cat-claw pulls, and a nightgown that had seen any number of better days. She lifted the hem of the robe for a closer look and shook her head in dismay. *Add new nightgown and bathrobe to the list.*

Olympia was rounder in the chin and tummy than she would have preferred. Her practical, wash-and-wear hairstyle framed a fair-skinned, freckled face that pleasantly reflected her Swedish-Irish-English heritage.

He'll have to take me as I am, she thought, *but then, he already has. Well, not quite.* There were one or two avenues left to their mutual exploration.

Enough, she scolded herself and refocused on what needed to be done. Start by changing the bed. No, buy new sheets. Then clean the house, go on a fruit and water crash diet, and hope for the best. Olympia was as foolishly excited as any sixteen-year-old — and equally as terrified.

The delicious anticipation replaced some of the fear and anxiety she had been feeling over Bethany Ruth and the Fellowship. Frederick would be here for Christmas and the New Year, as well. For the first time since the boys had moved out, she would not come home to an empty house on Christmas Eve. She wondered if Frederick was allergic to cats and how he and Jim would hit it off.

Her brain was gyrating, but her heart was thoroughly enjoying the ride. The tensions of the last month had taken a large bite out of her normal *joie de vivre,* and as much as Olympia hated to use the cliché, she knew in the end that time would indeed tell, and hopefully, where Frederick was concerned, not too much when it did.

I suppose he'll come to church with me. If he does, my collection of self-appointed church grandmothers will be clucking over it well into the New Year – and what in God's holy name am I going to tell my kids?

Olympia put her myriad questions on hold and picked up the new, blue toilet cleaner she had bought for special occasions. Houseguests, especially articulate Englishmen, certainly qualified as special. Her mother always said, "When in doubt, clean."

Oh yes, thought Olympia with a start, *Mother, and what about Miss Winslow?* She laughed out loud at the thought of it. *How do you introduce your gentleman friend to a ghost?*

The rest of the day was a happy *mélange*: part cleaning frenzy, part shopping binge for new underwear and a nightgown, part panic attack, and a lot of convincing herself that she'd made a wise decision accepting Frederick's offer of help.

By the end of the day, she was pleasantly exhausted, and the house was presentable. That night, Olympia slept like one of the logs she had piled by the woodstove.

On Sunday after church, Olympia continued with the cleaning and scouring, creating what she hoped would be a welcoming, but not overly suggestive, atmosphere. Yes to the scented candles in the great room, but no to red satin sheets. The thought of red satin sheets made her think of her sons. As old as they were, they were still uncomfortable with the idea of their mother and a man in a relationship, especially when said relationship included sharing a bed.

"But Frederick and I don't have a relationship yet," said Olympia to the steamy mirror on the bathroom wall.

In their letters and phone calls, she and Frederick had never discussed or defined any parameters of their relationship, and however intricate those possibilities might be, until he or good fortune proved otherwise, he was a pen pal coming for a Christmas visit. He was just someone she met.

Sure he is.

Olympia was not doing a great job of divesting herself of delicious and naughty anticipation of that visit. *Oh, well,* she thought, *it will all sort itself out in less than twenty-four hours.* She wondered if Frederick preferred red wine or white.

Forty-Six

Bethany Ruth was alone in her room. The other three occupants, including Yellow Bee Pollen, who was also an aspirant, were all down at breakfast. She had finished making the bed and was lingering, picking at things that didn't need her attention and thinking about Yellow Bee Pollen's coming baby. By anyone's best calculations, she was due in early June, and Bethany Ruth was counting the days.

She loved babies, loved holding them, even changing them. She couldn't let herself think about her twin nephews back in Oklahoma. She missed them desperately, and even the thought of them reduced her to tears. Having a new baby in the house to love and help care for would help to fill the hole.

Bethany Ruth tiptoed to the door and checked to see if there was anyone in the hallway. Then she slipped her hand under the bedding and took out the envelope containing the photographs. She knew she should be rid of this attachment, but this would be the first Christmas she'd ever been away from her family. Sitting on the edge of her bed with a picture in each hand, she didn't hear the door open.

"What have you got there, Sister, may I see?"

Startled, Bethany Ruth looked up to find Sister Sarah standing beside her.

"I … I … oh, God." She hung her head, rigid with fear and guilt.

Sarah sat down beside her and put a reassuring arm around her shoulders.

"Its okay, Little Sister," she said softly, "I won't tell. We all have our secrets. Is this your family? Your dog? I love dogs. What's his name?"

"Her name is Betsy," whispered Bethany Ruth, "She's …" She couldn't finish the sentence.

Sarah moved a little closer and began rubbing the back of Bethany Ruth's neck, comforting her, calming her fears. Sarah's body felt warm against hers. She smelled of soap and shampoo.

"Tell me about Betsy."

The gentle motion of Sarah's hand on the back of her neck felt so good. Bethany Ruth remembered how her grandmother would massage her neck and shoulders when she was sick or upset.

"We got her at the pound. She had a broken leg. We paid to have it fixed."

Bethany Ruth was afraid to speak above a whisper, afraid someone would come in and see them, afraid she would be denied her precious place in the First Circle of Commitment. She drew a deep breath.

"She's scruffy, part terrier and part something else, mostly black." Bethany Ruth looked over at the door.

"It's okay," said Sarah, "they're all downstairs at breakfast. I want to hear more about Betsy and more about you, too, but not right now."

Sarah lifted her arm from Bethany Ruth's shoulders and kissed her gently on the cheek. Then she stood, checked her headscarf and spoke in a low voice.

"Sometimes I think the rules are too strict around here, but I'll never say it where anyone could hear me. I've been disciplined too many times for speaking my mind." Sarah smiled and shook her head. "Women aren't supposed to have opinions here, but that doesn't' mean we don't." She lowered her voice even further. "Keep your eyes and ears open, keep your head down, and watch out for Brother David. He's tough."

Bethany Ruth sat looking up at Sarah, not moving, not knowing what to think about what she was hearing.

"The discipline is strict, but we do good work, especially with the poor and the homeless. That's why I'm here. I want to serve God, but I remember how it feels to be new. If you need anything, or you just want to talk about your dog, you can always come to me."

Sarah turned and started toward the door, then stopped and retraced her steps. "You'd better get down there before they notice you're missing. Use the back stairs. I'll wait a few minutes and then come down the other way." She paused in the doorway. "Don't let them catch you with the pictures, Little Sister."

Later that morning, Sarah and other members of the Third Circle were sitting around the conference table for the morning meeting. David was speaking.

"We got a message on the answering machine from Professor Brown saying she wouldn't be having any more contact with Bethany Ruth." He smiled in Sarah's direction. "Sister Sarah, I think your little mission over at Meriwether had the desired effect."

"I don't think I understand," said Sarah, unconsciously feeling for stray curls.

"It's a good thing you didn't get thirsty," said David with a low chuckle. "You would have puked your guts out all over Harvard Yard."

"What do you mean, puked?" asked Sarah. "Wait a minute, what was in that tea bag?"

"Ipecac." said David. "We've used it before. It delivers a messy, unpleasant warning that can't be ignored. Too bad Olympia didn't get it, though."

"I still don't understand," said Sarah. "Who got what?"

David got up and started pacing. "A friend of hers used the teabag and landed in the Emergency Room." He made a dismissive gesture with his right hand as if to indicate the hospital trip was of little importance. "She was out in a few hours. Message delivered, no harm done. Bethany Ruth heard it from one of the students and told Sister Miriam. She has no idea we were behind it."

David shot a warning glance at Joshua, who looked as if he might be going to say something.

"Wait a minute," said Sarah, her voice rising despite her attempts to control it. "You mean I almost poisoned somebody?"

"Not at all, Sister Sarah," David was talking to her as though she was a person of limited intelligence. "You merely delivered the first half of a message designed to get her attention," he half-laughed. "We called her later that evening with the other half. She won't bother us again."

Sarah fought to keep any hint of emotion out of her voice. "Well, that's a relief. I'd hate to see Bethany Ruth thrown off course." She looked at the people sitting around the table and said carefully, "She's coming along beautifully."

"I'm glad you agree, Sister," said David. He had a curious expression on his face. "I can see why you've found favor with the Abba. I've been talking to him. He tells me he has plans for you. But let's finish up with Bethany Ruth."

Sarah stiffened at the mention of the Abba. Her mouth went dry, and she licked her lips, but it only made them sting.

"Bethany Ruth wants more than anything to be admitted to the First Circle," said Miriam, anxious to speak on her behalf. "She's been working so hard. I think she's ready."

"I agree with Sister Miriam," said Joshua, turning towards David. "She's really committed. Even with the food, it's hard, but she's doing it."

"Don't let her get too enthusiastic." David stopped moving as if to emphasize his point. "Don't forget what happened to that other one."

"She was anorexic before she came here," said Miriam. "We couldn't have known that."

"True enough, Sister," said David, pacing again, "but that kind of thing can arouse curiosity. We encourage interest in our good works but not about our inner workings. There's a difference. In some ways, as much as we want to encourage the recruitment of new members, the more I think about it, it might be better if this one doesn't stay. Either way, we need to keep a careful eye on her and keep her healthy. If the weekend regimen is working, then we'll leave it at that for now."

David was looking at Sarah again, but his expression was unreadable.

"If Olympia Brown and the dean over there at Meriwether start asking too many questions, it could be awkward. The woman says she's not going to have any contact with Bethany Ruth, but I'm not sure I believe it."

Sarah maintained her outward composure, but her hands were clenched in her lap beneath the table top. "So what about Bethany Ruth?" She kept her voice level.

"She'll make it, no doubt about that," said Joshua. "We'll let her worry a little bit, then reward her. You know, the usual technique. It always works. She'll be grateful and dutiful, the way we like them."

Sarah couldn't believe what she was hearing. It was so cold and calculating. *These people must have discussed me this way when I was an aspirant.* She recalled how they would encourage her progress but quickly slap her down if she took any independent action. Bethany Ruth was a lovely and spirited young woman. The Fellowship would smother that spirit and make her conform. Total submission was a requirement of the process.

Sarah's own early training as an aspirant and later a member ascending the circles never really worked. Over the years, she had learned to control her passionate and rebellious spirit, to keep it hidden just like her hair. She was a quick study and a good actor. She joined the Fellowship to get away from the world and a church and a family that had condemned her and all her kind.

All of this flashed through her thinking when she realized that she cared far too much for Bethany Ruth to let her be crushed and controlled by anyone.

Forty-Seven

British Air Flight 734 lifted off at 2:30 p.m. English time and was scheduled to arrive at Boston's Logan Airport shortly after four that same afternoon. After the drinks and the mini-meal had been served and removed, Frederick was left with three and a half hours of sitting in a cramped space with his half-finished book, the *Guardian* crossword puzzle, and a bubble of postprandial gas nosing around his midsection. He allowed himself the most discreet of belches, tucked the crossword puzzle, book and pencil into the seat pocket in front of him, and instantly fell asleep.

"How would you like a nice cup of tea, sir?"

The red-blue-and-white-uniformed flight attendant was gently tapping him on the shoulder. "We're less than an hour from our destination."

Frederick opened his eyes. They felt like someone had poured rock salt in them.

"Just the thing to set you up before you come down." The man standing in the aisle beside him put his fingers to his lips and giggled. "Little joke sir? Set you up before you come down?"

Frederick ignored the joke but said yes to the tea. He was English. Tea was part of his DNA. It was five months since he'd seen Olympia, and before that, he had experienced a long period of lonely, celibate, bachelorhood. Frederick felt around on the floor for the complimentary travel pack, pulled out the miniscule toothbrush, and headed for the lavatory. While he might not be able to do very much about his travel-weary clothing and bleary eyes, at the very least, he owed the woman a clean face and brushed teeth.

When he was wedged back in his seat, Frederick began to collect his paraphernalia. He could feel the plane beginning the long descent into Boston. The captain came on and announced they would be landing in twenty-five minutes, and the temperature outside the airport was fifteen degrees Fahrenheit. Frederick was used to the Celsius scale and wondered how cold that might be, but he was far too preoccupied to do the calculations.

The landing gear dropped with a metallic thud, and Frederick wondered how long it would take to clear customs. Other than the two-bottle allotment of the best champagne he could afford at the duty-free shop, the only other gift he had with him was a pair of red, fur-lined leather gloves, recommended, selected, and gift wrapped by his younger sister. She had recommended black, but Frederick insisted on red with fur trim.

"You want a personal gift without overtones," she had said when Frederick asked for her assistance. Come the right moment he might well be disposed to a few overtones, but he prudently confided nothing of that to his sister.

The plane hit the tarmac with a bone-rattling thump, and the flaps on the wings came up, forcing Frederick forward as the roar of the reverse thrust brought them to an eventual halt. When the seat belt sign went out, Frederick twisted out of his seat, stretched as best he could in the cramped space, and then edged into the weary crush moving toward the exit.

At the same moment, Olympia was inching through gelatinous traffic, gripping a travel mug half-full of tepid coffee. It seemed as if everything possible had conjoined to interfere with her efforts to arrive on time. The pre-holiday traffic was a tangled mess, the roads were still dicey from the big storm, more snow was forecast that afternoon, and the clock was ticking. A huge plane flew low overhead on its final approach to Logan airport.

"That's probably him," said Olympia to the windshield, "and I'm going to be late. Damn, damn, damn!"

It was after four-thirty when she found a parking space and jammed the van into the angled slot. Although it was too old to steal, she locked it and took off at a dead run toward the entrance of Terminal E and an Englishman named Frederick Watkins. She knew he would still be there, because he had no idea how to be anywhere else.

As it turned out, clearing customs took longer than expected, and Frederick was just coming through the doors and scanning the crowd when Olympia, red faced, teary and wheezing from the cold, catapulted into view.

After one of those awkward, nose-bumping, eyeglass-catching, thoroughly chaste kisses, she stepped back and looked up at the wispy-haired, blue-eyed man standing in front of her. He was lovely.

"Have you been waiting long?" she asked, preparing to apologize.

"Not at all," he said, smiling and smoothing his thinning hair. "I'd just come through the doors when I spotted you crashing through the crowd. I must say, you look rather like you've just completed a triathlon."

"I feel like it." Olympia wiped her eyes and blew her nose as her breathing and heartbeat returned to something approaching normal. "Is this all you have with you?" she asked, reaching down for the carry-on. "Just this and the one suitcase?"

"We solitary bachelors don't have many material possessions, but I counter that with a rich inner life," said Frederick, waving away her offer of help. His quick humor eased Olympia's adolescent awkwardness

"Don't you have a hat? It's colder than hell out there," said Olympia starting towards the door. "What time is it your time? You must be exhausted. I hope you're hungry." She was babbling.

"In the order given," he said, doing his best to stay with her, "I must have left my hat on the plane. I don't know what time it is, but my watch still does. It's almost ten in the evening on my body's clock, and I'm exhausted. I've been in transit for almost twenty-four hours, and I must admit I didn't sleep well last night. I'm too tired to know if I'm hungry, but if confronted with food, I can probably give you an answer."

Olympia and Frederick walked out into the freezing cold after doing a little you-first-no-you-first minuet at the revolving door that sent them both into fits of self-conscious giggles. A light snow was beginning to fall.

"Crikey, it's cold," said Frederick reaching for her hand.

"It's not far," she said, "and the engine should still be warm. We'll be toasty in minutes."

When the two of them were loaded up and belted in, Olympia backed up with the skill of a long-distance truck driver and carefully wound her way out of central parking. It was likely to be a long, slow drive, and

Olympia had a tired, hungry traveler and a whole lot of unspoken possibilities sitting beside her.

Mercifully, the traffic was lighter than she had anticipated, and by seven o'clock they were home, chatting away like old friends as they carted in Frederick's suitcase and the groceries Olympia had picked up on the way. They stepped over the cats, dropped Frederick's things in the living room, and made straight for the kitchen and one of the bottles of really nice wine Olympia had laid in for the evening.

"Let me do that," said Frederick, moving closer and holding out his hand. "Where's the cork-screw?"

"Top drawer, left-hand side," said Olympia, opening a can of cat food. "The clean glasses are in the cabinet directly above."

"Jolly good," said Frederick.

Olympia chuckled under her breath. *Wow, they really do talk like that.*

As Frederick poured the wine, Olympia went into the next room and touched a match to the fire she had set earlier that afternoon. Then she lighted the bayberry candle she had artfully placed on the coffee table. As she turned to go back into the kitchen, she almost bumped into Frederick, who was setting the glasses down on the coffee table. The collision almost turned into an embrace, but they both stepped back before it did, and Olympia managed to find something important to examine on the strap of her watch.

"Let's just relax for a bit," said Frederick, breaking the unspoken tension. "Where do you usually sit? I don't want to get off on the wrong foot by usurping your favorite chair."

"I usually sit in that one," said Olympia, indicating her well-used armchair with the overflowing basket beside it, "but maybe I'll break with tradition and sit on the sofa beside you."

"An excellent choice, Madame," said Frederick patting the cushion beside him.

"Before I actually make landfall, give me one more minute to put supper in the oven. I made a vegetarian eggplant *moussaka*. I did tell you I'm vegetarian, didn't I?"

"You did, but don't rush." Frederick covered a yawn. "We have all evening."

When Olympia walked back into the living room ,Frederick had abandoned his half-empty glass on the coffee table and was stretched out on the sofa, snoring softly. The fire, the wine, and the jet lag had joined forces, and the man on the sofa was no match for them.

Olympia unfolded a granny-square afghan her mother made and spread it over him. She stood, relishing his peaceful contentment, and finished off the rest of his wine. Empty glass in hand, she retrieved the eggplant from the oven and put it back in the refrigerator. Then, with a dispirited sigh, she picked up a book.

At about nine, Frederick mumbled something in his sleep, turned over, and continued breathing deeply and evenly. At that point, Olympia abandoned ship and got out a second blanket. After checking the locks, stoking the fire and closing down the damper on the woodstove, she blew out the candle. Frederick was down for the count.

"Tomorrow is another day," whispered Olympia to the recumbent lump on the sofa, "and while I'm no Scarlett O'Hara, and you're hardly Rhett Butler, come the dawn, my sleepy English friend, I see distinct possibilities."

Olympia was blushing and humming "Rule Britannia" as she and the cats made ready for bed.

Forty-Eight

Bethany Ruth was settled into a comfortable routine of housekeeping, study, and the rituals of cleansing and releasing that were required of all aspirants. Her daily duties kept her busy and prevented her from thinking too much about Christmas and Oklahoma.

One morning, with a few rare minutes alone and without chores, she was sitting by the fire reading her Bible. Later in the day, as a special privilege, she was going to be allowed to go out with other Fellowship members to deliver food and blankets to the needy. She was sitting in a warm glow of well-being, reading the book of Ecclesiastes, when she came upon the familiar passage in Chapter Three, "To everything there is a season, and a time and a purpose under heaven."

How perfect, she thought. *In this holy time of Jeshua's birth, this is exactly where I am supposed to be ... every purpose under heaven.* Bethany Ruth looked up and smiled as Sarah entered the room.

"Good morning, Sister,"

"Oh, for God's sake, call me Sarah," she said smacking Bethany Ruth playfully on the shoulder, "at least when nobody's listening." Sarah sat down on the sofa, and Bethany Ruth shifted to give her more room.

"That Sister-Brother stuff seems so affected sometimes." Sarah turned more toward Bethany Ruth. "I'm sure the nuns at Saint Catherine's went by their first names when we weren't around. They were so weird. We always wondered what their hair looked like under those stiff white things they wore around their faces, their wimples. God, what a silly word, *wimple*, rhymes with pimple. You can imagine what we did with that."

"Saint Catherine's?"

"Part of my repressed Irish Catholic childhood, long before I came here," said Sarah. "My parents sent me to Catholic schools because I was such a tomboy. They thought it would make a lady out of me." She looked bemused. "Didn't work, though."

Bethany Ruth smiled and looked away.

"I'm still strong willed," she said, "but like my hair, I keep it covered up." She made a face and nudged Bethany Ruth gently with her elbow. " David makes sure of that." Sarah leaned closer and dropped her voice. "I don't like all the posturing and the discipline, but I do like what we do for the poor. I wanted to be a nun when I was younger. I never wanted to marry. Children would have been nice, but I didn't see a way of having children without being married, not in my family anyway. Oh, no."

Sarah chuckled again, took Bethany Ruth's hand in her own, and changed the subject. "So we're off to the big city this afternoon on one of our food-for-the-homeless outings. It's going to be very cold, so make sure you dress warmly." Sarah was drawing little circles on the palm of Bethany Ruth's hand with the tips of her fingers.

"We—are you coming?" asked Bethany Ruth, not knowing quite how to retrieve her hand. "I thought you worked upstairs.

"I do mostly," said Sarah with an impish grin, "but once in a while they let me out to play with you guys.

Besides, I can drive the van. Not even some of the men can do that. The thing is a pig. The workload is always huge before the holidays, and there's so much need. We all pitch in."

Sarah stood up, put another log on the fire, then walked over to the rocking chair and sat across from Bethany Ruth.

"Anyway," she said, rocking back and forth, "seeing the lights and hearing the music will be fun. We're not supposed to pay attention to such worldly affectations, but ..." she grinned. "I won't tell if you don't."

Bethany Ruth looked over at Sarah and wondered if she was missing something. Before she could ask, Sarah changed the subject again.

"I really love doing the Savior's work," she said. "It's why I joined to the Fellowship. Third Circle members are really middle management," Sarah winked, "but for heaven's sake, don't tell anyone I said that either, because if you do, I'll deny it."

The two women were laughing when Miriam and Joshua came into the room.

Sister Miriam spoke. "It's good to see you laughing, Sister Bethany Ruth. You've been looking too serious these last few days. What's the joke?"

Sarah spoke before Bethany Ruth could respond. "She was studying the book of Ecclesiastes when I came into the room. I asked what she was reading, and she said the book of elastics. Of course, it was just a slip of the tongue, but we both couldn't stop laughing. Then I asked her if she wasn't stretching the point, and that made us laugh even harder. My fault for being silly."

Behind Miriam's back, Sarah looked hard at Bethany Ruth and lifted a warning finger to her lips.

"I just came in to say we'll be cooking extra food for our mission this afternoon," said Miriam looking first at Bethany Ruth and then at Sarah, "so we have to start lunch early."

Bethany Ruth marked the place in her Bible and followed Sister Miriam into the kitchen. She wondered why Sarah made up the story about Ecclesiastes and elastics and then motioned for her to be quiet, but she knew better than to ask.

After they left, Sarah stayed on alone in the rocking chair staring into the fire.

When lunch was finished and the dishes cleared up, the Brothers and Sisters began the task of loading boxes of food and bags of blankets and clothing into the van. As she tramped back and forth, Bethany Ruth shivered in the icy chill.

"You're not dressed warmly enough," said Miriam. "Go back and get yourself another sweater and a hat, one that covers your ears."

"I'm still not used to this kind of cold," said Bethany Ruth. "I think even my fingernails are frozen."

"I have extra things in my room," said Sarah, turning back toward the house. "I'll go and get them. Do you need an extra pair of socks? I'll get some just in case."

"Sister Sarah is very kind to you." Miriam was pushing the last of the boxes into the back of the vehicle. " I hope you appreciate her taking such an interest in you, being so new and all." Sister Miriam had an odd look on her face. "Too bad she might not be here much longer."

"Sister Sarah's leaving?" Bethany Ruth was slapping the sides of her arms to keep warm.

"Well, I don't know for sure," said Miriam, dropping her voice, "but we hear she's found favor with the Abba. That usually means one day she'll move on to one of the family compounds. That's where Sister Yellow Bee Pollen will be going to have the baby."

"She's going, too?" Bethany Ruth felt like she'd been punched in the heart. The two people she liked the most. She had been looking forward to the baby's arrival more than she dared admit. "How come?" was all she could say.

"We have a facility out in the western part of the state," said Sister Miriam. "We don't have facilities for a baby here. She'll be well cared for."

"I could help out," said Bethany Ruth, keeping her voice steady. "I love babies."

"Oh, dear little Sister Bethany Ruth," said Miriam, reaching over and patting her arm, "you have such a good heart, but your work will be here with us. You'll be helping poor forgotten souls on the streets, feeding their bodies and bringing their souls to Jeshua. The Fellowship will provide a home for Sister Bee Pollen's baby. We always take care of our own."

"Everybody in!" called Joshua.

"Here you go," said Sarah, running lightly out of the house, "one heavy sweater, one woolly hat, and one pair of thick knee socks. Will your boots fit over them?"

"I think so," said Bethany Ruth as she clambered into the van. "If not, I'll make them."

It was the second time in ten minutes that Bethany Ruth had made a modest attempt at humor and the second time it was greeted with silence. She made a mental note to be more circumspect.

With everything loaded, there was little sitting room left. Bethany Ruth was wedged half on Sarah's lap and half on Miriam's. The two women put their arms around her, because there was no seat belt that would fit around the three of them. It was tight, but it made for a merry ride as they bumped and lurched along. In the happy tangle of all their arms and legs, Bethany Ruth was trying to put on the extra clothing. At one point, Bethany Ruth said she wasn't even sure she was putting the socks on her own feet, a remark which this time did send them all into gales of laughter. Finally, when everything seemed to be buttoned and zipped into place, the three young women sat heaped in a pile like puppies, arms around each other to keep warm in the cold, noisy van.

Sarah had both arms around Bethany Ruth and was resting her head against her shoulder. Beside her, Miriam had her right arm hooked through Bethany Ruth's left elbow and was bracing herself on the seat in front of her with the other. As they bumped along, Bethany Ruth could feel the warmth of Sarah's breath on the back of her neck.

But Sarah wasn't smiling any longer. She lifted her head from Bethany Ruth's shoulder and turned her face toward the window so no one would see the single tear roll down her cheek and drop silently into the rough gray wool of Bethany Ruth's winter coat.

Forty-Nine

Olympia forgot about her houseguest until the aroma of freshly brewed coffee wafted into her bedroom, and she heard the sound of footsteps in the kitchen. "Oh my God," she gasped, fumbling around and trying to read the bedside clock without her glasses, "Frederick. Oh, shit, what time is it?"

Olympia briefly allowed herself to think she could get used to someone starting breakfast for her, but just as quickly she reminded herself that his was a friendly, supportive visit, no less and no more. With the self-administered dose of caution firmly under her belt, she eased Whitefoot, the older cat, out of the way and padded barefoot into the bathroom. Standing in front of the mirror, she smoothed down her bed hair, brushed her teeth, tugged at the pale blue, padded bathrobe she had bought for the occasion, and set off bravely to greet the day and her gentleman friend.

"Well, good morning, Missus," said Frederick. "I hope you slept well. I apologize for passing out on you, but there didn't seem to be anything I could do about it. Coffee?" He poured a cup and held it out. "Black or white?"

"Black or white?" asked Olympia, accepting the cup

"White coffee has milk in it. Black doesn't."

"Black, please. Have you had some already?"

"Brits often start the day with tea," he said, holding up his mug." I'll switch over for elevenses."

"I can see I'm going to need a phrase book," said Olympia, enjoying the warmth of the cup in her chilly hands. "Would you like some breakfast to go with your tea? When did you get up? I assume you found the bathroom."

"I found the bathroom," said Frederick, "availed myself of the shower, put on clean clothes, and thank you, I've not eaten. I thought I'd wait for you."

Olympia put her coffee cup on the wooden sideboard and started poking around in the refrigerator. Then she started handing out a variety of bowls and plastic containers.

"How about yogurt with fresh fruit, strangled eggs, and toast?"

"Say again? What kind of eggs?"

"Family joke. My younger son Randall couldn't pronounce *scrambled*."

"This looks like a breakfast fit for a king," he said, laying everything out on the counter beside the stove, "or in present company, a queen."

Olympia giggled, reached for the skillet, and asked him if he had slept well.

"Like a baby," said Frederick, leaning on the sink to watch her assembling their breakfast, "or maybe more like a rude, inconsiderate lout who wasted a perfectly good opportunity to spend an evening with a beautiful woman. Is that where I'll be sleeping?"

"I didn't have time to clear a room for you," explained Olympia, picking at the sash of her robe. "There are a total of eleven rooms in this house, and eight of them are still full of antiques—or junk, depending on your perspective. The place was a wreck when I got it. That's how I could afford it. I'm living in three rooms for the moment, the kitchen, the great room and my bedroom. I'll sort something out before tonight."

The unspoken remained unspoken, and the two of them suddenly busied themselves with the intricacies of meal preparation.

"Is there something I can do?" asked Frederick.

"Will you cut up the fruit and put it in dishes while I cook the eggs?" asked Olympia, thinking for the second time that morning she could get used to this.

When they had finished breakfast and cleared up the kitchen, Olympia said she was going to get showered and dressed. Frederick asked if Olympia minded if he poured himself a second cup of tea.

"*Mi casa, su casa,*" said Olympia, starting out of the kitchen. "It's Spanish. It means my house is your house. In other words, you don't have to ask for anything. Just help yourself to anything you want."

"In that case," said Frederick, moving around the corner of the counter, "may I help myself to this?" He stepped forward and slipped his arms around Olympia and kissed her the way she'd wanted him to since she first saw him in the airport. *Was it only yesterday?*

"Good morning again, pretty lady," he said after they had awkwardly but reluctantly stepped back from one another. "Now go have your shower. I never discuss serious matters with women in dressing gowns."

When Olympia returned, Frederick was sitting comfortably on the sofa, and there was a fresh cup of coffee sitting beside her chair.

"Before we talk about this student of yours, can you tell me why that beautiful old clock on the mantel is facing the wall?"

Olympia looked over to where he was pointing and giggled. She hadn't laid a finger on that clock.

Frederick looked confused. "What's so funny?"

"I was trying to find the right time to tell you about this, but it would appear that I've been preempted by Miss Winslow. I think she wants to make your acquaintance."

"What on earth are you talking about, and who, pray tell, is Miss Winslow?"

Olympia took a sip of her coffee. *Where to begin?*

"I don't know if you're going to believe this, but it seems that I, or we, have a ghost. I think it's a woman named Leanna Faith Winslow who lived her entire ninety-one years in this house. She was born in the mid-1800s and died in the early1900s. I found that clock at the same time I found her diary. I've been reading it in bits. I haven't had time to really get into it. This business with the cult and the girl at the college has literally consumed me."

Olympia regarded Frederick over her coffee cup. "That clock seems to have a mind of its own. On the other hand, it might be how Miss Winslow gets my attention. Whatever the case, I haven't been anywhere near it in the last week."

"English history goes back to Stonehenge and before," said Frederick, smiling but not laughing at her. "Ghosts are ten-a-penny over there."

"Ten-a-penny?"

"It's English for lots and lots." Whereupon Frederick stood up, doffed an imaginary hat, bowed low in the direction of the clock, and said, "How do you do, Miss

Winslow? I'm Frederick Watkins, and I'm pleased to make your acquaintance. I'll be here for a while, so how do you like *your* coffee?"

Olympia burst out laughing.

"I think she likes me," said Frederick, returning to his seat, "but let's get back to this student of yours. If you don't mind, I'd like to hear it all again so I can make notes."

Olympia nodded at the man over the top of her coffee cup. "You're right," she said, "it might well produce some new insights."

For the next two hours, starting with Father Jim, and what he'd managed to uncover, Olympia reviewed the facts of the situation. From time to time, Frederick interrupted, asking for dates, times of day, sequences of events, names of the deceased students, and other specific information she might have gleaned from her conversation with the cult expert at Harvard. Finally, they went over Malcolm's observations on the day of the blizzard and his unexpected overnight stay at the Renewal Center.

When they finished it was long past noon, and both were hungry.

"Let's just sit with this for a while," said Frederick, getting up and collecting their cups. "I find that if I just let things roll around in the grey matter for a while, new ideas will sometimes ooze to the surface."

"Good idea, Mr. Watkins. Are you sure that your name isn't Watson?"

"Elementary, my dear Olympia, elementary," called Frederick from the kitchen where she could hear the clatter of the cups and spoons in the dishwasher, "or is it alimentary? I'm feeling a bit peckish. Uh, that's hungry in

English. Why don't you allow me take you to lunch? After that, I believe you mentioned something about a Christmas tree? That would make for a lovely afternoon. We can revisit Bethany Ruth over sherry or after supper. Maybe we can have another go at that moussaka I heard rumors about before I so rudely passed out."

Frederick took their coats out of the closet and helped Olympia on with hers.

"Remember how cold it was yesterday? We should probably buy you a hat while we're out, and what about a scarf?" she asked him.

Frederick made a face. "I don't have a scarf," he said. "Maybe we can get one of those as well."

"I could knit one," said Olympia as she closed the door behind them, "but not by Christmas."

"You are a woman with lofty intentions," said Frederick, walking behind her down the snowy drive. "I wish I could say the same for mine."

"Get in the car, Frederick," said Olympia, not bothering to hide a very agreeable smile.

The afternoon was delightful. Lunch was tasty and the conversation more so, with lots of eye contact and lingering touches of fingertips effectively building a delicious and heady tension between them. They made short work of picking out a tree *because it was so cold*, they told each other. They giggled over Frederick's unfamiliarity with American money and his occasional horrified gasp and sideways lunge in the passenger seat in an attempt to avoid cars coming toward them from what was to him the wrong side of the street.

Back home, Frederick lit the fire. Olympia fed the cats and poured the wine. Together, they decorated the tree, had more wine, and then sat side by side to admire their handiwork.

Olympia got up and made a good show of putting the moussaka back into the oven and setting a bottle of Retsina into the fridge to chill.

"So, my dear professor and minister person," said Frederick, patting the spot beside him when she returned. He slipped his arm over her shoulders as she leaned into the comfort of his musky proximity.

"You know," he said softly into her hair, "I don't think I'm as hungry as I thought I was. Maybe we could, um, relax a bit before dinner."

"Whatever do you mean, Mr. Watkins?" asked Olympia, feigning an innocence neither of them believed.

"I think, my dear girl, you know exactly what I mean. I suggest you turn off the oven and let the moussaka … mature for a while."

Olympia needed no convincing.

Fifty

The next morning, Olympia stood outside the kitchen door with her winter jacket buttoned over her new bathrobe, scraping the untouched moussaka onto the snow underneath the bird feeder. *The crows and blue jays will love it.* Between the tomato-cinnamon-mint sauce and the slippery chunks of eggplant, it had all the appearance of the remains of a chainsaw massacre, *but birds don't really care about presentation,* Olympia told herself with a huge, pink-faced, post-coital grin on her face.

"You're going to catch your death out there," said an equally flushed Frederick. "Get back in here before I have to take you back to bed."

"Dream on, dear boy," Olympia shot back. "I've been doing this for years. It keeps me young."

"It works for you, maybe," he said, stamping his feet, "but I'm freezing to death."

"Then go back in the house," she said, coming back up the steps, "I don't need an audience."

"I like watching you do anything. Coffee's ready."

"Thank you, Frederick," said Olympia. "You are a most accommodating houseguest, but to quote the bard, I fear these all too brief hours and days will pass by much too quickly. We need to talk more about Bethany Ruth before we're out of time."

"There are a number of issues I'd like to talk about with you, Olympia," said Frederick, "but we can begin with Bethany Ruth. By the way, this is a wonderful house, ghost or no ghost. It will be great fun restoring it."

"It's a lot of work," said Olympia, sidestepping the implied offer, "but it keeps me off the streets."

The two went into the living room, and while Frederick added another log to the fire, Olympia set out their respective cups and relished the unpretentious hominess of it all.

"This is the picture I have so far," he said. "Tell me if you agree with it."

Olympia nodded.

"The Fellowship has a carefully orchestrated hierarchical and patriarchal structure requiring a strict dress and behavior code." He scratched out something on his pad and continued. "They present themselves as a group of traditional Christians with a mission to help the poor and afflicted, which by its obvious lofty ideals effectively discourages any outside investigation.

Olympia tucked her bathrobe tighter around her knees and ankles.

"So," he continued, "these people approach Bethany Ruth at one of their concerts and she starts visiting their residence. She tells you about them, you ask a lot of questions and tell her to be careful. Then one day, she says she can't talk to you anymore."

Olympia nodded in resignation.

"Then somebody gets into your office and leaves a Bible verse warning you that the guardians will protect the good, and the evil ones will be made to suffer, or something like that."

"Close enough."

"Then you start getting hang-up phone calls, but after Malcolm gets into their residence, your pal Margie drinks some tea, probably intended for you, and ends up in the hospital. That evening you get a call from someone in the Fellowship telling you in no uncertain terms to stay away from Bethany Ruth."

"That's when I knew they meant business," said Olympia, hugging her arms to her chest.

"So you called the residence and told them you'll have nothing more to do with Bethany Ruth?" said Frederick. "Where'd you get the number?"

"Would you believe the phone book? I figured if they thought I was dropping out of the race, I could still snoop around without them watching my every move — which, it appears, is exactly what they were doing. It's been very unsettling."

Olympia looked at the man seated across from her, "I'm glad you've come here, Frederick. I don't feel so alone with all of this anymore."

"I hope you'll always call me when you need something."

"I think," said Olympia, stretching and repositioning herself and once again not responding to his invitation, "we have to find out what is really going on inside that place, and if there is something rotten in the woodwork, expose it for what it really is."

"How on God's green earth do you expect to do that?"

"I don't know, yet."

"I have an idea," said Frederick, "and it has nothing at all to do with God's green earth and a bit more to do with exposure." He held out his arms. "Why don't you come over here, and let's reflect on something else for the next few minutes."

Olympia could see an unmistakable bulge under his dressing gown. The man was right. It was an excellent idea.

Sometime later, they were shaken out of a perfectly wonderful afterglow by the persistent jangling of the telephone. Olympia snatched up her discarded bathrobe and made a dash for the phone. It was Malcolm, saying he had some kind of a flu bug, and he couldn't stop throwing up, and what should he do?

Olympia went cold.

"When did it start?" she said, trying not to scream with panic and rage. "Did you eat or drink anything different today?"

Frederick came over and put a protective arm around her shoulders.

"Ma, the only thing I drank this morning was some tea, and then everything started coming up."

"Oh, my God, what kind of tea? Where did you get it? Who gave it to you?" Olympia gripped the phone with both hands to keep from dropping it.

"For God's sake, Ma," said her son, "you're overreacting as usual. We had a big party last night, and maybe I had a little too much to drink."

"What kind of tea did you drink?"

"Something my girlfriend likes, she gets it all the time. We keep it in the house. I had some, and then I started throwing up."

Olympia relaxed her vise-grip on the telephone. "Okay, so it's probably a stomach bug, or ..." she made a face, "more likely, you're hung over. It's just that there have been some strange goings on ever since you went to that Christian Fellowship place. You haven't been there again, have you?"

Malcolm confessed he'd gone back to the Boston Common that past Sunday.

"They barely spoke to me, Ma. You don't think they found out who I am, do you? Oh, yeah, and some bastard spray-painted Revelations 20:15 on both sides of my car and across the windshield last night."

"Oh, Christ, Malcolm," said Olympia, stamping her foot. "I told you to stay away from them."

She put her hand over the receiver and whispered to Frederick, "Malcolm's car has been vandalized."

Olympia spoke slowly and deliberately into the receiver, "When did you find it, and what exactly did it say?"

"I just told you what it said, and I found it when I got up this morning. You don't think it has something to do with those Fellowship creeps, do you?"

Frederick started to speak, but Olympia held up a warning finger.

"I think it might have," said Olympia. "Listen, you've got a camera, haven't you? Go take some close-up pictures of the car and the graffiti, and then get them developed at one of those one-hour places." She had grabbed a pencil and was writing the words on a scrap of paper towel. "Malcolm, don't ask me why, just go do it. For God's sake, you're twenty-two years old, and you're still asking *why*. I have an idea, that's why."

Olympia's panic had dissolved into maternal exasperation. "Look, Honey, you're going to have to believe me and not ask any questions—and stay the hell away from the Boston Common. And," his mother continued, her voice returning to a more normal level, "drink lots of water and clear liquids, nothing acidic. Warm, flat Coke is the best. That's what I gave you when you were little."

"I'll go take the pictures," said Malcolm.

"Call me later and let me know how you're doing," said Olympia. "Be careful, Honey. I love you."

Olympia put down the phone and looked at Frederick. "This is getting ugly," she said, starting out of the kitchen and walking towards her bedroom. "Somebody spray-painted a scripture verse on Malcolm's car. Where the hell is my Bible?"

Olympia found her dog-eared King James on a shelf in her bedroom and in it, Revelations 20:15. *And whosoever was not found written in the book of life was cast into the lake of fire.*

"I'm scared," said Olympia.

Fredrick had followed her and was standing with his two hands on her shoulders. Olympia leaned back and rested her head against his chest.

"Get dressed," he said, smoothing her tangled hair. "Don't you think you should call the Dean of your college?"

"Not him, Frederick," Olympia turned in her seat and looked up at the man who had come so far to help her. "For some reason, Will is deliberately trying to keep me out of this. Jim Sawicki's the one we need to call, my priest friend."

Fifty-One

Sister Sarah and Brothers David, Aaron, Joshua, and Sister Miriam were reviewing the previous day's street mission and the attendance at the rock concert.

"The numbers were really low," said Aaron, making notes in the ledger on the table in front of him. "It's probably a combination of the cold and the Christmas break."

"I think we should hold off on any more until the students come back after the holidays," said David. "Maybe even until the spring and the weather's better. There's plenty for us to do for the hungry and homeless this time of year, and it's high visibility for the Fellowship."

"I agree with Brother David. It's a better use of our resources," said Aaron. "Besides, we're still doing the Bible study groups, aren't we?"

"That Meriwether professor's kid was there again on Sunday," said Joshua," but we made short work of him."

Sarah sat forward. "You're kidding. What did you do? Not more Ipecac, I hope?"

"Not even close," said Joshua with a sneer. "We were polite, but we didn't invite him to play. He got the message. He wandered off before we finished." Aaron closed the ledger with a snap. He looked pleased with himself. "But the next day we had one of the brothers go over and spray his car with that verse from Revelations about being cast into the fire."

David looked troubled and started to speak, but Aaron stopped him with a dismissive wave. "Don't worry, Brother David, he'll just think it was some religious fanatic. I said to hit a couple of other cars, too, so it didn't look like he was being singled out. I told him not to do any real damage, just make a mess."

"Even if Malcolm doesn't get the message," said Joshua, tapping his fingers on the table, "you can bet his mother will."

"If he tells her," said Aaron.

"He'll tell her," said David.

Aaron turned to Sarah with an unpleasant edge of sarcasm in his voice. "No, dear sister, no Ipecac this time. Do you have a problem with that?"

Sarah's hand automatically went up to her headscarf. She spoke carefully.

"Not so much a problem as the thought that we don't want someone somewhere putting two and two together and have the answer point to us." She looked over at David and hoped she sounded convincing. "We need to be careful about doing the same thing too often. The spray paint was a good idea. We might want to come up with some other type of no-miss message in the future."

"Sister Sarah has a point," said David. "We can never be too careful, and it doesn't hurt to review what we do every so often." He turned and looked directly at Sarah, "It would appear that the Abba has chosen well. He's asked that you meet with him after our meeting."

Sarah felt herself going pale and tried to hide her distress with a coughing fit.

"Are you all right, Sister?" asked Miriam.

"The air is so dry in the wintertime," said Sarah getting up. "I'll get some water."

When she returned, the four of them were discussing Bethany Ruth and her readiness for membership in the First Circle.

"Well," said David, who was by nature a man of rules and regulations, "she's doing her best to hide it, but I think she's still too attached to her family and possibly that professor of hers, as well."

Miriam leaned forward and turned towards David. "I haven't sensed that, Brother David, and I'm the one supervising her."

A flicker of irritation crossed David's face. He didn't like it when someone disagreed with him.

"We can't have another accident," said Aaron, "especially with one from Meriwether."

Sarah raised her hand to speak.

"Really, Sister Sarah, we are not that formal here. What is it you would like to say?"

Sarah kept her voice even. "It's about Bethany Ruth. I've had more than one occasion to speak with her. She told me she's happier than she's ever been in her life. If we make it too hard, and she gets discouraged, we could destroy her sense of mission. Some of them take longer than others, Brother David, you know that. Go easy on her."

"And," said Aaron, "the Fellowship would lose her tithe money, let's not forget that. It's not our first priority, of course, but it is a consideration."

Sarah looked directly at David. "Bethany Ruth is totally dedicated. She's doing her best to leave the past behind, and she's working at making a new life with us. Her enthusiasm and her idealism will be a great strength to all of us and to the organization at large. I think we should do all we can to encourage her and not make the road too steep or rocky."

"Nothing worth having is ever accomplished without hard work and sacrifice," said David, getting up and beginning to pace around the table. "It's best she learns that from the start. Rules are rules."

Sarah lifted her chin. "Don't crush her spirit, David. If that happens, she'll just be another little robot."

"There is great merit in obedience," said David, looking down at Sarah, "especially in women. It is as Yahweh intended."

Sarah bowed her head, but her hands were fists in her lap.

"I'm inclined to agree with Sister Sarah," said Miriam. "Bethany Ruth is exemplary in every way. I think she is coming along beautifully. Wasn't it you who suggested that she go out on the last street mission with us? We don't often allow our aspirants do that. They can make mistakes."

David was pacing faster now. Sarah knew he didn't like losing an argument.

"You may have a point, Sister. I just don't want to make it too easy for any of them. It's important during aspirancy that they feel like they are on trial. It is a probationary period, is it not?"

"Bethany Ruth is exactly where we want her," said Joshua, "but as one of her guardians, I have to agree with Miriam. I'm ready to recommend her for the First Circle."

It was evident that David could see which way the tide was flowing. "So be it," he said. "Miriam and Joshua, it will be your privilege to tell her she is to be conditionally accepted to the First Circle right after the beginning of the year, but she will not have full membership until we're certain of her commitment."

David got the last word and Sarah hated him for it.

"There is one more issue to resolve before we adjourn," said David. "That pregnant one, what's her name, again?"

"Yellow Bee Pollen," said Miriam.

"We need to make arrangements to move her out to one of the family compounds to have the baby. Sarah, will you see to the arrangements?" David didn't wait for an answer.

"What then?"

"The child will be placed with a nursing mother, and she'll come back and complete the training."

"What about after that?" asked Sarah. "Will she get her baby back when she's a full member?"

"Only married women have babies. When she marries, she can have another one. It's not good for children to be moved around. They need stability and security." He stopped by the door. "Our meeting is adjourned, Brothers and Sisters." He turned to Sarah with a tight smile on his face. "I believe the Abba is expecting you."

Fifty-Two

"Take off your headscarf, Sarah. I want to look at your hair."

The Abba was sitting in a carved armchair. Instead of the tunic and loose trousers she remembered from before, he was wearing jeans and a light grey sweater.

Sarah reached up and slowly slipped off the triangle of fabric. Her long dark curls, free from the constant restraint, expanded and fluffed out around her face and shoulders. The Abba caught his breath.

"I want to talk about your future. Do, please, sit down." He gestured to a chair next to his desk. "I've asked to have some tea brought in. You'd like that, wouldn't you? Or maybe you would prefer cocoa. I understand you like cocoa."

"Tea, please." Sarah sat on the edge of the chair.

"Relax, Sarah." His voice was softer than she remembered. "I won't bite." He pulled up a chair and sat down opposite her, "At least not unless you want me to."

The man in front of her would never be called handsome or even good looking, but there could be no mistaking the magnetic power radiating from him.

"I don't think I'd want you to bite me," said Sarah.

"Oh, you might someday," he smiled, "under different circumstances, of course. A little nibble here and there?"

"I don't understand," said Sarah.

"You will." He pulled his chair a little closer to her as David entered the room carrying a tray with two cups of tea and a plate of cookies. Without speaking, he placed the tray on the desk and turned to leave.

"David," said the Abba, "come back in an hour, will you? There's a matter I need to go over with you before this evening."

David nodded in agreement and then looked down at Sarah before he turned on his heel and left the room. The Abba waited until David closed the door behind him.

"My dear, beautiful young woman, I believe that the time has come for you to have a husband."

Sarah put her hand to her chest. She was having trouble breathing.

The Abba continued, "You're an intelligent woman with a fiery spirit. I find this attractive and desirable."

Sarah folded her hands and pressed her palms together to keep them from shaking. Her eyes were fixed on the floor between them.

"Tell me what you're thinking."

Sarah paused, taking great care in composing her response. "I'm honored that you're pleased with my work, and I would like to continue. I have no particular desire to be married right now, but perhaps later. I have some ideas for the Bible study groups I'd like to develop. Maybe when I finish that." She prayed that she sounded convincing.

"Ah, my dear, and you shall have your wish." Abba picked up a cup of tea and held it out to her. "I want you to be happy. Here, have some tea with me."

Sarah looked at him, not knowing what to think. Might she really be able to stay here and avoid marriage to a man? Her hand was trembling as she accepted the teacup.

"Sarah." The Abba spoke as though he were talking to a child. "A woman needs to be married. It's the way of Yahweh. Didn't Jeshua himself celebrate the wedding at Cana? And Saint Paul tells us it is better for a man to marry than to burn for lusting after a woman who is not his wife. In the time when Jeshua walked upon the earth, a man took many wives." The Abba leaned forward and took Sarah's icy hands in his.

"Your hands are cold," he said looking into her eyes and leaning even closer. "Let me warm them, Sarah. I won't send you away, at least not until you are with child. Then you will move into the central compound with my other wives and children. You are a trusted member of the Inner Circle, and we value your work here."

The Abba tightened his grip on her hands and pulled her closer to him. "Sarah, my intense, beautiful woman, I have chosen you to become one of my wives. You will live with me in my rooms when I am in residence. Do you understand the honor and privilege of this?"

Sarah didn't dare look at him. She loathed this man and feared he would see it in her eyes. She took a long slow breath and raised her eyes.

"You'll understand if I am emotional," she said, hoping the catch in her voice would be seen as shy pleasure. "I … I don't know what to say."

"There is nothing to say, Sarah," he said quietly. "Your actions tell me everything I needed to know. Go downstairs and get your things. You will come to me tonight." He lifted one hand to her scarlet cheek and looked into her eyes. "We will have a formal ceremony after the start of the new year." He looked toward the door, "David knows, of course. He's always spoken highly of you."

"Abba," said Sarah, twisting her hands, "I can't come to you tonight."

"What do you mean?"

"I'm … unclean." Sarah looked at the floor and whispered, "I'm menstruating."

He grimaced. "How long does it last?"

"It just started this morning, five days."

"Then you will come to me on Saturday." He was smiling again. "It will be my personal pleasure to look at you out of that shapeless dress—and awaken your passion."

Fifty-Three

Sarah stood on the landing outside the door, gripping the newel post. She felt physically ill and didn't trust her legs to support her. After taking a couple of deep breaths, she took hold of the banister with both hands and started down.

"Feeling a little out of breath, Sister Sarah?" David was standing halfway up the stairs looking at her.

"Please let me by," said Sarah, covering her mouth and hoping not to gag in his presence.

"Anything for the Abba's chosen," hissed David. "Did you enjoy the tea I was instructed to serve you?"

Sarah tried to slip sideways past him on the narrow passage, but he held out his arm and blocked her. She could never speak the words that she was choking back.

"It's a great honor," she whispered, "but it's too much to take in. I need to be alone, please, David."

"Oh, you'll get used to it, Little Sister," he jeered, stepping back and letting her pass. "They all do. I hope you like it rough."

She could hear his low, mocking laughter as she walked down the stairs and headed for the privacy of her room. One of the few privileges of Sarah's Third Circle position was that she had a room to herself, and in that desperate moment, she had never been so grateful for anything in her life.

Sarah was literally vibrating with rage and panic. In the last hour, everything that she had been suspecting and not wanting to believe had become devastatingly clear.

"That fucking bastard," she hissed, punching the pillow beside her. "It's not about Jesus or doing good. It's about money and power and sex, and that horny, greasy little shit is in charge of it all."

I've got five days …

At that moment she didn't have an exact plan. She only knew that she had to gather as much information as she possibly could and then get out and blow every whistle in Christendom. And if there was any way on God's green earth she could do it, she was taking Bethany Ruth with her.

Sarah bowed her head, forcing herself to relax. Five days. If she was going to pull this off, she had to convince them all she was overjoyed at the honor which had been bestowed upon her. She needed to be the shy, virginal bride everyone expected her to be.

"Jesus, Mary, and Joseph," she whispered, familiar words of comfort from her Catholic childhood. "Hail Mary, full of Grace." Sarah dropped to her knees. With the tips of her fingers she made a sign of the cross, touching her forehead, breastbone, and each shoulder before continuing the prayer. "Pray for us, now and at the hour of our death. Amen," she finished.

She got to her feet and stood, holding on to her dresser for support. Her mind was whirling with thoughts she hadn't allowed herself to think for years. One by one she began to collect and weave those thoughts into a plan of action. There was no turning back, not now. She had been undercover all of her adult life, but this time the consequences of being discovered were deadly. She now knew what happened to people who tried to leave the Fellowship, but she had no choice. If she got out, at least she might have a chance at life. If she stayed, she'd die.

She would start in the office where she did her record-keeping. In the next four days, while supposedly attending to business, she would learn as much as she could and commit it to memory. There were at least fourteen Fellowship chapters in cities across the United States. How many members were there in each compound? How many couples, how many wives, children? How many women were there like herself, and how many so-called accidental deaths of people who tried to leave? It was staggering.

Worse than the ugly facts behind the pious façade was the fact that she, Sarah, had been a part of this terrible pyramid and its deadly mission until this morning. *Sweet Jesus,* she thought, *I'm the one who got Bethany Ruth into this. Please, God, help us both.*

However she managed it, she had to do it fast and without raising a whisper of suspicion. She stood up and automatically went to tuck her hair under her scarf, then remembered she had left it upstairs.

"He's probably masturbating with it," she snarled. She walked over to her dresser, took out another, and yanked it into place.

When she thought about it, she really only had four and a half days.

Fifty-Four

When David asked what was taking her so long in the office the next morning, Sarah told him she was reorganizing things because some of the files were out of order, and a number of the records needed updating and refiling.

By early afternoon, her eyes were bleary from reading, and her fingers were cramping from copying so much information. She was hungry because she missed lunch and outraged with what she was learning. Her absence from lunch wouldn't be questioned. Third Circle status bought Sarah a greater degree of personal freedom than the others, and she was going to need every scrap of it.

Too tired to go any further and in need of food, Sarah was walking down the hallway when she heard muffled sounds coming from Bethany Ruth's bedroom. This time, she knocked.

An indistinct, "Who's there?" came from the other side of the door.

Sarah pushed the door open. "It's me, Sarah. Oh my God, what's the matter?" She ran across the room to where Bethany Ruth sat on the bed sobbing.

"For God's sake, tell me," said Sarah. "Here, take my hankie, blow your nose."

Bethany Ruth took the offered handkerchief, covered her face with it, and cried even harder. Sarah sat and rocked her and smoothed her hair the way she would comfort a distraught child.

"It's going to be all right, trust me. It's going to be all right."

After a few minutes, the worst of the flood subsided. Bethany Ruth blew her nose again and in shuddering gasps poured out her pent-up homesickness, her fear of failure, the misery from the constant hunger, and now, the expectation that she would contribute five thousand dollars a year as her required tithe.

"I can't do it," she said shaking her head, "I just can't do it. All I ever wanted to do was to serve Jesus and walk in his path, but I'm not good enough. I'll never make it, and I tried so hard. I should leave now, but I'll wait until after Christmas."

Sarah unwound herself from the wretched young woman and closed the door to the room. Returning to Bethany Ruth's side, she took hold of both her hands.

"Listen to me, and don't ask questions. I have to tell you something."

There was an odd sound to Sarah's voice. Bethany Ruth sniffed and lifted her tear-stained face.

"I have to ask you to promise not to repeat what I say, no matter what you decide to do after I finish."

There was long silence before Bethany Ruth answered. "I promise."

Sarah leaned forward and spoke quickly. "You're going to have trouble understanding this, but this place is not what it pretends to be. There are some really bad things going on here."

"But I ..."

"Please," begged Sarah, "you can ask questions later. You have to hear it all, and I don't have much time. I don't know everything yet because I've just uncovered the first layer. You know all that money we contribute, like your five thousand dollars? It's not going to homeless shelters or food programs. It's going into the Abba's pocket or into an offshore account somewhere. I've managed to get into the private files. I've uncovered a whole bunch of information I'm not supposed to be looking at, top-secret stuff that's connected to something called John Marigold Enterprises."

Bethany Ruth stopped crying and stared at Sarah in disbelief.

"This whole operation is one great big lie." Sarah spoke quickly now. "The God they worship is money, and the Abba is the golden calf, the false idol. He's totally hollow, and I know for sure now that he and David are in it for the power, the profit and the sex. You'll be next. They don't care one bit about Jesus and walking his way. That's just to keep people from asking questions."

"But ..."

"Later," hissed Sarah, "just listen. You couldn't know this, but a couple of members actually died when they tried to get out. It was accidental according to the newspaper reports. So for God's sake, don't even mention that you are thinking of leaving. One of them that died was from Meriwether. Three others died when they started vomiting and choked to death. I happen to know they were given ipecac. It makes you puke."

Bethany Ruth was shaking her head in disbelief, but Sarah pressed on. "I put the teabag with ipecac in it in your professor's office. It was supposed to scare her off, but a friend of hers got it instead and ended up in the hospital."

"Oh, my God."

"I didn't know what it was," said Sarah. "I was being dutiful, doing what I was told. Not any more though, I'm done. I'm getting out, and I want you to come with me. This place is evil. But whatever you decide, remember what I said. Don't ever tell them you're thinking of leaving."

"I don't understand. What are you going to do? I can't just leave, but you, where … how …?"

Sarah waved her hand in dismissal.

"Hush. I haven't worked it out yet. I have three days for sure, maybe four. No one has any idea. Yesterday, the Abba told me he's going to make me one of his wives, his Boston wife." Sarah spit out the words. "In other words, his screw of the month. I told him I had my period. I don't really, but it bought me four days. I'm going to find out as much as I can about these two-faced bastards, and then I'm going to hang them higher than God's got trees." Sarah's eyes glittered.

"But …"

Sarah took hold of Bethany Ruth's hands. "They're going to chew you up, spit you out, and throw away the bones. They were discussing you yesterday morning like you were a piece of meat. They don't give a shit about you. It's about money and how much you can bring in, and then, which one of them will get you into bed."

Tears of rage pooled in Sarah's eyes, but she blinked them back.

"When all of this gets out, it will be the end of the Fellowship. I'm getting out of here, Bethany Ruth

McAllister, and I want you to come with me." Sarah looked at her watch. "I have to go. Now that I'm the Abba's intended, they're going to be watching me."

"How are you going to do it?" asked Bethany Ruth.

"I told you, I don't know."

"They seem so good and caring."

"Most of them do mean well," said Sarah. "The good ones, the First and Second Circle members like you, and Miriam and Joshua, have no idea what's really going on. They're going to be disillusioned as hell. They'll have to find places to live. Some may even have to be deprogrammed. It's the upper level ones, the ultra-inner Third Circle, that's where the rotten wood is, and that's who I'm after. I suspect your professor friend may have figured out what's going on behind all the Christian goodness crap. That's probably why they want to keep you away from her."

"Oh, my God," was all Bethany Ruth could stammer yet again. "She was trying to help me. Maybe you should try and get in touch with her and tell her."

"I'm hoping your goodhearted professor will be part of my plan." Sarah smiled for the first time that day. "I want to call her. You probably don't have her phone number, but do you know where she lives?"

Bethany Ruth screwed up her face. "Somewhere south of here. Let me think, Brookwell or maybe Brookwater? I don't know town names around here."

"Brookfield?" said Sarah.

"That's it, Brookfield. I'm sure of it."

"Great. I'm going to try and find her and ask if she'll help." Sarah stood and smoothed her headscarf. "If she says yes, then I'll have more of a plan." She took a long breath. "I want you to come with me, Bethany Ruth, but even if you don't, I beg you to keep your promise not to say a word to anyone. I'm counting on you. I can't do anything to raise suspicion."

Sarah stood and started for the door.

"Let's just hope your kindly Professor Brown doesn't have an unlisted number."

Fifty-Five

December 22, 1859
Storm clouds are gathering in the northeast. By feel and the smell of the air, we shall have snow by nightfall. The widower, Mr. Jackson, has invited me to have Christmas dinner with him and his parents. I like his children well enough, though they still grieve their mother.

But I think not. I don't want to encourage him. A quiet day with my books and my memories will be the best for me, this year.

More anon...LFW

"This is a collect call from Bethany Ruth McAllister. Will you accept charges?"

"Oh, my God, yes!" Olympia waved her arms frantically and pointed at Frederick to pick up the extension. "Are you all right? Where are you?"

"Professor Brown? My name is Sarah. I live at the Fellowship Center with Bethany Ruth. We're in danger, and we need your help. Please listen to me, Professor."

Olympia was instantly on guard. "I told you people I wasn't going to have any more contact with her. Who are you? What do you want?"

"I know what you must be thinking, but please, hear what I have to say, then decide for yourself."

"I'm listening." Olympia was tapping her foot and wishing she were recording the call.

Sarah took a deep breath "I'm a senior member of the Fellowship, and I'm getting out. I want Bethany Ruth to come with me. She helped me find your number, and she trusts you. May I continue?"

"How do I know this isn't another attempt to scare me off?" Olympia was trying to remain calm, but she started pacing around the big old kitchen, the wide planks of the floor creaking beneath her feet.

"You don't know," said Sarah, "but you're the only person who might believe me and then be willing to help us."

Olympia couldn't see Sarah's trembling hands or the tears of relief that were squeezing themselves out of her eyes and freezing on her eyelashes, but she could hear the quaver of desperation in the young woman's voice.

"I'm going to have my friend Frederick listen on the extension," she said. "If you are who you say you are, he'll be helping me, and if not, I have a witness."

"That's fine, anything," begged Sarah. "I've uncovered some ugly information about this operation, and I plan to go public with everything if I can get away. I'm in a pay phone in Cambridge, so I can talk but not for long."

"Take your time," said Olympia.

"When I get out, I'll have names and places, even offshore bank account numbers. Do you believe me now? This organization is totally evil, Professor. It's all about money and power. I have proof."

In the great room, Frederick dug a pencil out of Olympia's floor basket and was writing as fast as he could.

"We have to go to the police, maybe even a television station or the newspapers. These people are so bad." Sarah paused, catching her breath. "Professor, I'm the one who left the tea bag in your office, and I'm so sorry. I didn't know what it was."

"Call me, Olympia, Sarah, and tell me how we can help. I believe you."

Frederick, listening on the extension, spoke into the phone. "Hello, Sarah, I'm Frederick. I'm a good friend of Olympia's. I'm part of the team."

Sarah took a breath. "Hello, and thank you. I haven't got a plan yet. I wanted to talk to you first. I need someone on the outside we can depend on."

"We're here," said Olympia.

"Right now, I think the best thing, if Bethany Ruth will come, would be to make the break when I go out on one of my food runs. I'll drive somewhere south of Boston. You two meet us somewhere, and we'll go straight to the police."

"May I speak?" asked Frederick.

"Oh, please," said Sarah.

"If Bethany Ruth goes with you, and they start searching, it's likely that Olympia's house might be the first place they look. Perhaps you should drive in the opposite direction, north instead of south, then find a pay phone in a petrol station and tell them you've had a breakdown. Give them the name and number of someplace south of Boston. That way, you will have bought yourself some time and distance if they do go looking for you. Meanwhile, you go north and we meet you where you tell us to."

"That's brilliant," said Sarah, breathing an audible sigh of relief. "I'll try for the day after tomorrow. We're supposed to be going around to restaurants and hotels to get their leftover food. No one will question me. I do it all the time. I just hope I can get Bethany Ruth to come with me."

"That's two days' time," said Frederick, "not counting today."

"We should be here all day tomorrow," said Olympia. "Once you know exactly when and where you're going, call us. We'll be there when you arrive. If for some reason we don't answer, leave a message."

"Be careful, Sarah," said Frederick. "You're in very dangerous waters."

"I can swim," she answered. "I've been swimming against the tide all my life. I know how these people work, and I also know I get only one chance."

"Sarah," said Olympia, "tell Bethany Ruth you've talked to me and that I'm in this with you. That might convince her."

"I can't leave her there, Professor, she's so ..."

Olympia heard the catch in Sarah's voice. "I'll pray for you, Sarah. Call us as soon as you can."

Olympia hung up the phone and waited for Frederick to come back into the kitchen.

"Well, my dear sweet Englishman, my ancillary knight on a dingy charger, it looks like we call Father Jim and then the police."

"One step at a time, good lady." Frederick cast a warning glance at Olympia. "If these Fellowship people catch the slightest hint of this, Sarah and Bethany Ruth will be in grave danger. Another thing, what about your college Dean? Shouldn't he know what's going on now?"

Olympia shook her head. "That man's been keeping me at arm's length since this started. Frankly, I don't feel like dealing with him and his blasted ego when we're this close to getting somewhere. Besides, he might take it into his head to jump the gun. He would do it if he got half a chance, then claim victory for himself and fire me for breaking rank. How conveniently win-win for him. But you do have a point. Let me think about it."

Olympia turned and headed for the makeshift office she had set up in the south corner of her bedroom. "I'm going to call Jim. Do you mind feeding the cats?"

When she returned, she told Frederick that Jim was elated to hear about Sarah's call and that it might just be the break they'd been looking for. Now they could talk to the police. He said that if Sarah and Bethany Ruth were able to pull this off, there was finally a chance of exposing these people. Jim also suggested they get in touch with Malcolm and see if he had developed the photographs of the graffiti on his car. If so, Jim would go and pick them up.

In the meantime, she and Frederick should drive up to the rectory. That way, the three of them could go over the facts before they called the police. They could also look at the photographs and see if there was any similarity between the handwriting on Malcolm's car and the note found in Olympia's office. Jim knew that was a long shot, but either way, it would be one more piece of evidence they could present to the police.

When she had finished relating all of this, Olympia looked at Frederick and said, "Looks like we're going to

Boston, or more specifically, an austere room in a hardscrabble Irish Catholic parish in Dorchester. Do you need to use the bathroom before we go?"

"Matter of fact I do, Mummy," laughed Frederick. "Gosh, how have I managed without you all my life?"

"Can't help it," said Olympia, pulling on her coat. "Once a mother, always a mother." *With a daughter you don't know about yet.*

"I'm not looking for a mother," said Frederick.

Olympia waited by the front door, thinking about the rapid turn of events. If Sarah's escape plan was successful, God only knew what they would uncover.

She would not allow herself to think of the consequences if it wasn't.

Fifty-Six

On the Friday before Christmas, the brothers and sisters of the Boston Christian Common Fellowship were walking the frigid streets of Boston distributing food, blankets, and other simple comforts to the hungry and needy. With each offering they repeated the words, "Jeshua loves you, take this in His holy name."

The media said it was a desperately needed service that these humble Christian people provided. "So full of Godly love," the papers said, but no one ever got past the public image. Newspapers ran heartwarming pictures of Fellowship members going about their work, and a local television station filmed a two-minute news segment that included an interview with Brother David. They filmed different members working among, as David so eloquently phrased it, "Yahweh's blessed poor."

"Following in Jeshua's way," he would say, clasping his hands to his chest and lowering his eyes. "We are only doing what He would do Himself if he were here."

David put on a good face, and the media people ate it up. He said that these poor forgotten souls were the dregs of the dregs, too cold or old or confused to go to one of the soup kitchens at the nearby Arlington Street Church or the Pine Street Inn.

If anyone was curious as to why no one ever learned anything about the Fellowship beyond the image David projected so well, it was because no reporter had ever been clever enough to frame a question that slipped beneath his polished veneer.

Working alongside David and Aaron on Boston Common, Sarah was handing out food and counting each minute to when she and Bethany Ruth would be out of this forever. She looked at the clock on the façade of the bank across the street. *Less than twenty-four hours.*

The wind cutting across the Common was merciless. She pulled her coat tighter and bent into her work. Above all else, she needed to appear fully engaged in the mission. Then she stopped and tapped David on the arm. "I need to go to the ladies room. There's one in the parking garage. I won't be long."

"Take your time, little bride," David sneered. "We're almost finished. You might as well go straight back to the van when you're done."

Sarah hurried toward the garage entrance and around the corner to a public telephone. She called Olympia to say that Bethany Ruth was coming with her, and so far, anyway, everything was going according to plan.

Tomorrow they would drive north to the city of Lowell and try to be at the Greyhound Terminal between three and four in the afternoon, but they couldn't be sure of the exact timing. Olympia said she would be there by three but not to panic if they were late. Holiday traffic and New England weather were always unpredictable.

Sarah thanked her and hung up the phone. These last three days had been the longest and most fraught with fear and worry of her life. They had also been the most hopeful and joyous. She had never felt so alive. Even when she was squashed in with the others in the cold, drafty van going back to Brighton, she smelled the fresh air of freedom.

Later that day, when everyone was at dinner, David and Aaron were seated in Aaron's bedroom with the door closed.

"What tipped you off?" asked David. "I can tell you what's making me suspicious, but I want to hear what you think."

"It was something in the office," said Aaron, "or maybe something not in the office."

"What do you mean?"

Aaron lowered his voice. "Sarah's always been a good worker. She's a quick study, picks up things easily, works fast. Anyway, she's good, but she's not particularly neat, you know, leaves papers around, doesn't always put things back."

Aaron's habit of using *you know* as a space holder in a sentence irritated David, adding to his impatience.

"Exactly what was different?" David drummed his fingers on the nightstand beside the bed.

"Well, all of a sudden nothing's out of place," said Aaron. "I mean, you know, even the pencils were lined up. It started me thinking, why is she getting so neat all of a sudden? When people start acting different, and I start noticing, it usually means something's going on."

"What do you think it is?" David frowned and dropped his voice to a whisper.

"I don't know," said Aaron getting up and stretching. "Nothing in the office was out of place or missing or anything, you know, but in her position she has access to all of our private information if she wanted to get at it. But then I asked myself, why would she? After Saturday, she's going to know everything anyway. Maybe she's just nervous or something. You know what I mean?"

"I've noticed a change," said David, "particularly in the last two days. All of a sudden, she's the perfect little Fellowship Sister." His voice tightened. "She walks with her eyes downcast, doesn't look left or right, does what I say without her usual look or sharp retort. You may be right. If you ask me, I don't think she's too happy about bedding down with the Abba."

"You don't suppose she's going to take off, do you?" asked Aaron. "That could be bad news."

"I don't think so," said David. He got up. "It's probably nerves, but if both of us are thinking that something might be wrong, then one of us could be right. Either way, we can't take chances. Maybe I should say something to the Abba just to be on the safe side."

"Wouldn't hurt."

"Meanwhile," said David, "keep an eye on her, but don't let her catch you. She's quick. She'll spot it. I'll check back with you later. I think you're right that its nerves, but better safe than sorry, right?"

"I hope so," said Aaron. "Sarah's good. I'd hate to lose her."

"I know what you mean."

David closed the door behind him and started down the hall. Aaron was right, it would be a shame to lose her, but David already had.

Fifty-Seven

"Why did you wait so long, Professor Brown?" Boston Police Detective Robert Blackwell was leaning on the corner of a scabby oak desk in his office.

"I wanted to come weeks ago," she said, turning more fully towards him, "but who would have believed me? Would you have bothered to listen to me before now?"

Detective Blackwell shook his head. "Probably not."

"I would have sounded like a mean-spirited, paranoid, crazy lady." She looked up at him. "Remember something, Detective. "These people call themselves Christians. They want the world to believe they're on a mission to live like Jesus and care for the poor. How far do you think I would have gotten with a collection of vague suspicions and fuzzy allegations?"

"Not very," he agreed.

Olympia Brown, Father Jim Sawicki, and Frederick in the role of concerned consultant were seated at a battle-scarred wooden table at Boston Police headquarters. Olympia looked around at the high-ceilinged interrogation room of the Victorian building. The mustard yellow and coffee brown paint on the walls was layered with a dull haze of city soot and cigarette smoke. The room was uncomfortably warm and smelled of generations of human misery.

Jim had been able to convince Detective Blackwell to agree to the meeting by using his credentials as a priest and the Chaplain of Boston College, plus the promise of some new information regarding the unexplained deaths of four area college students. Now it was up to Olympia and him to present their case and convince the two men sitting across the table from them of the truth and immediate gravity of the situation.

As her entry point, Olympia handed Detective Blackwell the scrap of paper with the green crayon message and the photos of the Bible verse which had been spray-painted on her son's car. He took the two pieces of evidence, looked at them and nodded.

"I can't tell about the handwriting, but the fact that it's a Bible verse makes it worth looking into. "I'll send them to one of our forensic experts," he said, "but even if it checks out, this by itself isn't enough to issue a search warrant. We need hard evidence to be absolutely sure of the grounds for issuance. You can understand that."

Olympia nodded.

Blackwell took a small notepad out of his pocket. "Start at the beginning, and tell me everything as you know it."

When she finished, Jim suggested that they request a formal inquest into the four deaths, review the medical examiner's reports, and look for similarities.

They concluded by telling the detective about Sarah and her intention to escape with Bethany Ruth the day after tomorrow. She explained how the young women planned to drive to Lowell, where Olympia, Jim, and Frederick would meet them and take them to the police station.

"Why so far north?" asked Detective McQuade.

"I wondered that myself," said Olympia, "but Frederick suggested that she go someplace far enough away from Boston that no one could possibly recognize the van. As it turns out, Sarah has an aunt in Lowell, so she knows the city."

"I suppose," said Blackwell. "Could be nasty driving though. We've got another storm coming in tomorrow. I think we need get onto this immediately. From what you just told us, those girls' lives could be at risk."

It took some convincing, but in the end, Father Jim and Olympia were able to convince him that until the two women were actually reported missing, they were safe. Besides, Sarah was collecting information—valuable, incriminating information—which might be destroyed or lost if they moved in too soon. In the end, the detective was more or less convinced.

"So," said Detective Blackwell, "if Sarah and Bethany Ruth make their escape as planned, and we have word they're with you," he gestured to Olympia and company, "the search team will enter the Renewal Center in Brighton and take it from there. Either of you have a cell phone?"

Jim shook his head and looked at Olympia. "If something goes wrong, and they don't make it by five o'clock, we'll call you from a pay phone, and you guys go into action."

Detective Blackwell shook his head and went over to a storage cabinet. He pulled out a mobile phone.

"Police issue," he said, handing it to Olympia. "Keep it charged, and keep it with you. Here's a sheet with the directions and the numbers. When this is all over, I suggest you all join the present century and get one of these."

Jim pointed at the phone in Olympia's hand and said, "I'm getting you one for Christmas."

Blackwell nodded agreement and then added, "Meanwhile, we'll request the medical reports on those students you mentioned and see what I can do about authorizing a search warrant."

"That makes sense," said Jim.

"I hope the hell they can pull it off," said the Detective, "but I'm worried about those two girls. If what you say is true, and these people do have blood on their hands, I think we should go in first and ask questions later."

Jim held up his two hands in the classic *stop* gesture. "Detective," he said, "from what Sarah told Olympia, this so-called Christian Fellowship is a national operation, maybe even international. The more we can find out about the total scope and structure of how they do business, the more evidence we'll have before the rest of them across the country scatter or go underground, because that's exactly what they'll do after the raid in Brighton."

Jim stood, using every commanding inch of his six-foot-one priestly persona. "Gentlemen," he said, fixing the investigator in his line of vision, "Reverend Olympia Brown and I are convinced that at least four student deaths are directly connected to their involvement with this organization. Multiply that by at least fourteen more centers across the country, and God knows how many compounds or sub-residences ..." He held out his hands, palms up, letting the gesture complete the sentence. "I wouldn't have suggested this if I thought the two girls were in immediate danger. As long as no one finds out what they're planning to do, I don't believe they'll be in harm's way."

Olympia looked at Jim and then at the detective before she chimed in, "It's clear to me that the one thing this group fears more than anything else, and the thing that will destroy them, is exposure. For that reason, we've got to let Sarah finish her work." She paused, "Then you can get on with yours."

Blackwell took a long, slow breath and nodded assent.

Olympia and Jim had made their case.

Fifty-Eight

On the day Sarah planned to leave the fellowship, the weather was cold and raw with freezing rain predicted to begin by late morning. With her final departure imminent, Sarah made a good show of going over the surplus food pick-up route with Joshua. She was surprised that she had no trouble arranging for Bethany Ruth to accompany her. There was an awful moment when Joshua offered to go along and carry the heavy boxes, but David intervened, saying he and Miriam were needed for an extra street-run that afternoon.

Sarah noticed that Miriam and Joshua were often together and suspected they had developed a fondness for one another. She wondered what would happen to them after today.

When the preparations were complete, Sarah turned to Bethany Ruth and told her to get her coat. The girl was standing by the sink looking as though she might break if anyone so much as touched her. Sarah urged her a second time, gesturing with a free hand to get moving and looking hard at the white-faced young woman.

"Come on," she hissed, "we need to get started before the roads get too slippery."

Bethany Ruth bit her lower lip and slowly shook her head. "I can't. You go. I won't tell."

There was no time for pleading or cajoling. It was her worst-case scenario with only seconds to decide whether to plead with the terrified girl or go on alone. *Oh, God.*

Sarah reached into her coat pocket for the key to the van and whispered, "Tell them you felt sick, and I told you to stay home. They won't ask questions. Stick your finger down your throat, make yourself gag, and make a run for the bathroom."

Sarah stood for one last, agonized moment in the place that had been her home and her life for the last seven years, then turned and walked out the door.

The anticipated freezing rain was already falling when she climbed into the van. She sat, letting the engine warm up and trying to get control of the situation. If anyone came out, she would tell them she was checking the route. *Whatever you do*, she told herself, *act like nothing's wrong. They could be watching.*

Joshua's last words had been to remind her that the heater still wasn't working, so she might have a problem with the windshield fogging.

"I'll be careful," she said with a reassuring smile pasted on her face. "I've been driving this thing for years."

When she finally released the emergency brake and pulled out of the driveway, she was frantically trying to reorganize her thoughts into some semblance of a back-up plan. She swerved sharply to avoid a pothole and went into a slight skid. *Joshua was right, the roads are bad.*

The last four days had been pure, nerve-shattering hell. Now, instead of being relieved that she had finally done it, Sarah was still trying to decide whether or not to continue on by herself and meet up with Professor Brown or just pick up the food and go back to the Renewal Center.

That would mean going back to the Abba's bed, but if I keep going and connect with the professor and her friend, the police will take over, and I can still get Bethany Ruth out of there.

The sleety rain was falling faster now. Sarah flicked on the windshield wipers, positioned her freezing hands on the steering wheel, and stayed the course. She would go north and find Professor Olympia Brown.

It was still hard to comprehend everything she had uncovered in the last four days, and it was only the barest tip of a totally evil and convoluted iceberg.

The Abba's real name was John Marigold. For years he had been living two lives. Outside the Fellowship, he was a high-flying millionaire investor and entrepreneur, and the Fellowship was only one of his enterprises. It served as his washing machine. Under the guise of a nonprofit organization, he could launder money, get all the sex he wanted, and feed his inflated ego on the mindless obedience and adoration of his followers. *Two-faced bastard.*

As she went over all of this in her mind, Sarah successfully negotiated the back streets of Allston and North Cambridge and was now heading north on Route 93. She hoped the driving might be better on the highway and she would be able to pick up speed, but the worsening weather made that impossible. It took everything she had to keep focused and stay on the road.

The outside temperature was dropping, and it was getting colder inside the van. Despite the adrenalin rushes and white-hot excitement of her departure from the Fellowship, Sarah was starting to shiver. In her fierce concentration, she took no notice of the vintage silver Mercedes that had been following her ever since she left the Renewal Center.

Fifty-Nine

The Abba leaned back against the heated leather seat. It was all going according to plan, his plan.

"You didn't say anything to anybody, did you, David?"

"Not a word." David was driving carefully, well back of the Fellowship van but always keeping it in sight.

"After I talked with you, I told Aaron that you thought Sarah's behavior was nothing more than nerves. I told him to forget about it, that it was probably pre-wedding-night jitters."

"He wouldn't say anything to anyone else, would he?"

"Aaron's a yes-man," said David. "He does what he's told. I told him there was no point in starting rumors."

"Good thinking. Pity, though. I was really looking forward to that one. I like them feisty. It's more fun when they fight back."

David stared at the road ahead of him. For a long time, he had wanted to do the very same thing, but the Abba claimed first rights. As he tracked her in the ice storm, David thought about the woman on the road ahead of him. He recalled the vivid dreams that awakened him with a pounding erection and the shameful release flushed away in a handful of toilet paper. Now, even if the Abba did tire of her, and he would, David would never have the chance.

He shifted into a more comfortable position, grateful for his bulky jacket. In his fantasies, David imagined Sarah squirming against him, breathing faster, begging him to stop — and then not to stop.

The driving was getting worse. Despite the best efforts of the defroster, sleet and freezing rain were building up and expanding in grainy triangles at the corners of the windshield. David needed to clean off the wiper blades but was afraid to stop.

He glanced down at the black zippered case lying on the console between them. He hadn't used it since he had been asked to leave medical school. *But,* he told himself silently as he squinted at the road ahead, *you never really forget these things, do you?*

Sixty

Sarah signaled for a left and turned onto the exit ramp. The bus station was located away from the center on a side street near the Merrimac River. Traffic was surprisingly light, considering it was two days before Christmas, *but these days,* she reminded herself, *everybody shops in the malls.*

After a couple of wrong turns, she finally spotted the bus station through the ice-crusted windshield. Her sigh of relief was visible in the frigid air inside the van. Sarah pulled over and sat for a few minutes to calm herself.

Other than a silver grey sedan which continued past her and made a left turn, there were no other cars in sight. No sign of the blue VW van Olympia said she would be driving. She was over an hour late because of the road conditions. She couldn't believe they didn't wait, *but if they aren't here, then where are they?*

She was trying not to panic, but when she could no longer contain her nervous energy, she pushed open the van door and stepped out onto the slippery pavement and crossed over to the bus terminal. Once inside, she spotted a pay phone and blessed her ability to remember long strings of numbers. After five rings she heard Olympia's recorded voice saying to leave a message, and she would return the call as soon as possible.

Sarah replaced the receiver and said aloud, "I know she's on her way. She has to be."

As she walked out of the terminal back toward the van, she saw a silver Mercedes parked behind it and almost shouted with relief. *The Professor had said she would be driving a blue VW van. Maybe it broke down, and she borrowed this one.*

Sarah quickened her pace, anxious to meet a woman who would drive all this way in such awful weather to help a stranger.

Sixty-One

"Do you want me drive for a while, Olympia?" Jim looked up from the roadmap in his lap. "That way you can read me the directions, and Frederick can watch for road signs and clear off the rear windows."

"Right-o," said Frederick, "make the foreigner do all the work. Don't you people have immigrant labor laws over here?"

Frederick's attempt at humor did little to dispel the tension inside the boxy van. On the best of days, the top-heavy VW was not the most maneuverable of vehicles, and with the deteriorating weather and the critical importance of their mission, Olympia was stretched to the outer limits of her patience and her driving ability. Despite the fact the three had started out early, a skidding accident outside of the city had stalled them for over an hour.

"I don't want to lose any more time," said Olympia, looking down at the clock on the dashboard, "but I think I will pull off at the next exit and let you take over. Thanks."

When the three had changed seats and were back on the road, Olympia's anxiety continued to mount.

"What if they've had a breakdown or something? How would we know, how would we find them? We've got a cell phone, but who knows if they do? Hey, look, there's a gas station." She was babbling a froth of nervous chatter.

Frederick spoke up from the middle seat behind Olympia. "They'll wait for us. What else can they do?

They're probably inside the bus station having a hot chocolate right now."

"I'm sure you're right," said Olympia, "but they might think we've had an accident, or maybe something happened, and they never made it out."

"We have no control over that," said Jim, dodging and squinting, trying to see the road. "You need new wipers, Olympia. Meanwhile, we'll get there when we get there. I'm doing my best. Hang on, Girl. If we miss them, we call Blackwell. That was the agreement."

Frederick reached through the space between the front seats and took Olympia's hand.

"Maybe we should have had the police meet us there after all," said Olympia.

"If you're that worried," said Jim, "take the cell phone he gave us and call him."

"You know me, I always imagine the worst. A few more minutes isn't going to make a difference. We're almost there."

Sixty-Two

In the waning light of the afternoon, Sarah could see two figures sitting inside the van. *They must have known I wouldn't recognize the sliver car.* With profound relief, she yanked open the driver's side door and was ready to climb in when she saw Brother David sitting on the far end of the bench-seat, grinning at her.

She started to take a step back, but someone clamped a hand over her mouth and pressed something hard against her ribs.

"Don't move," hissed a voice from behind her. Sarah recognized the rasping voice of the Abba. "Get in," he growled. As she did, she looked into the back and saw Bethany Ruth sitting with her hands cross-tied to her knees and a rag stuffed in her mouth.

Oh, my God, how did they find out?

"This is really unfortunate, Sarah," said the Abba. "I was really looking forward to tonight." His eyes narrowed. "That won't be possible now. You didn't fool us. Nobody does."

Sarah sat, loathing her two captors and fearing the worst.

"But you've made it very convenient for us." The Abba gestured toward the street outside. "With the icy roads and a van with poor brakes and a handy, fast-flowing river nearby … Too bad about your little friend, though. You were too insistent that she go with you. We took her out the front way while you were still in the driveway."

"Where are you taking us?" Sarah was shaking violently now. "What are you going to do?"

"Ah, my dear, it will be very gentle. I see no need to make you suffer. I don't believe in needless cruelty, do I David?" He turned toward her and stroked her cheek with the back of his index finger. Sarah flinched and tried to pull away. He was wearing white surgical gloves.

"David is going to inject each of you with something to make you sleepy and immobile, and then we're going to drive you to a pretty spot beside the river, somewhere without a guard rail. We'll put the van in gear, release the brake, and ..."

He reached down and patted her knee. "Don't worry, you won't feel anything. The accident report will read that you lost control of the car and skidded into the river. Two Christian women on a mission of mercy drowned, and they were still wearing their seatbelts. So unfair, such a tragedy, and not a trace of ipecac, Sister Sarah."

The Abba was taking his time, enjoying the sadistic foreplay. David sat by, turning a small black-zippered case over in his hands.

"Let Bethany Ruth go," begged Sarah. "She didn't do anything."

"She didn't do anything," David repeated with a sneer, "but I've seen you talking to her. She was part of the plan, wasn't she, and that means she knows."

"She doesn't know anything. I don't know anything. I just wanted to leave, but she got sick ..."

"I suppose you were going to take a bus from here," said David, ignoring her. "Good thinking. If we hadn't followed you, you might have gotten a little farther."

"But not much farther," said the Abba. "We would have found you."

David unzipped the case and lifted out a syringe and a small bottle. He, too, was wearing surgical gloves. "Looks like you'll have to share a needle," he said, "but I don't suppose it really matters now."

Sarah twisted and looked down at Bethany Ruth in the back. *She doesn't deserve this.* Their collective breathing inside and the cold outside had fogged up the windows of the van. The occupants were invisible to anyone who might chance to pass by—anyone who might miraculously be able to help.

"How did you find out?" Sarah was desperately stalling for time. Every millisecond was one more breath. *Where in hell is Olympia Brown?*

"You got too nice and too neat," said David. "I noticed it, and so did Aaron. It was out of character. And you were far too careful organizing this morning's food pick-up, making sure that only Bethany Ruth would be going with you. You've never been a detail person, Sarah, but unfortunately for you, I am."

He held up the little bottle and slipped the syringe into the down-turned top, pulled the plunger back and flicked the plastic cylinder with his thumb and forefinger.

"They'll catch you," said Sarah, looking past the man with the needle, trying to see through the opaque windows. *Nothing, no one.*

"We didn't want it to come to this, you know, we never do. It's your own fault." The Abba shook his head. "You would have been very happy with me." He slipped his fingers under Sarah's skirt and began rubbing her thigh. "Ready?"

David nodded.

"Do her first, she's the fighter. I want to feel her lose control." He moved his hand higher.

David turned in his seat, holding the deadly needle delicately between his index and middle fingers, his thumb on the plunger. He was smiling. "I'm going to stick it in your thigh. That way I won't miss if …"

Sarah took a deep breath and in one final, desperate act spit in David's face and slammed her left elbow into the side of the Abba's head. David roared in disgust and lunged toward her as the two front doors of the van flew open.

"Police, don't move! John Marigold, you are under arrest on suspicion of murder, attempted murder and embezzlement. You have the right to remain silent and are hereby warned that anything you say could be held against you in a court of law. Get out of the car, and put your hands on the roof."

The Abba turned and smiled. "Whatever do you mean, officer? The girls seem to have flooded the engine. We stopped to help. We were just waiting until we could try starting it again. There's nothing wrong."

"You are accused of using a false identity, coercion and embezzlement."

A second officer grabbed David, who was still wiping the spit off his face, and dragged him out of the van.

"I'm not speaking to anyone without my lawyer," said John Marigold.

Through the icy mist, Sarah saw a blue VW van pull up and park behind the Mercedes.

"My friend's in the back." Sarah was leaning against the side of the van, trying to catch her breath.

A second policeman pulled open the side door and climbed in. He untied Bethany Ruth and eased the gag out of her mouth. "Do you think you can walk, Miss?" he said gently.

"I'm not sure," said Bethany Ruth, holding on to the officer with both hands as she levered herself out onto the cold, wet pavement.

That was when she saw her professor and two other men running down the sidewalk toward them.

Sixty-Three

John Marigold and Brother David, handcuffed and sitting in the back of the unmarked police car, listened as Detective Blackwell read them their rights. Then Blackwell used the police radio to give the go-ahead to enter and search the Fellowship Renewal Center. Jim, Olympia, and Frederick stood beside Olympia's VW with Sarah. Bethany Ruth was curled inside the van, wrapped in a police issue army blanket. She was pale and near to being in shock.

As they waited for permission to leave, Sarah was fishing around inside her jacket. Finally, she pulled out a plastic bag with a wrinkled yellow mailing envelope inside it.

"Here," she said handing it to Detective Blackwell. "Take this before you go."

"What is it?" he asked, turning it over in his hands.

"Proof," she said. "I decided that with what I had uncovered and what I know about other members who tried to escape, if something did happen to me, no one would ever know the truth." Sarah looked at the detective, then at Olympia and Frederick. "The last thing I did this morning before I left was to take some of the most important evidence, seal it in a plastic bag, and stick it inside my blouse. I prayed no one would notice, but the corners of the envelope kept poking me while I was driving."

She shook her head. "If they ..." She paused. "Well, I figured eventually somebody would find it."

"You're something else, Sarah." Olympia wrapped a comforting arm around her quivering shoulders. "I don't know if I could have thought so clearly or so unselfishly at a time like that. By the way, I'm Olympia Brown, and I'm honored to make your acquaintance."

Sixty-Four

The Christmas tree in the corner of the great room was beginning to droop, but the twinkling lights and the sounds of the fire in the wood stove were quietly comforting to the battle-weary group gathered in Olympia Brown's home.

"In England," said Frederick, addressing no one in particular, "the first day of the new year is called Hogminay. It's the day when …"

"Maybe we could hear about it later, Dear." Olympia reached over and patted his hand. "With all due respect for cross-cultural relations, I don't think any of us can absorb one more piece of factual information. You don't mind, do you?"

"Come on outside, and help me get some wood," said Jim, getting out of his chair and brushing the cat hair off his slacks. "You can tell me about Hogminay."

Olympia looked up and smiled at her two men, then turned toward Bethany Ruth and her parents sitting close together on the sofa. She had called the McAllisters the minute they were home from Lowell. Once they had spoken with their daughter and knew she was safe, they booked the next flight to Boston and arrived in time for a picture book New England Christmas. On New Year's Day afternoon , they were still trying to piece it all together.

Sarah sat on her heels on the floor next to the coffee table. The two cats were curled on the mat by the fire, purring into each other's necks. It was the image of post-holiday tranquility, only it wasn't. It was aftershock.

"I've made some mulled cider for everyone," said Olympia, getting up and heading for the kitchen, "with and without."

"With and without what?" asked Bethany Ruth.

"With rum and without."

When she returned carrying a tray of steaming mugs, the delicious aroma of cinnamon and clove floated after her as she passed out the fragrant, steaming drinks.

"I still can't get my mind around it all," said Bethany Ruth, selecting a *without* cup. "How could I have been so stupid?"

"You weren't bein' stupid, Bethie, honey." Her mother's soft Oklahoma accent softened the edges of her words. "Y'all were homesick and lonely. You worked so hard to get here. Those Fellowship people looked like what you was used to back home with us. Isn't that so, Daddy?"

Bethany Ruth's father sat beside his wife and daughter staring into the fire, nodding in response but saying nothing.

"That's what they look for," said Frederick, setting down his armload of wood, "lonely, innocent, idealistic young people."

"Or angry, disenchanted young people," said Sarah, glancing over at Jim. "I hope you don't mind me saying this, Father, but I was so furious with what the Catholic Church said about people like me that I left without ever looking back. I was a prime target for those people. I could have been the poster child. I never knew what hit me until later."

"We'll talk about that one day, Sarah," said Jim. "Some of us do understand."

"A very skilled operation, that Fellowship thing," said Frederick, "and we won't know the full extent of it all for months."

"I was part of it," said Sarah. "I still don't understand how so many intelligent people could have been so totally gullible. I didn't find the Abba attractive, just the opposite, but there was something compelling about him."

"Marigold was the ultimate con-man," said Jim. "He thought he could play God and got too confident. That's when he started to make mistakes. He was so sure of himself, he never changed his name. He even registered the Mercedes in his own name. The police had no trouble tracing the license plate. Between what we told them and what they had on record, they probably could have tried and convicted him right there on the street."

"Its unbelievable how well organized it all was," said Olympia. "All that money going straight into stock accounts held in the name of 2121 Revelator Enterprises."

"Your priest friend here figured that one out," said Frederick. "It's another Bible verse. Revelations twenty-one, twenty-one, something about the streets of the city being pure gold."

"There's a lot more gonna come out of that there mess." Bethany Ruth's father spoke the first words he had said all evening. "You're one brave lady, Miss Sarah. You saved my daughter's life. I don't know how ..." He stopped and shook his head.

"The police got there just in time," said Bethany Ruth, looking at the fire. "They really were going to ..." She looked down at the woman sitting on the floor by her feet. "You saved both of us, Sis … Sarah."

"I thought it was all over," said Sarah. "Spitting in David's face was a last-ditch effort. If the police hadn't yanked open the door when they did, I don't know what I would have done." Sarah turned to Olympia, "What made them come—the police, I mean? You told me they were going to wait until you called them."

"Once the police started checking on Marigold," said Father Jim, "they realized what kind of a man they were dealing with and decided it would be too dangerous to wait. They stationed themselves outside the Fellowship residence in an unmarked car until the van pulled out. When they saw the Mercedes pull out right after you, Blackwell had the good sense to follow it. I can only thank God he did."

"So what's going to happen now?" asked Bethany Ruth.

Olympia held her mug with both hands, warming them.

"Marigold and his strong arm David were arrested on the spot," said Olympia. "Once they were in custody, Blackwell radioed the men with the search warrant to move in."

"What about the others?" Bethany Ruth reached for the plate of Christmas cookies on the coffee table. "What's going to happen to them?"

"I don't really know," said Olympia. "I suppose there will be social workers and crisis counselors working with them. Some of them will probably need to be deprogrammed."

"But other than making sworn statements and having a long face-to-face with your upstaged dean, my dear Olympia, we are off the case." Frederick uncurled himself from his position on the footstool and reached for a log. "You have quite enough with your teaching and your ministry without playing detective. I don't mind telling you, I'm glad this is over."

Olympia shook her head. "I can't say I'm looking forward to that conversation with Will. The man is not happy with me for this, even though it all turned out well."

"You mean he wanted to be the avenging angel and the conquering hero all rolled into one," said Frederick.

"Something like that, and he's not going to forget this. Wilbur Jackson gets even."

"You said you were ready for a change, Olympia." Jim leaned back in his chair and looked at her.

"So I did, but I want it to be in my time and on my own terms. I might not have that option now."

With that, she leaned over, pushed another log into the fire, and blew on the embers. There was nothing else to say. *Well, there was, actually, but who to tell and when? Two days earlier, she had received a letter from the City of Boston Department of Records informing Olympia that her daughter had officially requested that her file be unsealed.*

Olympia shut her eyes. The only sounds in the gracious old room were the crackle of the quickening fire, the purring of the cats, and then the sound of a single slivery chime from the clock on the mantel.

January 1, 1860

Cold and bright this morning, but by midday the icicles over the door were already melting in the sun.

This most tumultuous year is behind me. It is a day when one cannot help but recall the past and ponder the future. The house is legally mine, and the land across the way is sold. I am free to follow my own pursuits, which I do confess in the privacy of this diary might not be what is expected of an unmarried woman of some small means. But times are changing, even in the provincial town of Brookfield.

More anon...LFW

Meet Author Judith Campbell

Rev. Dr. 'Judy' Campbell is an ordained Unitarian Universalist minister and author of several books and articles. She has published children's stories, poetry, and numerous essays on spirituality, the arts and religion.

Dr. Campbell holds a PhD in The Arts and Religious Studies and a Master of Arts in Fine Arts. She has presented writing retreats and spirituality workshops nationally and internationally.

When she isn't tearing around the planet, she lives on the island of Martha's Vineyard and in Plymouth, Massachusetts, with her husband and best friend, Chris Stokes, a Professional Englishman, together with their annoyingly intelligent cats, Lucy and Katie.

CPSIA information can be obtained at www.ICGtesting.com
Printed in the USA
BVOW040542230513

321439BV00001B/1/P

9 780982 589953